# Coming in Second

# Coming in Second

Bobbe Tatreau

**COMING IN SECOND**



*This is a work of fiction. All of the characters, names, incidents, organizations, and dialogue in this novel are either the products of the author's imagination or are used fictitiously.*

*iUniverse books may be ordered through booksellers or by contacting:*

*iUniverse*
*1663 Liberty Drive*
*Bloomington, IN 47403*
*www.iuniverse.com*
*1-800-Authors (1-800-288-4677)*



*ISBN: 978-1-4917-4789-6 (sc)*
*ISBN: 978-1-4917-4790-2 (e)*

*Library of Congress Control Number: 2014917208*

*Printed in the United States of America.*

*iUniverse rev. date: 10/06/2014*

# CHAPTER 1

CALLIE'S ARRIVAL WAS the last straw.

From the garden window above the sink, Hanna Sheridan watched her sister's faded red pickup pull into the driveway and park behind her own 2007 Civic. Ryan had spent much of the afternoon washing and waxing the Civic, trying to score mother points that might be converted into gas money. Since he'd moved home after graduating from the University of Colorado, he'd been half-heartedly trying to find a job, emailing his resume to likely online job listings. Without success. A degree in Psychology wasn't easily marketable, especially at the end of a recession. Hanna had, so far, resisted reminding him she'd originally questioned the wisdom of choosing that major. He was too old for *I told you so.* Two weeks ago, her ex—who always did his best parenting with money—had offered to pay Ryan's law school tuition, promising an internship in the Denver law firm where Michael was a partner, but Ryan was having none of it. No more studying or walking in his father's footsteps, in spite of having no means of supporting himself. The fact that Ryan didn't even have money for a haircut didn't seem to bother him. He was sleeping 'til noon, eating Hanna out of house and home, and occasionally taking care of Lexi's baby while she ran errands or took a nap.

A week after Ryan's return, her older daughter and three week old Marie had been delivered to Hanna's doorstep by Lexi's husband

Kyle, who was being deployed to Afghanistan. "Lexi's afraid to stay in Oceanside by herself with the baby," a baby who was thoroughly adorable but preferred sleeping during the day instead of at night.

Boomerang kids.

At forty-eight, Hanna wasn't in the mood to continue being a full time mother to three adult children and a grandchild. She wasn't in the mood to be unemployed either. Nevertheless, in early April, the Durango Public Library had cut back on the hours it was open and eliminated two part-time positions, one of which was Hanna's. By the time she'd picked herself up and dusted herself off, it was the week of Brooke's high school graduation. No time to feel sorry for herself. Michael and his significant other were flying in for the ceremony, and Hanna's cousins and their children were driving over from Colorado Springs. For three days, she had hungry people everywhere.

What amazed Hanna was that Lexi and Ryan behaved as though it was perfectly natural to head for home when the going got rough. Hanna did *not* think it was natural. At some point, children should leave the nest, returning only for holidays and weddings. She'd foolishly been assuming this summer would be *that point* until Brooke served notice that, instead of going to Colorado State in the fall, she was staying at home to attend Fort Lewis College with her boyfriend. This, after she'd been admitted to CSU and assigned a dorm room. Father and daughter were still deadlocked on the topic. Since Michael was paying her tuition and expenses, he believed he should have a say in her choice, but so far there were no signs of Brooke preparing to drive herself and her stuff to Fort Collins in time for Freshman Orientation. Technically, Brooke hadn't moved out, so Hanna couldn't accuse her of moving back home, but the result was the same. She'd be in the house four more years. The nest wouldn't be empty until Hanna was fifty-two.

Bottom line, all three children had settled in, expecting to be taken care of.

And now Callie was on Hanna's doorstep, barefooted, wearing a long, flowing pink skirt, and a man's white shirt rolled to the elbows. She walked to the passenger side of the truck to unfasten the seatbelt holding a battered guitar case upright like some headless alien. As she lifted the case out and turned toward the house, she saw Hanna watching her and smiled the killer smile that had melted the hearts of most of the males in her senior class, as well as two ex-husbands and countless boyfriends. Falling under Callie's spell usually ended badly for all concerned. Callie included.

"Hey big sister." Callie propped the case against the kitchen table and collapsed into the nearest chair. "I'm wiped. I drove straight through from Vegas."

"Hey yourself. Are the cops after you?" With her sister, anything was possible.

Callie laughed. "Not that I know of, though there's a motel manager in Henderson who might want to track me down. I owe him two months' rent." She pulled her shoulder length, dishwater blonde hair into a sloppy ponytail and slipped a black scrunchie around it. "Leo and our drummer got into a nasty fistfight three days ago; both ended up in jail and on the front page of the Vegas newspaper. The casino where we were appearing wasn't thrilled about the bad publicity—so here I am."

"Yes, here you are." Hanna recognized the familiar sibling-induced irritation crawling over her scalp. Undoubtedly Callie was short on cash, looking for free board and room until she found another gig. Not the first time. Because their parents had left this house to both Callie and Hanna, Callie didn't have to ask for crash space. But why now! The house was already full, and Hanna was tired of caring for people who should be taking care of themselves. Admittedly a politically incorrect attitude born of twenty-five years of being at everyone's beck and call. She was fed up with not having a life separate from the family. Years ago—when the kids were young and Michael was still hers—she'd loved being *Mom*, but the divorce changed everything. Since then, she'd felt unfairly burdened by other people's decisions and needs. Even though those needs were very real.

When did she get a turn?

For several months, Hanna had been flirting with the idea of running away from home. It didn't really matter where she went, just as long as it wasn't Durango. It had been years since she'd been outside of Colorado, she'd never seen the ocean, never gone to visit Zoey, or seen the balloon fiesta in Albuquerque. The dream of watching the sun set at the edge of the Pacific, wandering art galleries in New York City, or sketching the Maine Coast kept eluding her grasp. Michael's alimony would, in the short term, cover her living expenses. Fortunately, her parents had paid the house mortgage off years ago, and the property taxes weren't due until next April.

"We're rather short on space right now."

"I thought Lexi was in California and Ryan would be—"

"No such luck. All of them, including the baby, have settled in for the duration. Unless you can convince Brooke to share her bed, the best I can offer is the pullout sofa in the family room." Hanna's tone was anything but welcoming. She definitely did not want Callie sharing her room because her sister was a night person, needing the drone of the TV to put her to sleep and given to strewing her possessions everywhere.

Callie shrugged. "If necessary, I can sleep on the air mattress in the back of the truck."

No doubt. But Hanna really didn't want Callie sleeping inside or outside of the house. Another mouth to feed and probably a pile of dirty laundry to be washed. Loving her sister and tolerating her were two different things.

"I'm famished. Any leftovers?"

And so Hanna was scrambling eggs and fixing toast when Lexi came downstairs with a bathed and powdered Marie in her arms. "Aunt Callie! When did you get here?"

"Minutes ago, Darlin'. Let me hold Miss Maria." She pulled the pink-cheeked baby into her arms and planted a noisy kiss on Marie's cheek. Marie studied this new person—then favored Callie with a toothless smile.

"Her name's Marie, not Maria."

Ignoring the correction, Callie nuzzled Marie's neck, "I'm your Great Aunt Callie," and carried the baby into the dining room, singing *How do we solve a problem like Maria?*

"Marie never smiles at people that quickly. Aunt Callie has magical powers." Lexi took the chair Callie had vacated and helped herself to a piece of toast. Her hair was the same blonde/brown as her mother's and Callie's, her figure showing no hint that she'd given birth three months ago.

"Hey, you had your dinner. This is for Callie."

"I'm still eating for two."

"Then make more toast."

"Uh oh. Your Callie snarl."

"With good reason. I'm not a short order cook."

"It's great to see her. I don't understand what your problem is."

"Long story." Under her breath, *forty-four going on thirteen.* Hanna knew she was being bitchy. Callie always brought out the worst in her.

The house refused to quiet down. As soon as Lexi and Marie went upstairs, Brooke showed up with her handsome reason for not going to Fort Collins—the lanky Dennis, who moved with slow grace unless he was running sprints for the high school track team. "We were out with friends." They'd been dating since Christmas though Hanna was fairly sure more than just dating was involved. She remembered her own senior year with Walt Anders. There'd been more than dating going on then too. Dennis and Brooke made an attractive couple, her 5'9" just right for his 6'1". Brooke was the only one of Hanna's children who'd inherited Michael's black hair and dusky skin, compliments of his Mexican great-grandmother. Lexi and Ryan, however, burned and peeled in the sun, just like Hanna and Callie.

For the next hour, Callie concentrated on charming Dennis; she was always at her most entertaining with a new male, even one young enough to be her son. Because she'd played with many of the big name musical groups and knew a few of the current music icons, her stories easily captivated the younger crowd.

Dennis went home just as Ryan appeared, complaining that his truck was running on fumes. Hanna ignored the hint; she'd given him money for a tank of gas last week. What about getting a job—any job—did he not understand?

Callie had another male to hang on her every word.

It had been the same way in high school. If Hanna brought a date home to dinner, Callie soon had him in the palm of her hand, wondering why Hanna was upset with her. Their mother preferred not to interfere. *You'll have to sort it out with Callie yourself.*

Thirty years later, it was still impossible to sort anything out with Callie. She was impervious to criticism.

Tired of watching the *Callie Meeker Show*, Hanna retreated upstairs to take a leisurely bath and find a few minutes of peace and quiet. Callie could make up the pullout bed herself; she knew where the linen closet was.

For Hanna, moving to Durango three-plus years ago had amounted to admitting failure. The discarded wife in retreat. Staying in Denver after the divorce hadn't been an option. Too many people knew that the unfaithful Michael had walked out on his family for a twenty-eight year old paralegal. Hanna preferred to lick her wounds someplace where no one knew Michael, so she came back to her childhood home. Already engaged to Kyle, Lexi was finishing her senior year in Boulder, and Ryan was a freshman. Their day-to-day lives hadn't changed as much as Brooke's. She'd had to cope with a new high school and a town she hadn't visited since she was ten.

Once the house in Denver was sold, Hanna had enough cash to make repairs to her parents' house, which had stood vacant since her father's death. It needed painting inside and out, a new roof, and a new furnace. As soon as the house was finished, Hanna applied for a part-time job at the library, both for extra money and as a way to reenter life in Durango. Though a few of her high school friends still lived locally, after two decades in Denver, she no longer had much in common with them.

After the divorce, Hanna had learned she could survive on her own but, this last year, she'd begun looking beyond Durango, beyond her leftover life. Surely, there was something more. She had a degree in Art, had once been considered a promising artist, had raised three children, and worked at the library for two years. Yet everything and everyone were intent on holding her in place. Though she was dissatisfied with her current life, she had no idea how to fix it. Perhaps, she should simply settle for a more serious relationship with Walt or someone like him. Play bridge, join a bowling league and wait for—

What?

She'd spent twenty-five years paying attention to other people's "wants" without discovering what hers were. Hanna Elizabeth Meeker Sheridan was a mystery to herself, and her patience with others' expectations was wearing dangerously thin.

# CHAPTER 2

HANNA AWOKE EARLY. Even before she opened her eyes, she could feel the sun pushing against the bedroom shutters. The day was going to be hot. With the San Juan Mountains on the north and east and the Colorado Plateau to the west and south, Durango was balanced between the coolness of fourteen thousand foot peaks and the arid oven of the high desert. If there were such a thing as bi-polar weather, Durango had it. Today, the plateau was in charge. Since Hanna had moved into her parents' house, she hadn't been able to afford the luxury of air conditioning—just ceiling fans in the kitchen and living room. Fortunately, the nights usually cooled off, so sleeping wasn't a problem unless, of course, she was annoyed with her family.

Like last night.

Before her feet touched the floor, she was already thinking about today's grocery list. With extra adults in the house, she'd been shopping three or four times a week. The first month Lexi and Marie were at the house, Hanna had tried sending Lexi to Albertson's but, each time, Hanna had to go back later because Lexi had gone off-list, buying whatever she was used to buying, not what Hanna wanted.

And then there was the ever-present laundry. Currently, at least two loads of dirty clothes were spilling out of the hamper in the upstairs hall. Yesterday, Brooke was complaining that she was running out of clean Levis, a necessary part of the *Steamworks* uniform. It would have been worse if Lexi were still using the cloth diapers she'd brought with her from California, explaining that disposable diapers were too expensive on a Marine budget. Hanna's *too bad* had quickly settled that issue. Better to have additional trash than additional laundry.

Mrs. Biggs, the cleaning lady who came every two weeks, was due at nine, Hanna's dental appointment was at three o'clock, and her ex was flying into Durango late this afternoon. He'd unexpectedly texted Brooke last night. Typical Michael behavior. Assuming the world would adapt to his schedule. At least he wasn't bringing the ever-perky Sheri—very blonde and very size two.

The timing of Michael's visit undoubtedly coincided with the fact that next week was Freshman Orientation at CSU. Last stand at the College Choice Corral. Hanna hoped Michael would win the battle. She'd been looking forward to Brooke being at the university on her own and, more importantly, out of the house. But now, even if Brooke went to CSU, Ryan, Lexi, Marie, and Callie would still be underfoot.

Hanna needed space for herself. Did no one understand that?

The last two days, Callie had been playing Pied Piper with her nieces and nephew—*we need to reconnect*—using her credit card to pay for their trip on the historic Denver and Rio Grande steam train that ran to Silverton and a day climbing in and out of cliff dwellings at Mesa Verde National Park. It wasn't that Hanna wanted to ride the train or visit the park. She'd done both plenty of times, but she resented that her family was out having fun while she was babysitting. Admittedly not difficult since Marie slept most of the day, preparing for her nighttime insomnia. This new resentment was piled on top of the other resentments. A tower ready to collapse.

The one bright spot of the day was her regular Tuesday lunch with Walt, though she was going to be late today because the lines at the supermarket had been longer than she'd expected. She called to warn him—Walt Anders was punctual to a fault—asking him to order her the Thai salad and iced tea.

At ten after one, she slipped into the booth just as the waitress finished taking the order. "Sorry."

"Don't be," Walt's broad smile told her he wasn't upset. Tall and well-built, thanks to years of working construction, Walt had gradually graying brown hair that curled against the collar of his khaki work shirt and charcoal eyes behind bifocals that made him look rather scholarly. Tired of working for others, he'd begun his own construction firm a dozen years ago, and his clients sang his praises to anyone who would listen. He was solid and safe, her high school boyfriend. She was pretty sure he was in love with her. If pressed, she might have to admit to being in love with him too, but she was afraid of solid and safe. Afraid she'd never get beyond Durango.

Love versus independence.

"How're things at Hotel Sheridan?"

She made a face. "Michael's flying in later today."

"Oh, oh. Brooke?"

"Probably." The waitress brought two tall glasses of iced tea.

"The eye-candy too?" Walt had seen Sheri at Brooke's graduation.

"I don't think so."

Because Walt was a good listener, she'd become accustomed to confiding in him. He'd heard a lot about Sheri the home wrecker, about Brooke's rebellion—about everything except her own heretical thoughts about potentially escaping all things parental.

He deserved equal listening time. "How's the new job?" He was doing a kitchen remodel out on East Second.

"In rip out phase. Mindless but therapeutic activity. The lady of the house is already fussing about the mess. Same old, same old. I've also landed the job I bid on at the college. Six storage sheds adjacent to the football field."

"Have you heard anything about the hotel restoration in Silverton?"

"Not yet. The owner is buried in paperwork because it's a historical treasure."

They spent the next hour on local gossip, the weather, Walt's mother, who had just moved into an assisted living community, and of course Hanna's inconvenient boarders, including Callie.

"At least Lexi pays for Marie's formula and diapers—but that's about all. She promised Kyle she'd save half of every paycheck so they could get a place of their own when he comes home, and she does. Ryan doesn't have anything to save, and Brooke's job at *Steamworks* barely pays for her gas and clothing."

Walt frowned. "Are you running short of cash?"

"My alimony still comes every month. Michael's good at paying on time. But since I haven't found enough job listings to interview for, the State Unemployment Office is threatening to cut off my benefits." Here she was, unloading her problems on him again.

"I'd be happy to find work for Ryan. Only grunt labor for the moment, but it'll give him something to do and a little spending money until he gets the job he wants."

"Thanks," Walt was always trying to make things better for her. She didn't appreciate him nearly enough. "I'll mention it, but I think college has ruined him for manual labor. He seems to think he should get a job that starts at $80,000 a year with benefits, comes with a corner office and a company car. This generation doesn't understand starting at the bottom and working their way up." She sighed. "Don't pay attention to me. I didn't sleep all that well."

"Tell him to call me anyway." He reached for the folder holding the bill, "My turn to pay," and slipped cash inside.

He walked her to her car and kissed her on the cheek, "Try not to worry," then crossed the street to where his truck was parked.

She was never sure how to respond to his kisses; the brotherly ones on her cheek weren't a problem, but the more serious goodnight kisses after a movie or a night with mutual friends were tantalizing and definitely sexy—silently asking the question she pretended she didn't hear and he didn't pursue. After her divorce, when they'd started seeing one another for lunches and movies, Hanna hadn't wanted more than friendship and had said as much. Being dumped after twenty years of marriage had left scars that were slow to heal. To his credit, Walt hadn't pushed the envelope. Though she sometimes wondered what *more* would be like.

Still—it would be hard to trust her heart, her life, to another man. Even one she'd known since she was sixteen.

By the time she got home, she was exhausted. Having her teeth cleaned always wore her out, making her mouth tender and her head hurt. She just wanted to drink something cool and sit in the back yard staring at the red mesas that tucked themselves around Durango. She didn't feel like cooking. Nowadays she had no clue how many would show up for meals. Tonight Michael would surely take Brooke to dinner. One less.

When Hanna walked into the kitchen, Callie was the only one there and, miracle of miracles, she was adding a large jar of marinara sauce to a frying pan of ground beef and onions. Hanna slipped out of her shoes, opened a can of diet coke, and poured it over ice. "Where are the others?"

"Having dinner at Michael's expense. I told them to go to the Ore House and order steak and lobster." She grinned, "He can afford it."

"I thought he was coming to twist Brooke's arm about college."

Callie shrugged. "Search me. Do you want a salad with this?"

"I'll make it." Hanna swallowed more Coke, letting it cool the soreness left behind by a dental hygienist who took her job seriously. For the moment, it was rather nice to share the kitchen with Callie—to have the house quiet.

"How was your date with Walt?"

"Not a date." Hanna's tone was instantly defensive. "Just lunch and gossip. We take turns paying."

"Did he ever marry or is he gay?"

"You know perfectly well he isn't gay. He married one of the Peace Corps workers he met in Zambia. But after seven or eight years in Durango, she divorced him, then applied for another tour abroad. Two years later, she died of sleeping sickness in Kenya. Walt was shattered."

"He never remarried?"

"No. When I moved back here, he and Mitzi Bradshaw were an item, but she married an accountant in Farmington." Though Hanna wasn't quite sure why Walt and Mitzi broke up, she did know he was the one who walked away.

"Around here, I bet he's considered a good catch."

"Probably." Hanna changed the subject. "Is the pasta ready?"

Hanna was upstairs in her bedroom folding sheets, and Callie was in the back yard playing something mournful on her guitar when the children returned. They were unusually quiet. No bickering or joking, just car doors slamming, the back door screen, then feet climbing the stairs. Probably Lexi with Marie.

Hanna waited a few minutes before going to stand in the doorway of Lexi's room. "How was dinner?"

"Ask the other two," she was pulling Marie's t-shirt off, "I need to get her bathed." Subtext: *I don't want to discuss my father.*

Blown off by her eldest, Hanna headed downstairs. Something wasn't right but then Michael was an expert at upsetting his family. Before she reached the kitchen, she could hear Brooke crying and Ryan trying to calm her down. She must have lost the college battle.

"What's going on? What did your father want?"

Ryan was leaning against the kitchen counter, a scowl marring his still boyish good looks. "To tell us he's marrying Sheri in Montrose—a church wedding yet. Next Saturday. He wants us to come. Just imagine, she'll be Sheri Sheridan; what are the odds?"

Hanna felt her insides lurch. *Remarried!* Destroying one marriage allowed him to have a new one. She should have expected something like this when Michael brought Sheri to Brooke's graduation. Still cheerleader pretty at thirty-something, Sheri had been trying too hard to make friends with Lexi, Ryan and Brooke.

"So that's what he came for, not the college issue?" Hanna could hear the edge in her voice.

Tears continued to roll down Brooke's cheeks. "He said he didn't care what I decided to do—as if he *ever* cares what I do—but if I start at Fort Lewis, I have to stay for all four years—even if I hate it."

So was Brooke crying about Fort Lewis? That didn't quite make sense. Fort Lewis was what she'd wanted. Or was she crying about her father getting married? Knowing Brooke, she probably didn't know why she was crying.

"And," Ryan dropped the second bomb, "Sheri's pregnant. Really embarrassing. His grandchild will be a year older than his own kid."

Before Hanna could find a response, Ryan stormed out of the kitchen. She could hear his voice and Callie's, and then her truck pulling away. Callie was a soft touch.

Hanna sat down opposite Brooke, waiting for her daughter's tears to be replaced by words of some kind. Instead, Brooke gave her a furious look, "Don't say what you're thinking," stomped up to her room, and slammed the door.

So much for Tuesday.

Heavy silence on Wednesday. Not even Callie's good humor could jump start a conversation. "Are they mad or just embarrassed?"

Hanna shrugged. "Maybe grossed out by the idea that their father's been having sex."

Thursday, Brooke spent the day out at Fort Lewis registering for classes and buying textbooks with the check Michael had given her to cover the expenses. Hopefully, she wasn't giving Dennis the same silent treatment her family was getting.

Lexi and Marie were spending the day with another young mother who had three year old triplets. "A play date."

"Play? Marie isn't much on playing yet."

"Okay, okay. *I* need a play date."

"Don't take your anger with your father out on me," Hanna shot back and continued pulling clothes out of the dryer. She was tired of being caught in the middle. Her days of refereeing were over.

Friday morning, Hanna received notice that, because she hadn't gone on the requisite number of job interviews each week, she wouldn't receive any more unemployment checks. Three pages of regulations were attached along with a form to fill out if she wanted to appeal the decision. It wasn't that she hadn't known about the requirements, but what she wanted to do and what the Unemployment Office wanted her to do were quite different. Working at the Durango Mall food court was not at all appealing.

Perhaps she should cut Ryan more slack about his job search. She didn't want just any job either.

Callie spent a large portion of the evening on her cell phone with someone from the band that had been booted out of Las Vegas. Judging from Callie's side of the conversation, the band wasn't getting back together anytime soon because Leo still hadn't been able to make bail. Which meant the hotel hadn't paid up.

No one in the Sheridan Hotel was happy. Except perhaps Marie.

# CHAPTER 3

MICHAEL'S WEDDING DAY began with blustery winds that were yanking the last of the leaves from the trees. In the days preceding the ceremony, the children couldn't make a decision about whether or not to attend. They took two steps forward, then one step back. Ryan and Brooke agreeing to go, then Ryan refusing, then Lexi agreeing. In the end, Hanna waded in, using safety as an issue. At least two had to go or no one was going. To get to Montrose, they had to drive the Million Dollar Highway with its notoriously risky stretch carved into the side of the mountains between Silverton and Ouray. Eventually all three went, leaving Marie with Hanna.

Callie and her guitar disappeared after lunch with only a cryptic, "I'll be late."

Once Marie was down for her nap, Hanna climbed the narrow stairs into the attic to search for the boxes of the Meeker/Sheridan family photographs. Lexi wanted to start a family scrapbook for Marie, pictures of the great grandparents, grandparents, aunts and uncles on both sides. Kyle's mother had sent pictures of the Jorgenson side of the family just before Kyle left for Afghanistan.

Hanna was pretty sure she'd stacked the boxes near the attic's front window when she moved back from Denver. Because the divorce wounds had still been raw, she hadn't been interested in revisiting the photos of family picnics, birthdays, and Christmases that had been hastily jammed into manila envelopes or bound with rubber bands. Once the three boxes were on the dining room table, Hanna made the mistake of looking into one.

A Fourth of July picnic at Chatfield Reservoir—2002 was scrawled on the back of each photo. Lexi had been fourteen, Ryan almost eleven, and Brooke seven, her hair forced into braids that unsuccessfully tried to subdue the wayward curls that she hated. Photos of a baseball game and the kids on inflatable rafts. A picnic table covered with food.

On the surface, a picture postcard family day.

Curious, Hanna opened several more envelopes.

She stopped looking at her past when Marie woke up but, as soon as the baby was happily occupied on a blanket on the dining room floor, Hanna returned to the pictures.

It wasn't nostalgia or even sadness that drew her. She was searching for herself—literally and figuratively. She rarely appeared in the photos. Michael with the children, the children together and separately. Out of all the pictures, Hanna was only in seven shots. Seven. She was sorry she'd counted them. Michael had always been quick to hand her the camera. *You take better pictures than I do.* In those days, she'd been flattered.

Based on the photos, she almost didn't exist. There without being there.

Few visible footprints on the family's photographic history.

An overreaction perhaps. After all, they were just pictures. No one had intentionally left her out. She'd been perfectly willing to photograph her family. She should be happy to have such a sweet granddaughter, to have children who were reasonably intelligent and had stayed out of major kinds of trouble. But instead of being happy, Hanna was hurt.

It was getting dark when she took Marie into the kitchen for her dinner; then bathed her in the kitchen sink, sang a few lullabies, and put her in her crib, hoping she'd stay asleep. Hanna needed time to arrange her thoughts. And pack the car. At some point during her afternoon, she'd reached a decision. Back in April, she'd emailed Zoey that she might be able to come visit in the fall as soon as Brooke was in college.

Zoey's "Please come; we haven't had girl time for ages," had brought tears to Hanna's eyes.

It was time to make the trip.

When she finished packing, Hanna took a few minutes to look into each of her children's rooms. In Lexi's, Marie was on her back, sleeping. Good news. This bedroom had been a guestroom ever since Lexi got married. Callie was its most frequent occupant. Now Marie's crib was at the foot of the double bed, baby paraphernalia and toys crammed into every available space. No remnants of Lexi's cheerleader days, her passion for flowers or the color green. On Lexi's first day of kindergarten, Hanna had wept as her five year old in a bright green blouse and pants waved goodbye at the schoolroom door. Nearly twenty years ago.

Twenty years!

Ryan's room still had unpacked duffle bags and boxes of textbooks piled along one wall. Unpacking might admit he was actually living here rather than just passing through on his way to a career. Until now, everything had come easily to Ryan—girls, athletic trophies, good grades. It seemed her son wasn't prepared for hitting a rough patch. As always, his bed was unmade, piles of clean clothes on the dresser and dirty clothes littering the floor. The family slob.

She resisted walking in. If she did, she'd be picking up his stuff.

Conversely, Brooke kept her room obsessively neat. As early as primary school, she'd been overly concerned about how her clothes were folded, even how her school supplies were arranged on her desk. The walls still had the colorful travel posters she'd hung when she was fifteen, exactly ten inches between each one. Hanna remembered how long it took to get the measurements right.

Hanna holding the yardstick, Brooke putting tiny pencil marks on the walls.

In spite of everything, her kids had turned out well. She felt pride when someone complimented them or they won a prize. But whatever *glow* she felt never lasted long. The next day she'd still be making dinner, doing laundry, and listening to their problems. Mothers didn't get awards. Maybe a card and breakfast on Mother's Day.

She loved them—deeply, completely. Of that she was sure.

Were love and sacrifice synonymous?

She was running low on sacrifice. A subtle, insidious dissatisfaction had—in recent months—crept into her thoughts. At first, she blamed what she called *The Return of the Children* though Brooke had been there all along. Then the loss of her job. The money wasn't the issue; having a role outside the house was.

Her dissatisfaction had probably begun about the time Lexi went off to college. A child raised—a mini ending. Like the old Peggy Lee song. *Is That All There Is?* And Hanna began asking herself the same thing. Three years later, Ryan left for college, and then Michael left. Everyone gone except Brooke. That year, she'd been glad Brooke still needed her.

In theory, the children were old enough to take care of themselves. It wasn't as though she was turning them out onto the streets—though Brooke would think so.

When Callie showed up this time, Hanna realized she was actually jealous of her sister's freedom and her passion for music. Though Callie barely made a living as a musician, she was deeply committed to her music, was respected for her talent, and had a network of friends in the business.

Hanna had none of those things.

She closed the door to Brooke's room.

*It's time to enlarge the borders of my tent.*

She was sitting in the backyard when Lexi's car, with Ryan driving, pulled into the driveway. All three looked a bit bedraggled. The long drive and watching their father take a new wife had drained her usually energetic children.

"How'd it go?"

Brooke opened her mouth and pointed into it with her index finger. "Like gag. She wore white. Can you believe?"

Lexi sat down and slipped out of her high heels, "Get over it. No one worries about that kind of tradition these days. I thought she looked very pretty"—Lexi was always willing to see the positive—"and Daddy looked happy but—sort of—old." Hanna was tempted to remind her he was forty-nine. "The reception was mostly her friends and family. I don't think Daddy invited any of his friends or colleagues."

*Probably wise.*

Ryan started toward the house. "I'm gonna hit the sack."

Hanna sat up a bit straighter in her chair. "Before you go in, I want to talk to all of you about something."

He grimaced. "Please don't tell us you're getting married too. We've had enough of that for one day."

"No, but I am going to take a vacation; I'm leaving in the morning."

The silence was palpable. Ryan sat down alongside Brooke on the picnic table bench. "Why?"

*Why indeed.*

"Because—" She didn't add *I need it.*

"But what about the job interviews for your unemployment checks?" This from Brooke, who'd been worrying that her mother had lost her job.

"No longer a problem. My unemployment benefits ended yesterday."

"But if you leave, how will we—I mean—" Because the yard was dark, Hanna couldn't see Brooke's eyes, but they were probably ready to cry.

"You're smart kids. You can figure it out."

"How will we eat? Aunt Callie's charge cards are maxed out—and I was going to cut back my hours at *Steamworks* now that classes are gearing up, Ryan's stone broke—and Lexi won't part with a penny of Kyle's precious check." Brooke was working up to a good cry.

"You have a roof over your head. You'll have to cope with the rest." She knew she was being hard on them but, if she backed off, there might not be another chance.

Lexi ventured, "How long?"

"As long as it takes for me to figure out what the rest of my life should be."

"But—" Ryan this time.

She stood up. "I love all of you. I'll check in now and then." Before they could wear her down, she went straight to her room and closed the door, amazed that she'd actually had the guts to tell them.

No one had asked where she was going.

A little before 5 a.m., Hanna backed the Civic out of the driveway. Her children hadn't understood last night. They wouldn't understand this morning either. More conversation would only make her more defensive.

Why were men allowed to have mid-life crises while women who hit the same life-wall were written off as irrationally menopausal? Even in the twenty-first century, women weren't allowed to question whether their lives had meaning, whether they should change direction. Michael's crisis included a sweet young thing, a Harley, and a partnership in a new law firm, leaving Hanna to finish raising Brooke, assuming that shared custody meant 10% for him and 90% for her.

*Now it's my turn.*

In two years she'd be fifty. She'd lived more than half her life as a wife and mother. There had to be something more.

Self-pity carried her through Cortez, where she stopped for gas, but somewhere around Tec Nos Pos, Arizona, fear set in. She was alone, heading west across the empty high desert. Two suitcases, a couple of novels, her art portfolio and sketching pads, her laptop and a cell phone.

Other than seeing the Pacific Ocean and maybe Zoey, no specific plan. Scary and exhilarating.

# CHAPTER 4

BROOKE WOKE UP determined to talk her mother out of leaving. Mothers were supposed to stay at home. Ready to do battle, she threw on yellow shorts, a white t-shirt, and combed her hair.

The door to her mother's bedroom was wide open.

And empty.

As was the kitchen.

And the Civic wasn't in the driveway.

She stood at the kitchen window staring at the missing Civic. If ever there was a crying moment, this was it. She checked the family room, but Callie hadn't come home last night. When Brooke tried her mother's cell, the voice mail cheerfully invited her to leave a message. No help there.

She didn't have a clue where her mother would go—or why. The fact that Hanna might want to take a trip or live someplace else had never occurred to Brooke. This turn of events was even worse than the divorce. At least then she'd had her mother's support. Now she was standing on air.

Such bad timing. Her father was honeymooning with his child bride, so Brooke didn't dare call him yet. Though once he knew what Hanna had done, he might send money. After all, this was an emergency. He was always good about giving money to his children. However, if he refused to help them out, she didn't know how they'd survive. Ryan was broke. Probably Callie too. That left Kyle's check and her own salary; even combined, they couldn't feed four adults and put gas in four vehicles.

She headed for her brother's room. Ryan was just going to have to get off his lazy ass and find a job——any job. She was not going to support him the way her mother had.

Not bothering to knock, "Hey!" Ryan's head was buried beneath the pillow. No movement. She grabbed the pillow and pulled it off. "Wake up. She really left."

He rolled over, eyes closed, his hair tumbling every which way. "Give—me—the —pillow."

"No. Open your eyes. Listen to me. She left. Mom left. Not even a note or some cash. Just gone. Her cell's turned off," she took a breath, "and Callie didn't come home last night."

He grinned. "Maybe she got lucky."

"Don't be gross. Do you have Callie's cell number?"

"Nope. Ask Lexi."

"She's sleeping."

"So was I, dimwit."

"But you weren't up half the night with Marie."

Ryan extended his hand. "Gimme."

Brooke tossed the pillow at him, and he stuffed it under his head.

Her initial fury was draining away, leaving her shaky, tears threatening. She sat on the edge of the bed. "What're we going to do?"

"Don't pull that crying crap on me. I don't know."

"Should we call Dad?"

He shook his head. "He'll have me enrolled in law school and clerking in his office."

"This isn't just about you. We need money. I was going to cut back on my hours so I can concentrate on my classes. As it is, I barely earn enough to put gas in my car and clothes on my back."

"You could stop buying clothes."

"This from the person who's been sponging off Mom since May. At least I can afford a haircut. Pretty soon you'll be wearing a ponytail. Didn't I hear Mom tell you to call Walt about a job?"

"Yeah."

"Did you?"

"No. Why would I want to work construction? I have a college degree."

"Because you like to eat."

"Hey you two; stop yelling. You'll wake the baby." Wearing a tank top and faded pajama bottoms, Lexi was standing in the doorway, her puffy eyes suggesting she was short on sleep. "What's wrong?"

"Mom really left and turned her cell off."

As though she didn't believe her sister, Lexi walked into Hanna's room, coming back a few minutes later. "Both suitcases are gone and her laptop." Because Ryan didn't have a chair in his room, she sat on the floor, her back against the wall.

"What're we going to do?" Brooke's tears won out, streaking her face. "I start classes tomorrow. And I have a five hour shift today."

Lexi scowled. "Stop being such a baby. How is it you can always cry on demand?"

The room was silent except for Brooke sniffling and wiping at the tears with her hands.

Then, as if on cue, Marie let out a wail. "Damn!" Lexi stood up, "See what you've done?" and ran toward the sound.

"I get dibs on the shower." Ryan jumped out of bed, crossed the hall, and slammed the bathroom door behind him, leaving Brooke alone.

"Am I the only one who sees the problem here?" Back in her own room, she called Dennis.

Callie woke up in Bayfield, fully dressed, curled up on Louise Kroger's couch, which was definitely too short for comfortable sleeping. A high school friend, Louise owned a bar out on Highway 160 and, whenever Callie came to town, Louise let her entertain the customers. *I need to work on my own compositions*—as well as the folk songs and country western selections that were in her personal repertoire. When she was playing with a band, she had to play their material.

Her head hurt—too much beer—and she needed a shower and a toothbrush. Since Louise was still sleeping, Callie left a note on the kitchen counter and let herself out. It was still early enough that she might be able to take a shower and change her clothes before Hanna got a look at her. Her sister had never approved of Callie's somewhat casual lifestyle. "You're a talented musician, yet you walked away from a full scholarship at one of the best music schools to go on the road with that red-haired saxophonist."

"He was impossible to resist but, to our credit, we did get married—eventually." Though the marriage had lasted only three years.

An old argument. The conventional, respectable Hanna: husband, children, PTA, divorce. The unconventional Callie: two divorces, living out of suitcases, moving from band to band, never quite willing to go out on her own to find out whether her voice and compositions could support a solo career. Probably too late now. So many young performers out there.

Hanna's car wasn't in the driveway. Her lucky morning.

Brooke and Ryan were at the kitchen table, drinking coffee.

"You two look like someone died—no one did, did they?"

Ryan didn't look up from his cell phone, "Mom left."

Callie poured herself some coffee, accidentally adding too much sugar. "Left as in left?"

Ryan laid the phone on the table in front of him and met her eyes. "You missed last night's speech about taking a vacation and wanting to go find herself or something like that."

"So where's she going?"

"She didn't say. Left before we woke up." Brooke's voice cracked. "Just left."

"Imagine that!" Callie was pretty sure her reaction was going to annoy her niece and nephew. "Only took her twenty-five years to spread her wings." She lifted her coffee mug in a mock toast. "Good for you, big sister."

"How can you say that?" Brooke's tears were welling up. "She's left us in the lurch. I've got classes, we haven't got any money, and Dennis isn't answering his phone."

Callie wanted to ask what Dennis had to do with the issue but decided this wasn't the time for logic.

"There she goes again. Bloody waterfall." Ryan grabbed his phone and walked into the back yard.

"Where's Lexi?"

"Trying to get Marie back to sleep. Ry and I woke her up."

Callie climbed the stairs, sipping at the sugary coffee.

Lexi was just coming out of the bathroom, freshly showered, her chestnut hair pulled into a ponytail.

"They told you."

Callie nodded.

"Let's go into Mom's room. I just got Marie back to sleep."

Hanna's room—once their parents' room—had off-white walls with bold splashes of turquoise and green. Hanna'd always had a good sense of color, probably the reason she'd studied art at the university. But pursuing art must have seemed too risky, so she settled instead for Michael Sheridan who, at the time, seemed risk free. Callie'd preferred musicians with wandering ways. Definitely not risk free.

She didn't wait for Lexi's reaction to Hanna's defection. "I can understand why she'd take off."

"Well sure, that's what you do." Lexi's tone was matter of fact rather than disapproving.

"It is. I've probably done it too much." She was surprised at that piece of personal truth. "Hanna's never done it at all."

"So what are we supposed to do while she's out finding herself?"

Callie looked into her now empty cup as though it held the answer. "Get on with things."

"How?"

"How did you do it in California?"

She shrugged. "I had Kyle's help. When he was deployed, I came home. Staying in California on my own seemed too hard."

"When your mother came back here after the divorce, she didn't have a parent to help her. She had to do everything on her own. And you all survived." Defending Hanna seemed strange.

"You come here when you're out of work."

"Guilty. It's the only place I don't have to pay rent." And sometimes, she needed a safe place to regroup. Being a musician was all she'd ever wanted, but the lifestyle could wear her down. However, too much time in Durango was generally too much time in Durango.

They spent the rest of the day not talking about THE PROBLEM. Until her one o'clock shift, Brooke stayed in her room, talking on the phone, probably to Dennis. Ryan went running, washed his truck, then watched the Broncos' game. Lexi did laundry for herself and Marie while Callie took a long nap in Hanna's room. When she woke up at four, her head felt better but she was still at a loss about how to deal with her sister's children. A bad time to be out of work.

In years past, Callie would have loaded up the truck and taken off—let the chips fall. But she really didn't have anywhere to go. Though she had put out feelers about a job, any job, the music network was perversely silent, so fleeing the scene wasn't an option—yet. Usually she could pick up work in a week or two because Callie Meeker's skill with the acoustic guitar was respected, and she could do back-up vocal if necessary. Currently, she had about $900 in her checking account and very little room left on any of her credit cards. The Vegas hotel owed the band for the last week they'd played. Perhaps Leo had been paid and used the cash to make bail. It wouldn't be the first time.

Twice Hanna almost turned around. Once at a rest stop outside Kayenta, Arizona, and later near Tuba City. Both times, she sat with the engine running, imagining what it would be like if she drove home now and walked into the kitchen to face her family. There surely would have to be an apology for throwing an adult tantrum. Her mother credibility had been seriously damaged. Then she remembered it was the strictures of the mother credibility she was running from. Both times, the moment of uncertainty passed, and she pulled back onto the highway heading west.

For most of her adult life, when people asked *What do you do?* she had answered, half apologetically, *I'm a stay at home mom.* When the library hired her, she could at least say *I'm a librarian.* Of course she wasn't really a librarian; she merely checked out books and collected overdue fines. Truth be told, boring work, but she could get out of the house and meet other people two days a week.

Ironically, Callie always had a better answer to the question. People were impressed when she said *I'm a musician.* Yet Hanna often felt superior to Callie because Callie didn't have a marriage or children or a home. Now of course Hanna didn't have a marriage either, half of her home belonged to Callie, and her children wanted her to keep mothering and mothering and mothering. So much for being superior. If she didn't stop or at least reduce the day-to-day mothering, she'd never have a life of her choosing. Finding a man to take Michael's place wasn't necessarily in the equation because she'd probably end up taking care of him too. What she was feeling was undoubtedly heresy.

At Flagstaff, Hanna rented a room at the Holiday Inn Express, found a Chinese restaurant that did take-out, and spent the night in her room watching *Friends* reruns and eating spring rolls.

The second day, even though she'd slept soundly, she was exhausted, grateful she'd remembered to bring her old thermos for the waitress to fill with very strong coffee. She'd googled a map of Interstate 40 but had forgotten to check on the mileages between towns. She might not reach the Pacific Ocean today.

After that? No idea. She was running away from and toward things that were, right now, unexplainable—and enticing. In the moments when she wasn't uneasy about what she was doing, a humming excitement ran through her.

Was this what Callie felt whenever she had a new job or a new man?

Driving the Interstate was deadly dull. The scenery, after leaving Williams, equally so. High desert morphed into desert-desert—washed out beige dotted with occasional gray/green vegetation that looked half dead. Blue sky from edge to edge, so different from the mountains and mesas that defined the Colorado horizon. Though there was such a thing as having too much sky.

At Lake Havasu, she stopped for lunch, then pushed on to Barstow, where she spent the night. She wanted another night's sleep before running head on into Los Angeles.

The third day, she followed I-15 into the monstrous tangle of the L.A. freeway system, merging and crisscrossing lanes marked by enormous green signs listing destinations she'd never heard of. She'd rarely had trouble negotiating Denver traffic, but this raceway was ten times faster and more complex, drivers abruptly crossing three lanes to take the next off-ramp. Not a road for amateurs.

Uncertain about taking I-15 or 210, she gambled on 210, and later took 118, following the signs to a place called Ventura. Hopefully it was on the coast.

And once she'd seen the ocean, then what?

Hanna seldom let her emotions so totally govern her decisions. Even marrying Michael had been preceded by a list of pros and cons.

In hindsight, if she had to make the list, perhaps she should have passed on his proposal.

During their senior year in college, Michael Sheridan had swept Hanna off her feet. He was handsome and charming, wooing her as no boy in Durango had, not even Walt. Michael was always waiting outside the university library, where she worked four nights a week as a student assistant, walking her to the apartment she shared with Zoey. Maybe they'd stop for coffee or hot chocolate. Holding hands, kissing at the front door, if Zoey was home. Michael coming in when Zoey wasn't—staying over if Zoey was out of town. Going to his room was too complicated since he lived in a frat house where privacy was almost impossible.

At graduation, she finally introduced him to her family, proud of his dark good looks, the elegant way he wore clothes. His manners. A cut above Durango boys. He'd picked up the check the night they all had dinner, suitably impressing her parents, and for once Callie didn't flirt.

In September, Michael and Hanna were married in the Durango Lutheran church. His parents flew in from Denver; his brother and sister-in-law came from New Jersey. Hanna was sure it was the happiest day of her life.

As soon as the newlyweds moved into a small apartment in Aurora, Michael began law school and Hanna snagged a part time job at the University of Denver library. Her art degree and portfolio already on a back burner. Fledgling watercolorists weren't marketable. The month after he passed the Colorado bar, Lexi was born, Hanna stopped working to take care of the baby, and Michael was hired by a firm specializing in corporate law. By the time Ryan was born, they'd bought a small starter house, and Michael was on track for a partnership that ultimately helped pay for a five-bedroom house near the Denver Country Club. Brooke arrived four years later. Three children and an expensive home pushed Michael to work even harder. Most nights, he came home after the children were in bed. The American dream came at a price.

Oddly enough, Hanna felt that driving away from her family was—if not right—at least okay. She already felt lighter, her head clearer. Less anger. For months, she'd been angry, surprised that anger and love—she hadn't stopped loving them—could exist side by side. She wondered whether other women her age rebelled against their lives. Or was she abnormally selfish? She didn't have anyone to ask. Certainly not her sister. Though Hanna had a few friends in Durango, there was no one with whom she could share this kind of turmoil.

It was nearly dinnertime when Hanna parked at Ventura Harbor, her first sight of the Pacific Ocean, gray in the low light of a fog bank folding over the coastline. The air was moist and sweet, the breeze pushing her hair away from her face. Different smells, strange but not unpleasant. She locked the car and walked to the edge of a grassy park to look at the water stretching into the fog. She'd done it—driven all the way from Durango to the edge of the continent. A quiet satisfaction flicked over her thoughts.

She rented a room at another Holiday Inn and ate fish tacos at Rubio's. One thing Colorado and California had in common was a taste for Americanized Mexican food.

What would she do tomorrow?

Keep driving?

Stop here?

Call Zoey?

She'd been so intent on getting to the coast, she hadn't thought any further. Now she had to do more than escape. She was turning her back on everything that, up to now, had defined her. Jumping off a cliff. She couldn't continue spending this much money on rooms and food. If she wasn't going home for a while, she needed a job and a place where she could cook for herself.

Though she didn't sleep soundly, she at least slept, not waking until it was almost ten, barely enough time to check out, load her luggage into the car, and buy coffee at Starbucks. She drove back to the harbor parking lot to be near the soft swish and slap of the ocean while she drank her coffee. There was something soothing about the water sliding over the sand, then pulling back, as undecided about where it should be as Hanna was.

Having charged her laptop and phone overnight, she listened to the voice mail messages. Each child had left three or four monologues, ranging from furious to whining. Callie left only one, *You go, girl.*

She erased all of them.

On her laptop, she pulled up the file with her Christmas card list, scrolling to the S's and stopping at Zoey Seabrook. Zoey had been her roommate at Boulder, a tanned California surfer who had decided to see what living in ski country was like, transferring her natural athletic ability from the water to snow.

All four years at Boulder, they'd been fast friends, eventually sharing an apartment. Zoey was a bridesmaid at Hanna's wedding, then headed back to California. *I'm just a beach girl after all. I miss the salt air.* A few years later, she married her high school boyfriend. Hanna had been eight months pregnant with Ryan, so she hadn't been able to fly out for Zoey's wedding. In the intervening years, the only times they saw one another was at yearly class reunions. Somehow it was never the right time for Hanna to make a trip to California: Lexi needed braces, Ryan was playing football, Michael wanted a divorce. In the last two years, they'd been e-mailing less often. After Zoey's husband Jonathon died suddenly, she was busy running their successful catering business in a place called Del Mar. Hanna googled a map. To get there, she'd have to drive south through Los Angeles. An unappealing prospect.

# CHAPTER 5

INSTEAD OF CALLING ahead to warn Zoey that she was on the way, Hanna decided to surprise her. Once again, she braved the tangle of freeways, taking 101 South, switching to 405, and finally following I-5 to Del Mar. By the time she left Orange County and was driving along the barren coastline of Camp Pendleton, the Marine Base where Kyle had been stationed, it was mid-afternoon. Having skipped breakfast, she was starving, but there was nowhere to stop until she reached Oceanside. She ate a hamburger and fries in the McDonald's parking lot, then drove another twenty minutes south to Del Mar. After three days on the road, it was suddenly crucial that she find Zoey, that she connect with something or someone familiar. Being footloose had its downside, though footloose never seemed to bother Callie.

She assumed Zoey would be at work. Google told her to exit at Del Mar Heights for Seabrook Catering. On the right side of the off ramp was the Village Shopping Center parking lot. She stopped across from the CVS Pharmacy and entered the phone number for Seabrook, not at all certain what she'd say. Perhaps Zoey was out of town or had sold the business. In one of her recent emails, she'd mentioned the possibility of selling. Corporations and the wealthy residents of the beach communities had been cutting back on the kind of entertaining that was the heart and soul of her business. Zoey had sounded worried.

"Seabrook Catering. How may we help you?"

Zoey's voice. *Thank God.*

"Zoey, it's Hanna."

It took a moment for Zoey to process the words, then "Oh my God! Are you okay? You never call."

"I'm here." *I can't believe I'm here. Can't believe I've done what I've done.*

"Here? You mean here, as in Del Mar?"

"Yes. I'm parked in the Village Shopping Center at the Del Mar Heights off-ramp. How close is that to you?" *Please let it be close. After all those freeways, I don't think I can drive much farther.*

"Close. I'll be there in minutes. What're you driving?"

"A light blue Civic, Colorado plates of course. I'm in front of CVS."

"Stay put." The line went dead.

A few minutes later, Hanna saw Zoey walking toward her, wearing a white bib apron over denim slacks and a bright pink blouse.

By the time Hanna got out of the car, Zoey was in front of her, taking a moment to look at her intently, "Honey, what are you doing here? I'm so glad to see you." Then she wrapped her arms around Hanna. "Can you stay?"

The adrenalin that had propelled Hanna from Durango to the West Coast instantly vanished, and she felt tears sliding down her cheeks. As foolish as it sounded, "I've run away from home." Her voice broke.

Zoey stepped back. "Let's get out of this parking lot. Follow my car," she pointed at the red SUV with the Seabrook Catering logo on the door; "the kitchen is just across the freeway in the Highlands Shopping Center."

Callie'd rarely had to be responsible for another person. Neither of her marriages had required any kind of care giving other than administering hangover remedies. In the three days since Hanna's departure, Callie had inadvertently morphed into the head of Hanna's household. Not a position she was comfortable with. All of a sudden, her nieces and nephew were looking to her for direction. The blind leading the blind.

Instead of figuring out how to survive, Ryan, Lexi and Brooke seemed to be marking time, hoping their mother would come back to rescue them or that Michael would write a check to keep the wolf from the door. Brooke was gone eighty percent of the time, either working or attending classes or hanging out with Dennis. Ryan had at least cut the lawns without prodding but, inside the house, he was clueless. Because his truck still had no gas, he kept asking to borrow Callie's. The third time he asked, she refused. Let him walk.

On Tuesday afternoon, it fell to Callie to explain Hanna's absence to Walt. Looking worried, he came by the house a little after one. "I've been trying Hanna's cell all morning, but she's not answering and she missed our usual lunch."

Since the Sheridan house was out of milk and almost everything else, Callie was in the midst of making a grocery list—not something she was in the habit of doing, especially not for four people with healthy appetites. She'd asked Brooke and Lexi to turn over whatever cash they had—a total of $62.59. No sense asking Ryan. She would have to charge the rest of the grocery tab on one of her credit cards, but she wasn't going to be able to do that for long. She didn't want to touch her checking account until absolutely necessary. One other time, she'd been so broke she'd qualified for food stamps. She wondered if the kids could qualify.

Callie held the kitchen door open for him, "There's some coffee left, but it's been reheating all morning."

"No thanks. I'm mostly a tea drinker. Coffee tears up my stomach. Nice to see you, Callie. Been a while." He sat at the table. "What about Hanna? Is she okay?"

"Hope so. She left early Sunday morning, and we haven't heard from her since. She's not answering our cell messages—probably because we're the reason she left."

"A fight?" That didn't sound like Hanna's style.

"Not the knock down, drag out kind. More the *I'm fed up* kind. Having a house full of people who expect her to take care of them—again—would be part of the reason. But I'd guess there's more to it. When the kids got back from Michael's wedding Saturday night, she told them she was taking a break, and the next morning she was gone. I was playing Bayfield that night and stayed with Louise after closing."

"Where would she go?"

Callie shrugged. "Maybe Zoey's, her college roommate. She's always wanted to visit, but it never worked out. Zoey runs a catering business somewhere in Southern California. I'll try to find a phone number online. I get the feeling Hanna isn't going to call in on her own."

Taking note of the sink full of dirty dishes, he ventured, "How're things around here?"

"Excessive doom and gloom. Brooke's new mantra is *The sky is falling. The sky is falling.* Ryan's keeping out of the way in case someone forces him to get a job. Lexi's probably the most useful. At least she can cook for more than one person. My cooking skills are rusty, and it's too expensive to buy prepared dinners."

"Ryan never called me. I told Hanna I'd find something for him."

Callie frowned, "I didn't know that." She made a mental note to confront Ryan as soon as he turned up.

Walt handed her his business card, "In case Ryan wants to talk to me. He may not like the work, but it pays minimum wage."

"Thanks. If Hanna doesn't come back for a while, they'll need money. I'm going to have to find a gig somewhere since I have no other employable skills." She grinned wryly and pointed to the list. "I have no idea how much food to buy for all of us."

"Send Lexi."

"Can't. Marie's having a well baby checkup at the pediatrician's office."

He stood and picked up his car keys. "I'd help, but I'd be equally bad at four person shopping."

"I'd rather you figure out how to get Ryan to go to work. We have a roof over our heads and utilities. Everything else is up to us, and we're four of the most dysfunctional people you've ever met."

He laughed softly. "At least you haven't lost your sense of humor."

Walt had always been amazed at how different the Sheridan sisters were—Hanna, the prettier of the two, was more serious, the responsible one. Callie was the free spirit, flying in the face of convention. Both were still attractive women. Callie was wiry, a bit sharper around the edges than her sister, who had a softer, sweeter look. That sweetness was the first thing Walt had noticed about her. They'd dated in their senior year, but Hanna was headed for the university. Walt wasn't. Without the grades to get into a four-year college, he'd signed up for the Peace Corps. He loved the work. Loved the people in Zambia, and then there was Lily. Love in an exotic setting. But once their contracts were up, and he brought her to Durango, the ordinariness of Colorado took its toll on their marriage, and several years later Lily went back into the Peace Corps—to Kenya, where she died.

In the years since, he'd focused on his construction business and might have married Mitzi Bradshaw, the widow of Durango's police chief, if Hanna hadn't returned, beaten down by her divorce. While repairing the Meeker house for her, Walt realized the old attraction was still alive and well. To be fair to Mitzi, he'd ended their relationship even though Hanna had made it clear that, for the time being, she was only interested in his friendship. In hindsight, perhaps he'd given her too much time.

And so, once again, she'd disappeared from his life.

Seabrook Catering was in a separate building at the south end of Highlands Shopping Center on El Camino Real. The reception/office walls were covered with bold abstracts, bright orange, red and yellow upholstered couches were arranged around a low, highly polished table piled with books containing pictures of the kinds of events Seabrook specialized in. Behind an enormous glass window was the biggest kitchen Hanna had ever seen, gleaming stainless steel with a crew of three rapidly assembling trays of finger foods.

The moment Zoey and Hanna entered the reception area, a blonde woman wearing a red blazer with the Seabrook logo, hurried over, "Zoey, Mr. Curlew called. There'll be six additional people tonight."

Zoey frowned. "He always pulls that." She dropped her purse onto the curved desk near the door into the kitchen, "that's why we prepare for more people than he predicts. We're covered. Is Terry's crew ready?"

"They've already called in. George and I'll drive everything over and collect the final payment."

"Thanks. Kit, this is my friend Hanna. Hanna, my irreplaceable assistant."

Kit smiled and stretched out her hand, "Nice to meet you. I have to run."

Hanna peered through the window separating the kitchen from the office area. "The kitchen's huge."

"It takes a lot of space to do the cooking as well as the assembling. Then there's the storage for everything to serve large groups. Sometimes this building isn't big enough, and I have to rent extra space. Wait here for a minute and let me check my messages."

Hanna sat on the orange couch, watching as the kitchen crew loaded the trays into refrigerated containers with Seabrook logos and carried them to the panel truck parked at the front door. In the midst of all the activity, she began to relax. Maybe she could stay with Zoey long enough to sort herself out.

Hanna's first California week was heaven.

Every morning, the rhythmic swoosh of the ocean gentled her awake. Smooth white noise sliding into the guest room—its stark white walls complemented with soft beige and blue tones. In the days since she'd been at Zoey's, Hanna hadn't paid attention to time, enjoying a semi-vegetative state. Rising late, strolling the beach, sitting on the deck with iced tea or coffee, being mesmerized by the waves. For the first time in her life, there was nothing on her agenda except showering and fixing her own lunch. One day she never got around to having lunch.

And the world did not end.

Zoey usually left the narrow, two-story house on Ocean Front around seven, rarely returning until six or seven at night, bringing food from work for their dinner. So far, Zoey was giving Hanna plenty of time and space. On the surface, it looked as though Hanna was simply taking a break. But there were subtle layers beneath that surface, emotions and memories she'd ignored too long. Somewhere in her evolution, she'd skipped a significant life stage. Like a child who walked but never crawled, she'd gone straight from college to parenthood, leaving no time for Hanna-the-person to bloom. What that bloom would have been like, she had no idea. That might be the real reason she was here. Her children were simply the catalyst. Eventually, Zoey would ask what was bothering her—sooner than Hanna would have answers. In the meantime, she wrapped herself in peaceful communion with the Pacific.

Because most catering events occurred on weekends, Zoey worked on Sundays too. The Sunday after Hanna's arrival, Zoey was back at the house by eleven, full of purpose.

"Okay my friend. It's time to call your children or your sister or your boyfriend."

"I don't have a boyfriend." *Not exactly true.*

"They have all called me at work. Callie on Wednesday, Lexi on Thursday, Ryan on Friday, Brooke on Saturday and this morning someone named Walt. I don't want to push you, but I don't have time to fend off everyone in Durango. They're getting cranky because they're pretty sure I'm lying about your being here. You know I don't lie well."

Having just returned from walking on the beach, Hanna was wiping her sandy feet with the towel Zoey kept outside the sliding glass door. "I suppose I could call Walt."

"You just said you don't have a boyfriend."

"I don't, but Walt won't guilt me."

Zoey did an about face and headed for the front door. "I have three events today, but when I get home, we will talk."

Hanna lucked out. When she called Walt's cell, it went to voice mail. *Hi, it's Hanna. Yes, I'm with Zoey for the time being. I'd appreciate you telling Callie that Zoey's not happy about getting all the phone calls. Sorry I didn't give you a heads up, but I left unexpectedly. Thanks.*

She quickly broke the connection and sat staring at the phone in her hand. Not a very friendly message. Walt would be genuinely worried. The others were simply annoyed by her departure. If she let down her guard and went back to being the *good, dependable* Hanna, she'd be trapped again. No, it was too early to abandon *selfish* Hanna. *Responsible* Hanna would have to stay out of the picture for a while longer.

Because Walt had promised to drive his mother to Farmington for her annual two-week visit with her sister, his cell phone was off when Hanna called. He'd never gotten around to installing a hands free system in his truck. While he was at his aunt's, he returned Hanna's call but ended up in her voice mail again. Frustrating. She clearly did not want to talk to her family. Or him.

He drove into Durango around four o'clock and went straight to Hanna's. Barefooted, wearing a pair of shorts and a faded Broncos t-shirt that was probably Ryan's, Callie was washing dishes, a country western song blaring from the radio on the windowsill.

Walt turned the volume down, picked up a dishtowel, and began drying a plate. "She left me a message a few hours ago."

Callie rinsed the soap off her hands, "Let's have some iced tea." He finished drying the plates while she poured tea over ice. "I don't have anything to serve with it. Yesterday there were cookies. Today, no cookies. Ryan must eat non-stop during the night."

"Is he home?"

She nodded toward the family room. "The Broncos' game."

"Good. I'll corner him before I leave."

He sat down, taking a long sip of the tea. "Hanna left the message while I was driving my mother over to Farmington. But she didn't answer when I called back." He skipped the *I'm sorry* part of her message. It was meant for him, not the family. A positive note.

"What'd she say?"

"Just that she was with Zoey and to tell you Zoey didn't appreciate all the calls."

"Understandable. The only number we had was for her business."

"Have you ever met Zoey?"

"A few times when they were in college and at Hanna's wedding. Hanna usually brought her here for Thanksgiving. I remember she had short, wavy dark hair and the tan of tans. She grew up on the beach, loved surfing. Did some competitive skiing for the university. I was still in high school so they couldn't be bothered spending time with me. I think Zoey was widowed a couple years ago, but I might be wrong."

"This Zoey—will she let Hanna stay with her?"

"Probably. Hanna's had a thing about seeing the ocean. Zoey's influence, I suppose."

He concentrated on his tea. "I guess we wait."

"Apparently. When Hanna makes up her mind, she doesn't let go easily. It's taken her a long time to decide she wants time for herself. This phase could last a while."

"Are you going to stay with the kids?"

Callie shrugged. "Until I find work, and I do need work. I can't live on air."

"You'll go where the work is?"

"Of course." She met his eyes—almost black, compelling and straightforward. With Walt, what you saw was what he was. Not many musicians came with that quality.

"And then the kids will be on their own."

"They're good kids, but helpless as babes. Even Lexi, who has a baby of her own. It took me two days to convince them that Hanna's housekeeper had to be let go. We, they, can't afford her. You'd think I'd suggested selling them into slavery."

"Not much on housework?"

Callie half-laughed. "Hanna has spoiled them all. Brooke and Ryan have no idea how to manage money, how much things cost. Part of that is Michael's fault. His answer to everything is to write a check."

"Does he know?"

"I don't know. He may still be on his honeymoon." She made a face. "I never was a fan."

He drank the last of the tea and put his glass into the soapy water. "Let's see what I can do with Ryan."

Ryan was lying on the couch in front of the TV, eating popcorn, a can of Red Bull on the floor within reach.

Walt sat on the arm of the couch, "What's the score?"

"24 to 30, Chargers' favor. But there's still another quarter."

"Manning's had some good games."

"Ummmm."

"Are you interested in working for me until you find something else? I could use the help." It was actually the truth. The young man who'd been doing cleanup had moved to Grand Junction.

Ryan sat up and reached for the can of Red Bull.

"I don't know anything about construction."

"Not necessary for the moment. My crew will show you what they need."

"You mean like cleaning up?"

"And other things. Minimum wage. I can usually promise twenty to thirty hours a week, depending on the jobs. I'm assuming you're going to need gas money." Walt stopped short of saying *since your mother isn't going to provide your spending money anymore*.

For a few minutes, there was only the shouting of the football fans. Walt kept his eyes on the screen as though what Ryan decided didn't matter. In truth, it only mattered because of Hanna.

Finally, "How much is minimum wage?" Like that was a bargaining point. Walt wanted to laugh.

"$7.78 an hour."

"I'll think about it." Ryan lay down on the couch again. Conversation over.

Walt started back to the kitchen. "Don't think too long. I need an answer by five o'clock tomorrow." Having a deadline might light a fire.

Callie was scrubbing the sink. Softly, "Well?"

"He's taking it under advisement."

She clapped a soapy hand over her mouth to keep from laughing out loud.

He smiled in agreement. "Exactly. I'll keep in touch."

# CHAPTER 6

IN RETROSPECT, ZOEY'S debriefing had a surprisingly cleansing effect, encouraging Hanna to unload some of the conflicting emotions she'd been struggling with since she left Durango.

*Guilt: Mothers are supposed to mother, regardless.*

*Entitlement: At some point, I deserve time off for good behavior.*

When Zoey came home a little after four, she brought a bottle of expensive champagne and poured it into two glasses. "Left over from yesterday's wedding reception. A little bubbly to smooth the rough edges of the world."

Hanna took a sip of hers, "Very nice. Do you always get to keep leftovers?"

"No. But we've done several events for this family, so they wanted to thank us." Zoey was sitting in a white leather recliner, the footrest pulled out. "I'm not moving for the rest of the day. Feels like several trains have run over me." Another sip, "First, tell me about Lexi. How come she's back home?"

That answer was simple. "In May, Kyle was deployed to Afghanistan for six to eight months. He might come home in December, more likely February. In spite of being a bright and loving young woman, Lexi's never been very good at being on her own. She went from home to a sorority house to marriage. She panicked about taking care of Marie on her own, so they put their furniture in storage and he drove her to my place a week before he deployed."

"If memory serves, she's never actually lived in Durango. Does she have any local friends?"

"Not yet, but thanks to Marie's pediatrician, she's met a few other young mothers. One thing Lexi's good at is making friends wherever she is. She always sees the best in people, and that paves the way for friendship."

Zoey poured herself more champagne, "How will she fare with you gone?"

Hanna shrugged, "I honestly don't know. She's managing Marie fairly well and she has Kyle's paycheck. So long as nothing unexpected happens, she should be able to cope. However, she's never had to face an emergency on her own. Michael and I were always there to run interference. Kyle took over for us until his deployment."

"But you don't want to run interference right now." Zoey wasn't asking this time.

Hanna clamped her lips together, feeling as though she might cry but unsure what the tears were for. *Just like Brooke.*

"Sorry." Zoey poured herself more champagne.

They sat quietly, Hanna staring out the picture window at the soft gray fog rolling onto the beach, Zoey staring at Hanna.

Finally, Hanna walked up to the window, her back to Zoey, her hands jammed into the pockets of her cropped pants. "It's not rational—my being here—but I just—well—Callie showing up didn't help. She comes and goes at the most inconvenient moments. This time I was out of beds." Hanna sighed. "I've never had the opportunity to come and go as I pleased." Another sigh. "And Michael's going to be a father. Two weeks ago, he married the woman he divorced me for. It's not so much that Michael and the kids are the problem—well maybe they are. Then there were the photos." She knew she was making a mess of the explanation. "I wasn't in them much. If you only had the pictures to go on, it looks like I wasn't part of their lives, just recording what *they* did. Useful but not important. It sounds silly when I say it. Your family is supposed to matter more than anything. Family first. But suddenly, well, I wanted to come first, so I left. I've never in my life been irresponsible like this."

After a few minutes, "Tell me about Ryan."

Hanna walked back to her chair, picked up her champagne glass, then set it down without drinking from it. "He seems stuck. He worked really hard in college—great GPA—but the job market is still soft, and he refuses to try just any old job in the interim. He wants the *right* job. So he's broke, living off his sisters and me. Michael wants him to go to law school, but Ry isn't interested. I'm glad about that. I don't think he's cut out for the aggressiveness of the legal world. That said, I have no idea how he'll function now that I'm gone. I've been too easy on him, thinking he just needed time to unwind from studying. But it's been almost four months—" She couldn't throw him out to sink or swim. Being the bad cop was hard. Being the absent cop had perks.

Zoey looked at her watch, "I'm hungry," and pulled her cell phone from her pocket. "Pizza?"

"You order and I'll pay. I need to start earning my keep."

When the order was in, Zoey resumed her questioning, "What about Brooke? Does she still have that glorious halo of curls?"

"Yes, though she has to wear it tied back because she's waitressing at *Steamworks*."

"I remember how good their Gouda burger was."

"A thousand years ago." *Things had been so much easier when she was twenty.* "Brooke has more get up and go than Ry and Lexi. She's stubborn, fiery, bossy. A little bit anal. She's got a boyfriend—the ever-charming Dennis—so she's opted to stay home and attend Fort Lewis instead of CSU. Michael is furious, but Brooke has outlasted him. My mother used to accuse me of being stubborn, but Brooke is the poster child for stubborn. Of the three, she's the one who'll pick up her socks and get on with things—as soon as she stops crying. She cries over everything." After several minutes, "I'd been looking forward to some freedom. No day-to-day kid responsibilities and since I lost my job—"

"At the library?" Zoey interrupted.

"Yeah, in April. So I started thinking about taking some short trips. Maybe over to Santa Fe or driving here to see you. And then, wham. They were all back, expecting me to take care of them."

"Callie?"

"She'll stay until she gets a job, but substitute parenting isn't her style. She actually may drive the other three crazy."

"Do they really expect you to keep taking care of them, or do you just think they do?"

"Trust me, they expect it."

"And you're used to doing it."

Zoey was always good at cutting to the chase. Hanna didn't respond—couldn't. Fortunately the doorbell rang. She headed for the door. "I've got it."

Two days later, Zoey waded in again, not with questions but with a proposition. She'd slept late—a rare luxury—and was drinking a second cup of coffee on the deck.

Carrying a bowl of cold cereal, Hanna joined her. "You're still home."

"A lazy morning, I don't need to go in until noon."

"Do you ever get a day off?"

"Not often enough. It's a 24/7 job, kind of like parenting."

Hanna took note of the comparison and asked a question of her own. "How is Stephanie?"

Zoey shrugged. "Fair question, given my questions about your kids. She's doing her student teaching in Atlanta, preferring not to share the details of her day-to-day life with me. Yours are ricocheting home, mine rarely answers my texts. I'm barely on speaking terms with my daughter. I shouldn't be hassling you about your children."

"I probably needed to talk. Do you?"

Zoey shrugged again. "Steph took her dad's death hard—well, we both did—but in different ways. She was appalled that I kept working even as we were planning the funeral. I think she expected me to don sackcloth or go into a convent. I was appalled that she was appalled. It went south from there." Zoey abruptly changed the subject. "How are you at table decorations?"

"Following someone's instructions or dreaming them up on my own?"

"Both."

"I tried my hand at making centerpieces when Michael and I used to entertain his clients. Nothing terribly remarkable. Why?"

"One of the young women who's been doing them for me is seven months pregnant and has been put on bed rest for the next two months. I need someone to fill in until she can come back. Terry can't handle everything by herself. Not every client wants us to help with decorating. Maybe fifty percent. A lot of people hire their own florist or decorator. Some design their own events."

"I wouldn't know what to do."

Zoey continued as though Hanna hadn't responded, "Your art degree should give you a foundation to build on. And you can ask for help when you need it."

Zoey watched Hanna's expression move from resistance to tentative interest. Yesterday, when Isabel told Zoey she needed to stop working, Zoey had struggled to hold off the panic that threatened. *Not right now!* She did the managing, not the presenting. This morning, it had occurred to her that Hanna might be the solution. "I pay by the job. You'd do maybe three or four jobs a week. Heading into the holidays, most people will want seasonal themes; I already have a lot of supplies in storage, so it's just a matter of putting everything together. Isabel can offer advice so long as she doesn't get out of bed."

Listening to Zoey's explanation, Hanna felt her heart beat a bit faster than usual. The idea was intriguing. And daunting.

Late Monday afternoon, Walt was standing in what remained of the Mendozas' kitchen, making sure the crew hadn't missed anything. A blank slate ready for the new kitchen Walt had designed. Tomorrow, the electrician would start the rewiring. In two days the plumber, then the painting crew. The new appliances would be delivered next week, and Walt had just finished staining the cedar cabinets he'd built—he loved feeling the wood come alive in his hands. Installing them would come later. Depending on the subcontractors' unpredictable schedules, the job should be in the finishing stages in three weeks. But setting a specific completion date was never a good idea. The Mendozas were staying with their son's family—already complaining about being displaced.

"Walt?"

He turned.

Looking like he'd prefer being almost anywhere else, Ryan Sheridan was standing in the kitchen doorway.

"Hi Ryan. Can I help you?" Walt was fairly sure Ryan had come about the job, but he wanted him to ask. Lesson one in applying for work.

"You mentioned a job."

"I did. Are you interested?"

"Guess so. I need to earn some money. This morning the washing machine crapped out and, well, my aunt says there's no money to fix it or buy a new one so, since I'm not doing anything worthwhile, it's going to be my job to take all the laundry to the laundromat," he made *laundromat* sound like a dirty word, "several times a week."

Walt struggled to keep a straight face. Good for Callie; Hanna never laid down the law like that. She wasn't very good about disciplining her kids, preferring to inconvenience herself instead of making them do their share. The situation was funny and not funny.

"Come by my office tomorrow at 8 a.m. It's on 550, south of town."

Grudgingly, "I know where it is."

"Good. Talk to Gail; she'll help you with the paper work. Be sure you have your social security number and wear clothes that can get dirty. Then I'll send you out to the college." Cleaning up after a job was the best way to break in a green employee. Ryan undoubtedly would feel badly used. He probably had no skills beyond those needed for the classroom.

By Saturday afternoon, Ryan was beat. Every part of his body hurt, parts he didn't even know existed were screaming. Four days of back breaking work. Sweeping, bagging what he'd swept, hauling what he'd bagged. Then being a go-fer for the men hanging the doors on the storage sheds—*Hold this, get me that.* One of the men kept calling him Runyon, no matter how often Ryan corrected the mistake. His life had fallen into a rabbit hole. When he got home, all he wanted was a hot shower and to be left alone. Instead, Callie announced she wanted a family meeting after dinner. A meeting that did not go well.

Callie had hoped that openly discussing their collective plight might give her some idea about how best to get through the next weeks. Hopefully, it wouldn't be months. She wanted to be someplace else—soon—preferably working. However, instead of pulling together, the siblings resurrected a lifetime of wrongs, and the evening degenerated into childish squabbles, forcing Callie to play bad cop.

"Enough! Judas Priest. Six year olds behave better."

In a grand sulk because Lexi had just attacked her for being gone all the time and not doing her share, Brooke lashed out at Callie. "How would you know? You've never had six year olds."

With difficulty, Callie stifled a retort, which undoubtedly would only have made matters worse. Musicians were easier to deal with. No wonder she'd skipped motherhood.

Ryan was lying on his back on the living room floor. "Get to the point. I'm exhausted."

"Poor baby." Brooke stuck out her lower lip.

For the second time, "Enough! Give me five minutes of silence." When they were finally quiet, Callie outlined their situation. "Hanna's charge cards, the insurance, utilities and property taxes come directly out of her checking account, still generously funded by your father. Anything else we need is on our watch. I've already cancelled the newspaper and let Mrs. Biggs go"—a painful conversation she didn't want to revisit. "We'll be using a laundromat until there's money to fix the washing machine."

At the mention of laundry, Ryan sat up. "Now that I'm Walt's indentured servant, do I have to do ALL the laundry?"

"No. Each of us needs to be responsible for our own, including sheets and towels. I'll add the cleaning rags and tea towels to my stuff. And I'm moving into Hanna's bedroom. Sleeping on the pullout is killing my back."

Nobody objected—probably because it didn't involve money or work.

"Food and gas are our biggest problems right now. Lexi, we need more of Kyle's check and yours too, Brooke. As soon as Ryan gets a check, that will help. Until then, lots of pasta and beans, and no eating out. Ryan can pack a lunch for himself. Brooke gets fed at the restaurant when she's working. On the refrigerator is a cleaning schedule for the bathrooms and kitchen. Your rooms are your problem. Anything else can get cleaned whenever."

"How long are these rules going to last?" Brooke grumbled.

"Who knows? I don't see your mother coming back soon. We've got to function without that option."

From Lexi, "How long are you staying?"

"Until I get work. I have a little cash, but I've already drawn on it. Walt knows of a restaurant and bar between here and Purgatory that's looking for entertainment. He's going to get me an audition."

Ryan stood up. "Good old Walt to the rescue. Be careful. He's already rescued me, and I'm at least ten years older than I was last week."

# Chapter 7

It took Hanna only one day to understand that decorating catered events wasn't as easy as Zoey made it sound. Her first assignment was a small bridal shower scheduled for the third Saturday in September, a dozen guests, finger food and cupcakes. Should be a snap. But after poring over all of Zoey's photo files of past showers, buying bridal magazines, and surfing for ideas on the web, she had too much information and went into creative gridlock.

Panicked, she arrived at Seabrook just as Zoey was coming out of the kitchen, licking chocolate off a spoon. "Max makes the best ganache on earth. What's up?"

"I can't think of anything that's good enough for the Scarlotti shower."

Another failure. She was failing at everything. Her children couldn't function on their own, she didn't have a permanent job, and there wasn't anything or anyone she was passionate about. Running away hadn't solved anything. "You need to get someone else for Isabel's job. I don't think I'm capable of doing this. The shower's in five days, and I have no workable ideas."

"Nonsense." Zoey sat down at her desk. "You're scaring yourself. You aren't decorating Buckingham Palace. It's just a shower."

"But—"

Zoey was firm. "You can do it. More to the point, I *really need* you to do it. Are you not the one who left home to see what the world had to offer? If you're going to quit before you start, you might as well go back to Durango."

Harsher than Hanna expected.

Momentarily stunned, she wasn't able respond. She so wanted her life to be better, freer, more interesting. She'd come to Zoey's because—because she couldn't seem to help herself. Now Zoey needed Hanna's help.

"Have you called Isabel?"

"No. It seems like cheating." Hanna had never been good at asking for help.

"Call."

Hanna called and spent the afternoon in Isabel Tremont's bright yellow bedroom. Isabel was propped up with pillows, surrounded by books, the TV remote, and an iPad, her pale blonde hair braided into two pigtails. After only one week, she was already tired of lying in bed all day and was eager to help Hanna get her feet under her. "My mind's already turned to mush."

Isabel asked Hanna to bring her several files and a large newsprint pad from the desk in the dining room. With a black marker, Isabel quickly diagramed the kind of timeline she typically followed for each job and walked Hanna through a schedule for the shower. "For an event like this, Zoey probably has enough supplies—glue guns and pins and tape for assembly. There are various sets of China, as well as paper plates and napkins in all colors of the rainbow. Be sure to check on what Terry's using so you don't accidentally take what she needs. She's good at leaving a paper trail. You'll need to leave one too. If you're looking for special designs, the wholesalers will help you. For big events—fifty guests and over—we rent dishes and silverware." From her files, Isabel pulled out lists of florists, rental companies and paper product wholesalers in the San Diego area. "My 3-in-1 printer is in the dining room next to the computer. Make copies of these for yourself."

By dinnertime, they had a plan—mostly Isabel's plan—with some of Hanna's input. Baby steps.

The serving table would be covered with a white cloth—Zoey had dozens of tablecloths in all shapes and sizes. The napkins and paper plates would be in blues, greens and teal, the centerpiece a pair of sheer green butterflies outlined with wire. "The butterflies were ordered for a shower two months ago, but we never used them. The mother of the bride suddenly remembered her daughter hated green. The neurotic-people factor is the only downside to this job. Anyhow—use flowers, maybe blue daises, with the butterflies and you're in business. Be sure to take a picture for our files when you have everything in place. Zoey has a supply of throwaway cameras."

Her head spinning with lists and phone numbers, Hanna left when Isabel's husband Greg came home with their six-year old son, Charlie.

She just might be able to do this. With Isabel's help.

Even though the shower wasn't until 7 p.m., Hanna was at Seabrook by 9 a.m. Saturday, checking and rechecking every step of the process. Plates with teal flowers, silverware, cups and glasses, napkins in complementary greens and blues. A coffee urn and a variety of teas. Since the bride didn't drink alcohol, Hanna didn't have to worry about wine or champagne.

She'd enlisted the help of Lyn Brashers, a member of the kitchen staff who was always happy to work extra hours. At five o'clock, they carefully loaded everything into Hanna's car and headed to the house in one of the new tracts above Solana Beach, a two-story stucco with a red tile roof, a three car garage and professionally manicured landscaping.

When Hanna and Lyn arrived, the serving table was set up on the patio, strings of lights and Led candles softening the dusk. The evening was still pleasantly warm, even with the ocean breeze. By now it would be jacket weather in Durango, and no one would think of planning a party outside.

The woman giving the shower was the bride's aunt, a well-known criminal lawyer used to entertaining and giving instructions. Balancing what the hostess wanted Hanna to do with what Hanna had prepared required delicate dance moves. Zoey hadn't warned her about needing a degree in psychology. That made Hanna think of Ryan. *Had he found a job? What was he doing? What were all of them doing?* She couldn't seem to keep Durango out of her head tonight.

It took an hour and a half to arrange everything, taking special care with the centerpiece for the serving table and the miniature sparkly butterflies placed alongside the smaller tables arranged near the patio couches and chairs. As Lyn and Hanna were finishing, Kit and one of the cooks arrived to set up the food. Another crew would clean up around ten o'clock.

Kit surveyed the tables and smiled at Hanna. "Looks great." She reached for the camera Hanna was holding. "I'll take the pictures. You look beat."

Back in her car, Hanna laid her red Seabrook blazer on the back seat and finally let herself relax. "We did it. I've been so nervous."

Lyn smiled. "It'll get easier. Isabel was a bundle of nerves at first too."

It'd been five weeks since Hanna had driven away from Durango and her guilt about stonewalling her kids was beginning to fester. Though she regularly skimmed her emails and listened to her voice mail, she hadn't answered anything from her family. Brooke, always the most persistent of her children, was still emailing every day; yesterday she'd asked, once again, why Hanna had abandoned them. Hanna hadn't thought of her departure as abandonment. Mostly because she'd been focusing on herself. What she did or didn't have. What she needed.

The day following the bridal shower, she was sitting on Zoey's deck, her laptop open, ready to tell her family about this new life. Sending them all the same email, instead of calling, was undoubtedly taking the coward's way out, but telling them what she was doing seemed a safe way to reopen communication. She had to start somewhere.

Hi:

The last weeks have been really different for me. It took me four days to get to Zoey's in Del Mar. She has a two-story house right on the beach with steps leading from the deck to the sand. Beautiful sunsets. I love the sound of the waves.

I take a lot of walks and have begun running short distances. I'm up to three miles four or five days a week. Everyone out here runs or walks. I've learned that running on the sand is really difficult.

Zoey's catering company keeps her very busy. I'm helping out with the decorating for some of her events. I just finished working on a bridal shower. I'd love to hear what all of you are doing, *but I'd appreciate it if you'd not ask when I'm coming back or why I did this to you.*

All my love, Mom.

She hadn't explained her reasons for leaving or apologized. Still impossible. They probably weren't ready to understand anyway. She didn't write to Walt; explaining to him the real reasons for her flight would be harder. She wanted to say *I miss talking to you. Please don't give up on me. I just need time*. She did miss talking to him. Appreciated not having to explain herself or apologize. He always seemed to like her just as she was. Leaving may have hurt him more than the children.

That she did regret.

With her first check from Seabrook, Hanna went clothes shopping. October in Southern California was still warm, but subtle hints that fall would eventually arrive sent her in search of warmer clothing. In her rush to leave Durango, she'd packed only warm weather clothing and a rain jacket. There were plenty of sweaters and jackets in her Durango closet, but she didn't want to ask Callie or Lexi to send her anything. Didn't want to confess that she wasn't going home in the foreseeable future. So she drove north to the outlet stores in Carlsbad to shop for cool weather clothes: a cardigan, a fiber-filled jacket, a fleece top, and several long sleeved t-shirts.

Most important, a pair of running shoes to replace the Reeboks she'd been using. They weren't meant for long distance running. She'd forgotten how good she felt after a run, lighter, energized, and she was sleeping better than she had slept those last weeks in Durango. She was considering training for Carlsbad's half marathon in January. Which must mean she was staying over the holidays. She'd never missed spending Christmas with her children. But right now, not going home for the holidays seemed okay.

As soon as she sent the email, Brooke's messages disappeared but, three days later, she received a short email from Lexi, containing a recent picture of Marie in peach-colored pajamas. She was almost six months old, her fine fair hair, compliments of her father, now long enough for a pink barrette. She was smiling the same smile Lexi had smiled at that age. Hanna teared up. Her granddaughter was changing.

The email was "written" by Marie.

Dear Nana: I miss you. Most of the time, I sleep through the night now. My Mama's happy about that. I really like applesauce and cereal. Uncle Ry gave me some ice cream but it was too rich and too cold for my tummy so I threw up all over him. Marie.

The salt-scent and low rumbling of the Pacific Ocean enriched Hanna's days. Standing at its edge or relaxing on Zoey's deck, Hanna spent hours letting the surf hypnotize her, but she still hadn't tried swimming in it. Each time she ventured into the water, the waves relentlessly chased her back onto the sand. Frustrated by her timidity, she finally asked Zoey what she was doing wrong. "Kids swim in the ocean, so it can't be all that hard."

"This afternoon, if I get home before dark, I'll help you. I haven't been in the water since summer, mostly because the water isn't all that warm this time of year. At best, in mid-summer it's 70 degrees, probably several degrees cooler now."

And so at 3:30 that afternoon, they stood at the water's edge, Zoey in a bright pink bikini that she still looked good in and Hanna in a one-piece navy blue tank. After three children, no way would she have worn a bikini in any color.

"Keep in mind that you should never swim alone because there's no lifeguard here. To be safe, you should walk down to Powerhouse Park. The lifeguards can tell you when it's safe to swim or if there's a rip current."

"What's that?"

"A current that runs parallel to the beach and is stronger than most swimmers realize until it's too late. It will pull you where it wants to go, and you might not be able to swim back. Not a good idea to think the ocean's benign. I got caught in a rip a couple of times when I was a teenager."

"Maybe I don't want to do this."

"Sure you do. Just be wise. Of course, we're doing just what I told you not to do—swimming at an unguarded beach." Zoey grabbed her hand and began walking into the surf. When the first calf-high wave slapped Hanna, she paused. "Keep going," Zoey tugged, "walk through it." When a bigger wave came at them, Zoey released her hand, "Dive under it." With the skill born of living most of her life at the beach, Zoey disappeared beneath the water. Not quite sure how to dive into a wave, Hanna stood still too long and got knocked down, the wave washing over her. When it retreated, she scrambled to her feet, struggling for balance and breath, feeling like a fool. Zoey was already about fifty yards beyond her.

It took three more tries before Hanna got through the waves. Her dive was not pretty, but she sputtered her way to the surface on the other side, searching the horizon for Zoey, who was now about a hundred yards south. Since Hanna was already tired, trying to catch Zoey was a bad idea. She swam a few yards parallel to the beach to get the feel of the water, then turned back toward the shore, letting the waves push her in. When she could touch bottom, she stood up, her legs wobbly, and walked the rest of the way. As soon as she reached the spot where they'd left their towels, she sat down. She'd done it. Finally. She gave herself a mental high five. Next time, she'd do better, build up her strength. The sun was sliding into the fog bank sitting off shore, the breeze making her shiver.

Zoey reached the shore a few minutes later and sank down beside Hanna. "Did you like it?" Zoey had always delighted in the kinds of physical challenges that didn't come easily to Hanna.

"Sorta scary. But maybe it'll get easier." Like everything else in her new life.

Zoey stood up. "Let's go in; it's getting cold out here."

# CHAPTER 8

CALLIE HAD BEEN in Durango nearly two months.

Not since high school, had she stayed in town this long. Usually it took only two or three weeks for her music network to kick in, and she'd have a new job. This hiatus was different and—though she hated to admit it—worrisome. Every connection seemed to have vanished, including Jeremy Malik, her agent, who was rumored to be in London. It had been nearly a decade since she'd played with headliners, gradually working her way down to the likes of Leo's band. Living paycheck to paycheck or being temporarily out of a job had never bothered her before because she always landed on her feet. This time, she wasn't sure she could land at all.

And if she didn't?

Her parents' house had always been the safety net that kept her from sleeping in her truck or on the streets. Now, instead of spending a relaxing week or two between jobs, she was coping with her sister's adult children. Undoubtedly some sort of penance. Though she'd been quick to tell them they needed to shape up, help themselves and move on—she was a little afraid of her own advice. Afraid she might never get another job performing. She loved music. It fed her soul and body like nothing else, certainly no man, ever had. Unfortunately, she possessed no other marketable skills. The thought of having to resort to giving guitar lessons or working retail was interfering with her sleep. And Callie almost never had trouble sleeping.

Durango wasn't a terrible place, just seriously conservative and boring. This was *huntin' n fishin'* territory. Unless you were into outdoor sports, there wasn't much in the way of entertainment that interested Callie. Coming back here probably hadn't been easy for Hanna either. And now Hanna had gone looking for greener pastures. Responsible, conventional Hanna was hanging out on a Southern California beach, and Callie was stuck in Durango.

With children!

This afternoon, Walt was introducing her to the owner of Mountain Grub—an upscale restaurant popular with the ski crowd due to descend on southwestern Colorado. She'd spent the morning going through her sheet music files, picking out a few country western pieces, one or two folk favorites and some smooth jazz. Walt had no idea what the restaurant was looking for. All he knew was that the owner, Saul White, wanted live background music for the dinner crowd on weekends. She hoped he didn't want elevator music. Not that she couldn't play that type—and would. She needed the money. The Henderson Post Office was dutifully forwarding her mail, including the insurance renewal on the truck and two very large credit card bills. She hadn't been in such a financial squeeze since her first divorce when Billy had cleaned out their joint account and disappeared. Almost twenty years ago. In those days, she was younger and prettier—qualities that had probably helped her get work. Now, she was over the forty hill, still attractive, but middle-aged didn't sell as well as young.

She dug out her best denim pants and ironed a lemon/lime silk blouse. With her leather jacket and low-heeled boots, she looked Western-cool, not too reserved, not too hippy. She preferred hippy.

Walt picked her up just before three o'clock. She'd known him since he and Hanna had dated in high school, liked him. His quiet masculinity always suggested banked fires—and Callie was a sucker for banked fires—but she was pretty sure he was saving those fires for Hanna. Only helping Callie to indirectly help Hanna.

Today, she'd take any help she could get.

While Callie was setting up, Walt waited on a stool in the bar. Even though the bar wasn't open yet, Saul brought him a bottle of beer. "On the house. Consider it your finder's fee. You forgot to tell me she was pretty."

Walt smiled at his friend. "You didn't request pretty, just music."

Before she began playing, Callie and Saul talked for a long time; then he went to the other side of the dining room, and she became the guitarist Walt had heard about but never heard play. Curved over the guitar, deftly coaxing music from the strings, she seemed transported to some secret place. Whenever Callie was playing, deep calm wrapped itself around her—a warm confidence that the music was playing itself. At those moments, she was incandescent.

Her first guitar teacher—the lessons had been a Christmas gift when she was ten—told her parents she was a natural. "I've never had a student progress so quickly." Years later, as a music major surrounded by professors and students equally passionate about music, she knew she'd found her life. Nights and weekends, she played with any group she could find or practiced alone in a corner of the dorm's living room. Playing was all that mattered.

The summer between her freshman and sophomore years, she toured California with a university band calling itself *Mountain High*. The group's saxophonist had long fingers and a mop of dark red hair. Billy Whitmore could massage a melody so beautifully, so erotically, that tears would fill Callie's eyes. She was unabashedly in love with his talent and his charm. For most of her sophomore year, they lived in his bachelor-basic studio apartment off campus, skipping classes and playing gigs far into the night, sometimes getting paid, sometimes not.

Her parents had no idea she was flunking out of the university. When she and Billy were hired by *The Color of Sound*, a Denver band that had already cut a couple of CD's and was headed for the

East Coast, she called her parents to tell them she was dropping out and going on the road. They were not pleased.

She never looked back, never regretted her choice.

When Saul strolled from the back of the dining room to where Callie was sitting, she'd been playing for half an hour, lost in the familiar magic. He pulled a chair from one of the tables and sat facing her.

"You do know that you're probably too good to be playing in Durango." His voice was low and raspy. Rather sexy.

She looked into a face weathered by hours spent on ski slopes. Kind eyes that smiled. "Yeah. But I need the work." *No sense lying.*

"You certainly know what to do with that guitar. When can you start?"

"Yesterday." So hard to say straight out that she was almost broke, that for the first time in her life she was responsible for other people. She hadn't planned on being responsible. Looking after herself was occupation enough.

"I need music on Fridays, Saturdays and Sundays, five to eight. Right now, I can only pay scale. I assume you're in the union?"

"Yes." Though she wondered whether her dues were paid up. "You should know that some of my selections are my own." Actually, much of what she'd just played was hers.

"Even better. See you Friday." He reached out and shook her hand. "Is this enough for our contract?"

She could only nod, her throat suddenly tight, surprised that getting the job touched her that deeply.

As soon as Saul walked away, Walt slid off the bar stool and took the guitar case from her. "I've never heard you perform before. I'm impressed."

She gathered up her music and stuffed it into the worn black leather folder purchased back when she wasn't counting pennies. "Thanks, let's get out of here."

Once they were outside. “Is he going to call?”

“Doesn’t need to. We shook on it. I start this Friday.”

“Saul’s a good friend. When I was doing the remodel on the restaurant, he trusted me to do the job, stayed out of my way, and paid on time. Can’t ask for more.”

“At least this job will pay for food and keep my truck running. It’s making some strange noises.” She was aware she was underplaying the moment—afraid the job was too good to be true. Even though this wasn’t New York or Chicago or Vegas, she was again going to be paid for making music. She hadn’t felt this good since the afternoon before the bar fight in Vegas.

It had been three years since Lexi’d felt winter coming. While she and Kyle were at Pendleton, they’d been quickly seduced by the Southern California weather. Durango’s cooler days had sent her to Walmart to buy warm clothing for Marie, fleeces, a hooded jacket, leggings, sweaters and mittens. Her own winter wardrobe was still stored in her mother’s attic and probably out of style. But after she’d outfitted Marie, there wasn’t much left to spend on herself—except for a pair of rain boots.

Her retreat to Durango hadn’t turned out the way she’d envisioned. She wanted her mother to help with Marie, to teach her about babies and mothering, and to keep her company while Kyle was gone. Instead, after three months Hanna had decamped. Now there was only Callie, who had absolutely no experience with children. However, the guitar did have a calming effect on the baby and, when Callie practiced into the early morning hours, Marie slept through the night.

Lexi and Kyle kept in touch via email and used Skype whenever he could get access to a computer equipped with the device. The Sunday afternoon before Halloween, she dressed Marie in the tiny costume she’d bought—an orange jumpsuit covered with pumpkins that could double as pajamas after the holiday. She'd washed Marie's hair so it was softly curled against her face. "We'll let Daddy see how pretty your hair is."

Each time she saw Kyle, he looked older. The Afghan sun had given him a deep tan; his usually thick fair hair was cropped so close that she could see his scalp. She hated that look. But his gray/violet eyes were the same and, when they saw Marie, they softened. "Hi baby girl, remember me? I'm your Daddy."

Though the picture on the screen wasn't clear, Lexi thought she could see tears in his eyes.

As usual, Marie stared at the screen as if Kyle were a TV actor that magically knew her name. She pointed at him, but that was her only response. She pointed at all sorts of things lately. Lexi hoped Marie would smile for him this time. She moved the laptop closer so Marie's finger actually touched the screen. "It's your Daddy."

Kyle talked to her for a few more minutes and, finally, she smiled at him.

"Hey, a real smile." His face lit up, becoming the face Lexi loved.

She hugged her daughter. "She's getting the hang of this."

"I wish I were there." His voice dropped. "How are you Lex?"

"Okay—" A small lie. She missed him, missed her mother, wanted to kill her siblings. Those feelings did not add up to okay, but he didn't need to worry about her. He'd been so understanding about the move to Durango.

"Nothing from your mother?"

"Not since the last email. She loves her new job, and she's running every day with some guy she met at the beach. I'm beginning to think she's not coming back for the holidays." She paused, "Honey, I miss you." She always tried not to cry when she talked to him, but it was hard not to. Her throat threatened to close. "How are you? Are you safe?" A stupid thing to ask. A Marine in Afghanistan was not safe.

"Safe enough. It's getting really cold here."

“Here too.” She told him about the warm clothes she’d bought for Marie and held up the tiny lined boots.

“They’re so small.” His voice wavered a little.

“And she’ll grow out of them before spring. I tried not to spend too much for them.”

The rest of the time—others were waiting to use the computer—they talked softly, gently communicating their love even while others were listening.

Lexi had taught Marie to wave goodbye, and the baby almost managed something resembling a wave when their time was up. Lexi bit down on her lower lip to prevent the tears. No sense upsetting Marie.

# CHAPTER 9

HANNA WAS DISCOVERING that daily sunshine was addictive. No chilling winds tumbling off the mountains, no day-long rain—just occasional morning fog. Almost too perfect. So when the tail end of a hurricane slipped up the coast of Baja and dumped over two inches of rain during one weekend, she hurried out to buy an umbrella. "California actually gets rain!" she teased Isabel as they were discussing decorations for the upcoming Halloween parties that Zoey had booked.

"We don't often have this much rain early in the season, but sometimes storms sneak in from the south. The weather forecasters are always blindsided, as though the border fence should stop bad weather." Due to deliver in two weeks, Isabel was getting bigger by the day, anxious for this enforced rest to be over. Shoving another pillow behind her back, she shifted uncomfortably. "The only good thing about this bed rest stuff is that I don't have to figure out how to bend over to put my shoes on. When I was pregnant with Charlie, I could only wear slip-ons."

In two days, her mother and sister were giving her a baby shower. Isabel was looking forward to getting pink gifts for the girl she was expecting. Zoey, Terry and Hanna were invited. "My mother's doing all the cooking and decorating. For once, you guys can attend a party that you don't have any responsibility for. However, I'm not sure everyone I've invited is going to fit in this room."

Since her first Seabrook event, Hanna's angst had lessened somewhat. She'd begun to trust herself more and had pulled off four other bridal showers, a golden anniversary celebration for 123 guests, a house warming—actually a mansion warming—in Rancho Santa Fe and at least a dozen smaller affairs. For the anniversary and the house warming, Isabel and Hanna worked together but, for the smaller events, Hanna was pretty much on her own. Now, whenever Zoey gave her a new job, Hanna didn't panic. She'd discovered she liked the planning process, visiting the venues, fitting the pieces together, shopping for what wasn't in Zoey's storage, and doing the set ups. So far, she hadn't had to cope with crabby clients. Today, she'd dropped by Isabel's to share the glowing thank you note from the family of the golden wedding couple. Isabel was her third stop. Before breakfast, Hanna had gone for a run with Duncan, then checked on a delivery she was expecting at Seabrook. Now, she was standing at the foot of Isabel's bed.

"You ran in the rain?" Isabel was puzzled.

"Sure. It's just water. In Durango, no one stays home when it's raining. Only during blizzards or black ice. Besides, I'm in training."

"For?"

"The Carlsbad half marathon in January."

"Have you ever run that far?"

"No. Only 10K runs when I was in college."

"When'd you decide this?"

"I've been thinking about it for a while. There's a guy who runs on the beach at the same time I do in the morning. He explained what's involved, and so we're going to train together. He says training's easier with another person. To qualify, I have to be able to average a 27-minute mile. That's doable."

Hanna was still surprised at herself for taking on a project that would commit her to staying in Del Mar over the holidays. She'd always been the one trying to get all of her kids to come home for Christmas. Now she was contemplating Christmas at Zoey's. Missing Marie's first Christmas. Having sun instead of snow.

"A guy?" Isabel grinned.

"Don't give me that tone, just a guy."

"Name please."

"Duncan."

"Age?"

"How do I know? You're as bad as Zoey. She acts as though I'm being stalked by an online predator."

"You didn't answer my question."

"Probably late thirties or early forties, a nice pair of legs." The first thing she'd noticed about him. Surprised that she'd noticed.

"Hanna Sheridan, what would your children say?"

"Plenty and I don't intend to share any of this with them."

In truth she wasn't sharing much of anything with her children these days. A year ago, she'd never have believed she would know so little about their day-to-day lives, though Callie had emailed to tell her she'd landed a job out at Mountain Grub, thanks to Walt, who'd even taken her to the audition. Just like Walt.

Because Hanna was busy with the Halloween parties, it was a day or two before she examined the implications of the Walt/Callie connection. Was it simply Walt being Walt? Or was he interested in Callie? Was Callie interested in Walt? Hanna had no one to blame but herself if they were—whatever they were.

She was having trouble completing her thoughts on the topic. For three years, she'd been holding Walt at arm's length, knowing he wanted more from her than she was willing to give—yet. *Face it. Men don't wait forever, especially men like Walt. Attractive, solid.* But if she let their friendship become more, then she'd be accepting Durango as the boundary of her existence. Of course, there would be love inside that boundary. It wasn't that she needed to travel to exotic places or perform daring feats, but she did need to find out what she could do. Walt had at least spent some time in Africa, had tested himself in the outside world. Had his own business and he seemed satisfied. She wanted to feel that kind of satisfaction. But that might not be possible in the shadow of someone else's life.

The possibility of Callie moving in on Walt danced at the edges of Hanna's thoughts, regardless of her attempts to ignore it. High school revisited. But she wasn't ready to go back. Not yet. The penalty for staying away might be not having Walt in her life, even as a friend.

She should, however, email him. He didn't deserve being ignored.

Hanna had noticed Duncan the first morning she ran on the beach. She'd never run on wet sand before. After only a mile, her calves were screaming, but the chance to run with the ocean at her side was too wonderful to pass up. On the third morning, he slowed his stride until they were side-by-side. "Great morning." The fog was breaking up, letting the sun polish the wet sand.

"Sure is." Because she wasn't in the best of shape, talking and running weren't easy for her yet. And so they ran in silence until they got to Powerhouse Park. He stopped. "My car's parked here. Do you need a lift?"

"No. I'm staying in one of the houses back there on the beach." She pointed in the general direction of Zoey's.

"My name's Duncan McAllister. I haven't seen you running out here before this week."

"Hanna Sheridan. I just got here. I'm visiting a friend."

"Maybe I'll see you tomorrow." He pulled car keys from his pocket, "I have to get to a class," and hurried toward a silver SUV.

Had she just been picked up? How interesting. She smiled to herself and walked back to Zoey's. That would never have happened to her in Durango.

The only other time she'd been picked up was the day she met Michael. They were both juniors, and he was running for ASO president. The students in Hanna's photography seminar—an elective for her art major—were assigned to follow all the candidates around to chronicle their campaigns. Each student was responsible for a portfolio of campaign photos. Michael was at the door of the Norlin Library, handing out flyers for a political rally. When he spotted her taking his picture, his body language—his tall, well-built body language—clearly said he was annoyed. "You're the third person today who's chasing me with a camera. What's going on?"

"It's a class project."

"Me?"

"All the candidates."

"Then follow someone else."

"I've already photographed them." Michael was very good looking, crisp black hair, a good jaw, and dark eyes that locked on hers as though they were interrogating her. Even before law school, he knew how to intimidate. But that afternoon, she was completely captivated. She raised her camera for a headshot.

"Hey! I thought I told you to quit."

"You're a good subject." She turned to leave.

After a moment, "Do you want to go for a coke or something?"

She stopped. Surprised. It might be fun to spend time with him.

"I would. What about your flyers?"

"I'd rather talk to you."

A line impossible to resist. She fell hard and fast. Two months later, she was sleeping with him, and a year later they were engaged.

In those days, Michael had the ability to fill up all the spaces in her life. When their marriage ended, she didn't know what to do with those spaces. Even before he'd moved out, he'd begun building a new life, leaving her to pick up the bits and pieces of herself. Was her journey to California a delayed reaction to Michael's defection? Trying to prove that she didn't have to be satisfied with bits and pieces and could strike out on her own too.

When she left Durango, she thought escaping was about too much mothering. Maybe it was about needing the time to mourn all the things she'd lost when Michael left. Keeping Walt on the sidelines might be her way of preventing another loss.

# CHAPTER 10

BECAUSE ISABEL'S PREGNANCY had been problematic, she was scheduled for a C-section on Friday afternoon. Greg had been instructed to call either Zoey or Hanna as soon as the baby was delivered, which was why Hanna had kept her cell turned on. The first time she'd done that since she left Durango.

And, of course, Michael called.

"Hanna?"

At the sound of his voice, her heart tightened. Had something happened to one of the children?

"Is something wrong?"

"I called to ask you the same thing. Why in God's name are you staying in California so long?"

"The kids are all right?"

"As far as I know, though Brooke is desperately upset that you walked out on them and left Callie—of all people—in charge. Brooke should be concentrating on her classes instead of working to pay *your* household bills." He was using his courtroom tone to bully her. Obviously, Brooke was exaggerating her financial role. Ever the drama queen.

"I didn't leave anyone in charge. Callie just happened to be there, and the only bills—," she stopped herself. Michael was a master at putting her on the defensive. He was spoiling for a fight.

"When are you going back?"

*Stay calm. Don't play his game.*

"No idea."

"What if Callie gets a job and leaves?"

"Then she leaves." Her response sounded more confident than she felt.

"Ryan should not be cleaning up construction sites. A complete waste of his education. What's happened to you? I've never known you to be so irresponsible, so uncaring about the welfare of the children."

*Like you shacking up with Sheri was responsible. Please!*

"That's the problem. I've been too damned responsible too long. If you're so worried, you go down there and cook and clean for them." Which of course he'd never do in a thousand years. He just wanted her to go home so he could get Brooke off his case.

"I certainly can't walk away from my clients to babysit my adult children."

*Of course not. Clients had always taken precedence over family. Sheri, watch out.*

"The key word is adult. They need to learn to fend for themselves. They've never had to. I took care of their physical needs and you wrote checks."

"What are you doing in California?"

"Working for Zoey." He wouldn't remember what Zoey's company did—wouldn't care.

"Why do you need to work? I still send a substantial alimony payment every month."

*As though it were a favor to her.*

"I'm having my very own midlife crisis. You already had yours." Before she said something he could use against her, she hung up.

And immediately called Brooke. Amazingly, her youngest answered after the first ring.

"Mom?"

"Yes." Before she lost her courage, "Brooke, please don't call your father about me." *Then he won't call me about me.*

“I don’t have anyone else to call.” A hint of whine. “You never answer your phone.”

“Because the only reason you call is to get me to come home, and I’m not ready to do that.”

“Why would you do this?” Full blown whine, “Do you hate us?”

“No, but this conversation is why I keep my phone turned off.”

“We could all die and you’d never know. Or care.”

“I would care.” *Care? She would be absolutely destroyed but no sense telling Brooke that.* “Is Callie there?”

“No. Walt drove her up to Mountain Grub. He’s been doing that a lot lately.” Brooke’s whine was replaced by a conspiratorial tone, “I think there’s something going on between them.”

Hanna chose not to take the bait.

“How’s college?”

“Hard.”

“Your brother and sister?”

“Annoying. I wish I were an only child.”

“No more calls to your father.”

“At least *he* sent a check.” Brooke broke the connection.

*Of course he did.*

At dinnertime, Zoey called to tell Hanna that Isabel’s baby was healthy, and Isabel was in the recovery room. Six pounds, seven ounces. Susannah Lee. Greg had gone home to pick up Charlie and bring him to see his mother and baby sister. Zoey and Hanna could visit the next morning. For the rest of the evening, Hanna concentrated on what she needed for tomorrow’s events and tried to keep Michael out of her head.

Brooke was furious. How could her mother be so unfeeling and selfish! Didn’t she understand that Brooke needed her at home? Needed that touchstone—that safety net—whether she actually ever had to ask her mother for help or not. Her mother had rarely ordered

Brooke to do or, in this case, *not* to do something. Mom was the easy one. Her father, when he was still living with them, had been the one to set the rules. But since the divorce, neither parent had done much disciplining, so Brooke had pretty much had things her own way—staying out past curfew, avoiding chores. Her friends liked spending time at the Sheridan house—envied Brooke her cool mom because Hanna was willing to cook for them, clean up after them and, until they got their own driver's licenses, take them wherever they wanted to go.

Now the mom who was so easy going had stopped being mom. So Brooke was left with her siblings and Callie, who for all her free spirit reputation had become a force to be reckoned with. She complained about dirty dishes in the sink and the wet towels on the bathroom floor—Ryan's fault of course. Callie was especially quick to remind them about handing over cash for food and household expenses. Brooke was now paying for her own cell phone and credit card bills. Mom had never expected that. Brooke was surprised at how much the cell bill was and was already shopping around for a cheaper plan. She hadn't been able to buy new clothes for weeks and could barely afford gas for her car, which was due for an oil change. A low level of unease followed her around. She'd been tempted to keep the check from her father for herself, but fear that her siblings would find out at some point made her give them their share, all of them agreeing not to tell Callie about the extra cash; otherwise, the entire check would have ended up in the household budget.

Brooke had never before been short of cash. If she wanted a coke or a bag of chips, she bought them. Now she'd become tight fisted. When a high school friend suggested they see a movie on the weekend, Brooke turned her down. The last of the cash from her dad had gone for new windshield wiper blades, which were surprisingly expensive.

"Can't. I'm broke." She wasn't embarrassed about being out of money, just annoyed.

"It's only eight dollars on Saturdays."

"Which is five more than I have right now."

"Come on. I'll loan it to you. I really want to see the movie."

"Amy, I can't. Ry may be willing to be in debt to everyone on the planet, but I'm not."

Everything she was used to was backward. Brooke was already questioning the wisdom of carrying a full load of classes. She had passing grades in everything, actually a B+ in Calculus, but she was spending hours and hours on homework, leaving little time for Dennis, who was juggling his own classes, the track team, and the weekend job in his father's veterinary clinic. The whole point of attending Fort Lewis was to be with Dennis. Because they were having trouble finding time and space for privacy, they hadn't had sex in over two weeks. The cold weather made it impossible to find a place to be alone and comfortable. Having sex in the back of Dennis's Explorer was not especially romantic. Brooke found herself wishing they had their own apartment. She needed to talk to Dennis about getting a place of their own. She was tired of her siblings treating her like she was twelve, even sick of Callie who, in years past, was often her ally. Getting around Callie wasn't as easy as getting around her mother.

It had taken every ounce of control for Hanna not to call Brooke back and tell her she was sorry she'd spoken so harshly. She wasn't really angry with Brooke. She was angry with Michael. He didn't want her but still wanted to tell her what to do. It had been a long time since she'd cried over him. She'd thought she was done with crying.

By the time Michael told Hanna he wanted a divorce, everyone at his law firm, including the two wives who were supposedly Hanna's dearest friends, knew about the affair. Seemingly, the only one who didn't know was Hanna. She'd instinctively felt that something was off kilter with Michael but, in the past, whatever was wrong in their marriage would ultimately get sorted. But not this time. He was working even longer hours than usual and, when he was at home, they were only talking about family issues. How well Brooke's braces were working, the need to change the pool cleaning service, when to put new tires on her car. Safe topics.

Most significant, he seldom touched her, even casually, and they hadn't had sex in months. Often, when he came home late, he'd sleep in the guestroom. The *I didn't want to disturb you* excuse. She should have paid attention to the clues, should have known they were on a slippery slope, but she was busy with Ryan and Brooke's activities. Michael had never been involved in the day-to-day grind of piano lessons and soccer games and doctors' appointments. He'd enjoyed teaching them to ski because he loved skiing. The rest he left to Hanna.

After his declaration of departure, it took a week or so for Hanna to admit to herself she would gladly tar and feather him. Amazing how quickly twenty years of what she'd believed was love turned into hate. Dismembering a family and a life that had at least been comfortable, if not perfect, encouraged thoughts of revenge. The divorce laws and lawyers encouraged vicious behavior on both sides. Hanna made Michael tell the children he'd been cheating. *This is your mess; you can explain yourself to our children. I'm no longer your spokesperson.* She was shocked that she could sound so harsh and feel so harsh, surprised she could—in one rage-filled afternoon—move all of Michael's things into the garage and then change the locks on the house. After the deed was done, she poured herself some of his very expensive scotch—she rarely drank hard liquor—then poured herself more.

That night, she slept better than she had in some time.

The children learned to stay out of her way, having discovered a mother they'd never met. One who had little patience for any thing. Who vacillated between crying and shouting. By the time the house was in escrow and the movers were driving her possessions to Durango, Ryan was at the university, Lexi was engaged to Kyle, and Brooke was left to cope with her mother and a new school where everyone had been friends since kindergarten.

Hanna didn't set eyes on Sheri—bottle blonde, cute, young—until the day escrow closed. She and Michael met at the real estate office to sign the final papers. Sheri stayed in the car. Hanna pretended she hadn't seen Sheri, but of course she had.

A year later, Michael wisely attended Lexi's wedding alone; otherwise, Hanna might have embarrassed herself and ruined her daughter's big day. Two years later, when Michael brought Sheri to Brooke's graduation, sharing the day with his mistress was only slightly easier for Hanna.

# CHAPTER 11

By November, Hanna's California life had settled into something resembling normal. New normal.

She focused on one day at a time, no looking back or, for that matter, forward because she still had no idea where her life was going. Staying in the present was, admittedly, tricky. A window display of brightly colored baby clothing made her think of Marie; guitar music on the car radio reminded her of Callie.

*Stop it.*

*They're not your responsibility right now.*

But family was always a responsibility. No way to sever that intangible cord, though she was giving it her best shot.

Isabel had decided to wait until the first of the year to return to Seabrook, so Hanna was still working for Zoey, getting better and better at creating designs on her own and, with Lyn's help, doing the set ups on site. Zoey's approval—*You're getting the hang of this*—and compliments from clients were doing wonders for Hanna's confidence.

Duncan McAllister was doing wonders for her in other ways. During her exit from Durango, Hanna had assured herself that adding a man to her life was not part of her agenda, but now she wasn't so sure. At 6:30 every weekday morning, Duncan was waiting for her at the steps below Zoey's deck. His first computer class didn't begin until ten o'clock, so they could run for an hour, stop for coffee at the Secret Café, then walk back to Zoey's house. Hanna was intrigued by the soft pleasure she experienced each time she saw him leaning against the railing. Other than Walt, it had been a long time since a man had paid attention to her though, so far, Duncan's attention was only friendship. She guessed he was seven or eight years younger than she. Like many Californians, he was deeply tanned, with the leanness of the dedicated runner. His hair was dark blond, his jogging effortless, forcing her to work on smoothing her own stride. To pay attention to her arms and regulate her breathing. So much running sent her shopping for additional clothing. Longer pants for chilly mornings, shorts for the winter days with summer temperatures. Plenty of t-shirts, a hoodie, socks and sun screen.

Jogging didn't allow extra breath for conversation, but she found the silence comfortable. Just the sound of their feet on the pavement and sand. Over coffee, she was gradually letting her guard down as well as learning about him. A vegetarian who ate fish, an engineer who taught computer science at Miramar College in San Diego. A recently divorced father of two teenage girls, who was struggling with only seeing them every other weekend.

"Sam—Samantha is thirteen. Full-blown drama. She hates her braces—which are costing a fortune—her freckles, her sister, and me. Actually, there's not much she does like these days. My older daughter Paula is graduating in June. She's something of a nerd. Wants to be a physicist and doesn't much care how she dresses or whether she's popular. Paula ignores both of us, preferring to read whatever books she's loaded on her Kindle. Weekends at my condo feel like punishment to Sam because she wants to be with her friends, and her sulking spoils whatever I plan for their entertainment. Even worse, they have to share a bedroom. I look forward to their coming and am emotionally exhausted when they leave."

Brooke's sulks came to mind. "Being a teenager isn't easy on them or us." Hanna smiled in sympathy.

"Did your kids have trouble with the whole visitation routine?"

"Lexi and Ryan were legally adults and both at the university in Boulder, so they could do whatever they wanted about seeing us. Brooke was the only one involved in a custody arrangement. Initially, Michael would fly from Denver to see her rather than have her travel by herself. But by the time she was sixteen, she was comfortable traveling alone; she'd fly up for Easter week or her birthday. There was never a real schedule because Michael's work took precedence. He cancelled more visits than he kept."

And then there was Sheri. Once she moved in with Michael, Hanna wasn't happy having Brooke stay with them. She hadn't meant to dump her history with Michael into the discussion. An easy trap. "Thirteen sort of comes with drama."

"Good to know. I was lucky that Paula never seemed to have stages."

"Maybe she's saving them for later." Hanna was trying to lighten the discussion but remembered too late that Duncan didn't always get lightness.

"Not encouraging," he paused, "I'd like you to meet them sometime."

"Sure." *So long as I don't have to cook for them or do their laundry.*

As practice for the Carlsbad run, Duncan had signed them up for a 10K race in mid-December. Beginning at Balboa Stadium, following Florida Canyon, and ending back at the stadium, the race would attract top athletes. Hanna wasn't certain she was ready for that level of competition. "You can handle it, but I've only been seriously training for five or six weeks."

"This race is just a warm up. It'll give you a feel for what organized races are like. Regardless of the race, I never focus on winning. I just run my own race. For myself. To improve my time, sometimes just to survive the course. Running keeps me sane. Turns all those endorphins loose. I missed this 10K last year because we ended up back in court arguing about the Christmas holidays." Duncan's divorce and custody battles were never far from his conversation. "Karen wanted to take the girls to Orange County for the full two weeks. By the time we settled the issue, I got the girls for one week but missed the race and had to pay all the legal fees."

He and Hanna only saw each other in the morning. Her schedule was never the same two days in a row, and Seabrook's event set-ups often occurred at the dinner hour. In addition to his day classes, Duncan taught one evening class, "An overload to help me with legal fees, child support, and alimony." His ex had been a stay at home mother and was dragging her feet about getting a job.

*Shades of Ryan.*

And there was Durango, creeping back into her head.

Because December would be Seabrook's busiest month, Zoey never scheduled events during Thanksgiving week, giving the staff a much-needed week off because everyone would be working six or seven days a week until after New Year's.

On the company's white-board calendar, Zoey was crossing off the fourth week of November with a black marker. "I'm going to Atlanta for a few days."

"To see Stephanie?"

Zoey nodded. "She isn't thrilled about my visit, but I'm going anyhow. I haven't seen her for a year. This is my best chance to spend some time with her because she's planning a ski trip with friends at Christmas." She put the cap on the pen. "Are you going to Durango?"

Hanna shook her head. "Callie emailed that Michael's paying for the kids to fly to Denver for two nights. It seems Sheri wants to cook for them. New-bride-nesting mode, I suppose. But I wasn't planning to go anyway. I'm afraid if I get near Colorado, some huge gate will close behind me, and I'll be trapped."

On the other hand, she wasn't sure how she felt about Michael playing father in such a tangible way. His casual fathering had always allowed her to feel rather smug about her diligent mothering.

Of course, diligence only got her more mothering. Being responsible was vastly overrated.

A whole week on her own. A test of sorts. A major holiday without a family. The media would be filled with happy families eating lavish meals, enjoying each other's company. Romanticized images but discomforting nonetheless. Few family holidays lived up to Hallmark card expectations. In some ways, Hanna had been on her own last year too. Lexi had called on Thanksgiving morning while Hanna was fixing dinner with all the trimmings for Ryan and Brooke. Lexi and Kyle were having a potluck dinner with three other couples on the base. Ryan flew home Wednesday night and left Friday morning to go skiing with friends. Brooke spent Thanksgiving night with Dennis's family, and Walt had eaten dinner with his mother at the assisted living facility. Though Hanna's family had been on different paths that weekend, in May their paths had ended up at her house.

When Hanna told Duncan about Zoey's departure, he was instantly full of plans. "Let's play tourist. You haven't seen much of the county. My girls will be with their mother and grandparents in Orange County. I know a great place in the mountains for Thanksgiving dinner."

Hanna loved the idea of having something completely different to look forward to—instead of visualizing her family spending the day with Michael and the other, pregnant Mrs. Sheridan.

After her Monday morning run with Duncan, Hanna drove Zoey to Lindbergh Field, dropping her in front of Terminal 2 for Delta's noon flight to Atlanta. The rest of the day was hers. She'd been in the city a few times on shopping trips for Seabrook but hadn't taken the time to explore on her own. From the airport, she followed the Pacific Highway to Seaport Village. Zoey had suggested Hanna would enjoy the picturesque shopping complex beside the bay, its architecture a mix of coastal New England and Spanish architectures, a collage of boutiques and restaurants clustered alongside a working carousel.

Zoey was right. It had charm. Hanna strolled along the bay for a while, then stopped at *Upstart Crow*, a bookstore serving coffee and pastry. She bought a latte and a cinnamon muffin, remembered to get her parking ticket validated, found a table by a window overlooking the water, and pulled out her laptop to answer Callie's email about Thanksgiving. She sipped at her latte, watching an aircraft carrier crawl across the skyline.

Though she'd spent much of her life being annoyed by her sister, she was grateful Callie was still in Durango. Now Hanna was the one avoiding responsibility and expanding her horizons. She had time to pay more attention to what was going on in the world, had more time to read—she'd just finished Zoey's copy of Sonia Sotomayor's memoir—and had applied for a library card. She'd lost weight, thanks to all the running, and had even acquired a faint tan. She felt younger, more attractive, and was contemplating a different haircut. She clicked on New Message.

Hi Callie: I'm surprised Michael is hosting Thanksgiving. Hell may be ready to freeze over. I'm on my own this week as Zoey has shut down for a few days to go visit her daughter in Atlanta.

I'll spend Thanksgiving with Duncan, my running friend. My first holiday outside of Colorado. No cooking. We're going to the mountains for the day.

What are you doing since my kids will be gone? Working?

How is Walt? *A loaded question based on Brooke's hint that Callie and Walt were spending time together.*

I probably won't be home by Christmas. Duncan and I are going to run a 10K in a couple of weeks and a half marathon in January, though I may walk more than I run. Then I'll take a look at—things. Zoey's business is doing so well that it's wearing her out. She's had a couple of buy out offers, but she's uncertain what she'd do without the company she and Jonathon built.

I'm sitting in a charming, funky bookstore on San Diego Bay. I can see the Coronado Bridge crossing to the island. There are all sorts of watercraft going by, plenty of tourists shopping and taking pictures. It's about seventy degrees.

Are you still at Mountain Grub?

It was tempting to thank her for staying, for keeping an eye on Hanna's old life, but she didn't. She suspected Callie wasn't staying to help her.

Other than her morning runs with Duncan, the next two days gave Hanna plenty of alone time. Not as hard as she'd imagined. Actually soothing. She spent one day in La Jolla, walking along the bluffs from the Cove down to the Children's Pool where the seals had taken up permanent residence. She window shopped on Girard Avenue and had lunch on the deck at Pannikin. The next day she did chores around the house.

Duncan picked her up late Thanksgiving morning, and they drove an hour and a half northeast to a Nineteenth Century gold mining town tucked into the Laguna Mountains. Twenty-First Century Julian was mostly a tourist destination. Half an hour before they arrived, Duncan asked Hanna to phone the restaurant and put his name on the waiting list. "We'll get there just about the time my name comes up. The cafe's the only game in town on Thanksgiving, but it doesn't take reservations."

They emerged from the oak and pine forest onto a wide street with high curbs and false front stores. Hanna was reminded of some of Colorado's restored mining towns, but this one was less pretentious.

"It's a real town."

"Real?"

"It isn't gussied up, pretending to still be a mining town. It just is what it is. I like it."

"I thought you would." Duncan locked the car and took her hand as they walked a half block to the Julian Café, where several people were clustered on the sidewalk, waiting for their names to be called.

"Stay here a minute; let me see where we are on the list."

He was back quickly. "They're ready for us."

The café was smaller than she'd expected, maybe twenty tables, the walls covered with historical photos of the town, as well as rusted ranching tools and old lanterns.

The hostess seated them at the only table that had a view of the street. "How lucky is this!" Duncan held her chair.

Most of the Thanksgiving menu was set, with only a choice of ham or turkey, pumpkin soup or salad. Both of them chose the turkey and the pumpkin soup. If she were eating with Walt, they would probably have ordered one salad and one soup and then shared. But she and Duncan hadn't reached the food-sharing stage.

"Do you come up here at other times during the year?"

"Not as often as I did when I was younger. Nowadays, the weekends are seriously crowded and, when there's a dusting of snow, it's a zoo."

"Snow?" The hills, even though they were called mountains, didn't seem high enough for snow. Her Colorado genes talking.

"Because Julian's at four thousand feet, a storm has to be really cold before the town gets snow, but a few of the mountains behind us are six thousand feet so they get snow several times a year. On our way back, I'll take a different route and stop at Inspiration Point, where you can see the desert. San Diego likes to brag that you can drive from the ocean to the mountains to the desert and be home by dark."

After dinner, they walked along Main Street, a light breeze shaking golden oak leaves onto the pavement, and Hanna bought an apple pie to put in Zoey's freezer. When they stopped at Inspiration Point, the afternoon haze interfered with their view of the desert. Duncan was disappointed. "Bad timing."

By the time they reached Zoey's, it was dark. They'd been too stuffed to eat their dessert at the Café, so they warmed the slices of apple boysenberry pie the waitress had boxed up for them and opened a bottle of wine.

"Very nice house." Duncan had never been inside.

"Easy upkeep. Zoey likes the simplicity. I love the openness." Especially the high ceilings and white walls with just a few dynamic prints."

"Not like your house in Colorado?"

"Not even close. My sister and I inherited the house after my dad passed on. It was built in the seventies. Very traditional two-story floor plan. My mother favored French country furnishings, flowery wallpaper and ruffles. I haven't done much to it except make repairs, paint, and add some of my furniture. It's a hodge-podge. I've been making it up as I go along. Sort of like my current life."

They talked about running for a while and made plans to run in Balboa Park in the morning so Hanna could practice on the terrain for the 10K run. Maybe they'd visit one of the museums afterwards. At the front door, Duncan kissed her cheek, "It's been a great day. Thanks for joining me." Hanna waited until his SUV pulled away before closing the door.

It had been a good day; she hadn't thought about her family even once.

# CHAPTER 12

WITH THE SLEEPING Marie on her lap, Lexi watched the carpet of mountain peaks beneath the plane, the highest ones dusted with early snow. Though she'd often made the one-hour flight between Denver and Durango, the Rockies never failed to captivate her. She'd missed their silent splendor. The one thing Lexi hadn't missed, however, was the wind that swooped over the Front Range and buffeted the airplanes flying into Stapleton.

Looking forward to being in Denver again, she'd emailed three high school friends she hadn't seen since her wedding, suggesting they have breakfast together Friday morning since the return flight to Durango didn't leave until three. She hadn't decided whether to take Marie with her or get someone to babysit—maybe Sheri. She wanted to show off her daughter—Lexi was the first in the group to have a baby—but, if Marie was fussy, Lexi wouldn't be able to enjoy the reunion.

She was not exactly looking forward to spending up-close and personal time with her father and Sheri. Everything was bound to be awkward. Lexi, Marie, and Brooke would be sleeping in the guest room at the condo out near Cherry Creek. Ryan had opted to stay with a college friend instead of spending two nights on Michael's living room couch because the third bedroom had already been converted into a nursery for the baby boy Sheri was carrying. A half-brother who would be almost a year younger than Marie. Lexi didn't intend to mention the new baby to her friends. The whole second family situation was faintly embarrassing. Lately, her family seemed bent on doing the unexpected. Telling her friends about her mother running off to California would be even more embarrassing.

When the clouds cut off her view, she switched her attention to Ryan and Brooke, who were seated together across the aisle. Ryan had been playing a game on his cell phone ever since the pilot gave the okay for electronic devices, and Brooke was reading a textbook. *Can you believe I have a history test next Monday—like all I should do during the holiday is study.* From the time she was little, Brooke had always been quick to complain—or cry—about almost everything, both behaviors effectively getting her what she wanted—at least within the family. The power of being the youngest.

Since her parents' divorce, Lexi hadn't spent much time with her father, even less time with Sheri because, as soon as she graduated from college and married Kyle, her world was centered on him—and now on Marie. She'd finally stopped being angry about her father's affair. Most of the time, what he did or didn't do had little impact on her day-to-day existence, but tomorrow would involve impact. She could probably cope. Whether Ryan and Brooke could was another matter.

The Thanksgiving invitation had surprised Ryan. Refusing wasn't an option, especially since his sisters were eager to go to Denver to see their friends. However, being face-to-face with his father would necessitate discussing law school. The longer Ryan was without a real job—specifically the kind of white-collar job Michael assumed his son should have—the weaker Ryan's reasons for not considering law school became. Of course working construction was not how Ryan saw his future either. Since graduation, his life had become more complicated. People suddenly expected more of him. Good grades and good looks weren't enough anymore.

He'd been working at Walt's for two very long months. In addition to cleaning up job sites, he was learning the basics of construction—how to cut and fit mitered corners, install sheetrock and replace windows. He especially disliked getting up while it was still dark to be at a job site by seven or eight, and most nights he was too exhausted to do anything but crash on the couch in front of the TV. He did, however, like having money for gas, a new Broncos sweatshirt, and game apps for his phone. He didn't like having to turn over half of each week's check to Callie. He missed the old *let's have fun* Callie. But at least there'd finally been enough cash to fix the washing machine—no more visits to the laundromat—and to buy a cord of wood for the fireplace. Unfortunately, he was the only one who knew how to split the wood.

On the plus side, he was getting used to the calluses on his hands and was secretly proud of the muscles he was developing, the way his shoulders and neck had filled out.

By Brooke's measure, everything about celebrating Thanksgiving at their father's was weird—starting with Sheri, the woman her mother hated, waiting all by herself outside the baggage claim area, watching her stepchildren straggle toward her. Ryan was pushing the trolley loaded with Lexi's two large suitcases, Marie's car seat, stroller, and the small carry ons he and Brooke had brought. For just two days, the baby seemed to need everything she owned. At least Lexi thought so. If Lexi could have figured out how to carry it, they'd have been saddled with Marie's high chair too.

In her stylish red wool coat, Sheri smiled tentatively, "How was your flight?"

Lexi shifted Marie's weight from her right hip to the left. "Bumpy as always."

"Your father's working late."

Brooke couldn't resist, "No surprise there."

Sheri frowned. "Really Brooke, he wanted to be here to greet you, but he's swamped at the office. The only way he could take tomorrow off was to finish a deposition tonight." She reached out to stroke Marie's cheek, "She's growing so fast," then laid her hand on the curve of her own stomach, "I'm growing too. Come on. I'm parked in the front lot. It's not far."

With Marie in her car seat, the luggage, and four adults, Sheri's SUV was overflowing. The pre-holiday traffic between Stapleton and the condo was frantic, everyone intent on getting home to start the holiday. Even though Marie was crying and the traffic was pressing in on every side, Sheri remained calm, keeping up a monologue about some of the recent changes in Denver, definitely trying to make up for Michael's absence.

Because Ryan had called from the airport to give George directions to the condo, his friend was already parked at the curb when Sheri pulled into the driveway. Ryan and George carried the luggage inside; then Ryan picked up his small duffle bag, "I'm outta here." A half wave.

"Dinner's at two tomorrow," Sheri called after him. "Your friend is welcome too."

Lexi had to give Sheri credit; she was sincerely trying to make them comfortable, be a good hostess. Having to entertain your husband's grown children, whom you hardly know, had to be hard. Leave it to her father to absent himself during difficult family moments. He hadn't changed his behavior, only his wife. Lexi was pretty sure Kyle was going to be a better father than Michael. Wouldn't be hard.

She gave Marie her dinner and a bottle while Sheri went to get Chinese takeout for the three of them. "We'll be doing enough cooking tomorrow."

Worn out from all the excitement, Marie fell asleep on the couch and, as soon as Brooke finished eating, she went upstairs to call Dennis.

Sheri tossed the take out cartons into the trash and wiped the table. "It's my first Thanksgiving as part of your family. I'm really excited about fixing a traditional dinner. Michael didn't want me to go to all this work, but I need to get to know you better. I've never been much of a cook. I was an only child, and my mother sometimes worked on holidays."

So the dinner hadn't been Michael's idea. Lexi might have known.

"With my mother gone, we'd probably have hamburgers or pizza. My aunt isn't all that good in the kitchen, and Brooke would have been at Dennis's house. I watched my mother cook a turkey every year, but I've never cooked one. Let's get online and see what we can find. Is the turkey defrosted?" Lexi was pretty sure Sheri had no idea how much work the dinner would be.

"Oh yes, I bought a fresh one this morning and potatoes and vegetables and a couple of pies at Marie Callender's."

"We should be able to figure it out." At least Lexi hoped so.

For the first time since their arrival, Sheri seemed to relax a little.

Marie, as usual, woke at 6 a.m. but had miraculously gone back to sleep after her bottle. While Sheri made a run to a supermarket for chicken broth, boxes of prepared stuffing, and a meat thermometer, Lexi rubbed butter on the turkey inside and out, then salted and peppered it. The Internet instructions suggested thirteen minutes per pound unstuffed. If they put it in a little before ten, it should be done by two o'clock. She was rather enjoying this adult role. No mother to take over if she was doing it wrong. A rite of passage.

Lexi was washing the butter off her hands when her father came into the kitchen. "Hey Lex," he kissed her cheek, "Happy Thanksgiving. Sorry I couldn't get home earlier last night."

Michael Sheridan was still handsome, a salting of gray in his black hair. The classy new glass frames making him look rather sexy. Sheri's influence? No one would guess he was close to fifty. Working out at the gym in his office building didn't hurt either.

"Happy Thanksgiving, Dad."

"Where is everyone?"

"Sheri's at the store getting some of the things we didn't know we needed. Brooke and Marie are asleep, and Ry is at a friend's."

"Any coffee?"

"Sheri fixed some, but you're on your own for breakfast. We need to get all this food organized." She knew that *on your own* was not what her father wanted to hear. He was used to having someone—his mother, Hanna, his daughters, and now Sheri—wait on him. At least Kyle could scramble eggs and make toast. Lexi had always vowed not to marry a man who expected to be waited on hand and foot like her father.

Michael poured himself coffee and wandered into the living room to read the morning paper. Not even asking *How's Kyle.*

As soon as Sheri returned with the groceries, her cheeks rosy from the cold, she quickly fixed Michael toast and two soft-boiled eggs, carrying a tray into the living room. From the kitchen, Lexi watched them, the way Sheri touched Michael's back, his smile at something she said. Actually rather sweet.

She missed Kyle so much.

Fixing dinner kept everyone busy. Once Brooke was up, she sullenly agreed to set the table, taking her own sweet time about it. If they'd been in Durango, Lexi would have yelled at her, but this was Sheri's territory. No sense ruining the day.

Marie, having mastered skooching on her butt, was underfoot all morning. In desperation, Lexi talked Michael into taking his granddaughter for a walk in her stroller. "You need the practice, and we need Marie to be somewhere else." Surprisingly, he did as she asked. Lexi couldn't remember ever before giving her father an order—even a gentle one. She felt quite grown up.

Without Marie to watch out for, Lexi and Sheri put dinner together easily. The traditional green bean casserole that Michael liked, mashed potatoes with garlic, sweet potatoes with marshmallows—Sheri's favorite—, canned cranberry sauce, packaged dressing, gravy, and pies.

Ryan showed up just before two o'clock with George in tow, and everything was on the table by three o'clock. Not bad for amateurs.

The two women who hadn't been sure they could prepare a Thanksgiving dinner for six pulled it off with only a few stumbles—the marshmallows were closer to black than a toasty brown and Sheri had forgotten to buy dinner rolls. Since her parents' break up, Hanna's snide remarks about Sheri had colored Lexi's attitude about her stepmother but, by the end of the day, Lexi discovered she rather liked her. Sheri could laugh at her own mistakes, didn't fall apart when she burned her thumb, and wasn't afraid of hard work. They'd gotten along rather well.

By 6:30, they collapsed at the kitchen table with cups of steaming herbal tea, leaving the other adults watching football and, hopefully, watching Marie, who was enjoying the bouncy chair that Sheri had bought for her own baby. "Michael laughs at me for buying baby things so far ahead. But the chair's come in handy today."

"Marie has one of those back at my mother's. Callie bought it so Marie could be in the kitchen and not get into trouble."

"I don't think I've met Callie."

"The family black sheep, if a female can be a black sheep. We never know when she's going to show up because she has to go where the jobs are. She's a superb musician, but she's never gone solo until now. I think she likes playing at the Grub, though she doesn't like being a stand-in for my mother."

"She's younger than your mother?"

"Four years."

"Michael just rolled his eyes when I asked about Callie."

"They're from different worlds. Dad always thought Callie was a flake, and the divorce didn't help Callie's opinion of Dad."

She instantly regretted mentioning the divorce, but the words were already out.

"If your mother were still at home, would you have come here for Thanksgiving?"

"Probably not, but she's not at home and everything's different. I don't think she's planning to come back for Christmas either."

# CHAPTER 13

THOUGH CALLIE AND Saul had been dancing around the attraction between them since she'd been performing at the restaurant, she hadn't planned on spending Thanksgiving night in Saul's bed.

Soon after she began working at the Grub, Walt mentioned Saul's interest in her. Walt had driven her to the restaurant because her truck's transmission was being overhauled.

"He likes you, Callie."

Usually no one had to tell her when a man was interested. Evidently, she was out of practice. But she had noticed Saul always made sure he was nearby during her breaks, bringing her coffee or a plate of food. Courting her a night at a time.

"Is he married?"

"Divorced—but there's still some sort of connection. Once a month, he drives to Pueblo to see her."

"Why?" She hoped it wasn't a booty call.

"No clue."

"Not surprising. Men never ask each other personal questions."

He laughed, enjoying Callie's straightforward response. "You've got that right."

"Which explains why you haven't said something to Hanna. About how you feel." To Callie, Walt's feelings for her sister had been obvious from the moment Hanna moved back to Durango. Even more obvious when he and Hanna were dating in high school.

He swung into the Grub parking lot, turned off the engine but didn't get out. Now he wasn't sure he liked straightforward.

"No good answer. For a while, it was too soon after her divorce and then—well I'm not good at pushing. Which is probably the reason I've been single since Lily left." He fumbled with the handle as he opened the door for Callie. "And now, I may have waited too long."

"Have you thought about a trip to California?"

"Yeah." He'd hardly thought about anything else since Hanna's departure.

"You should go." Short and to the point. Callie reached behind the seat for her guitar case and music folder, and slammed the passenger door. "Thanks for the ride. One of the bus boys will give me a ride home. He lives a few blocks from the house."

Though she hadn't planned to stay, in the last few weeks Saul had made it quite clear that he wanted her to stay.

A week ago, he'd said, "Your call," his smile saying much more than the words.

It was time.

It had been a while since she'd been this attracted to a man. A couple of one-night stands in Vegas didn't count. Sex without attraction. Sleeping with Saul, however, would be sex and attraction rolled into one. They laughed together, enjoyed talking about music. Her mother—cautious about almost everything—would have said he was a keeper.

But before they went to that level, she had to ask, "What about your wife?" Callie had never knowingly slept with a married man. That was looking for trouble.

He sighed. "Ex-wife. Not something that's going to be solved anytime soon." When Callie didn't respond, "She's in the psychiatric hospital in Pueblo. Diana's dangerously bi-polar." He paused, "She needs supervision. While we were still married, I tried to keep her at home, but the medications don't control the manic stages anymore. I never knew what I'd find when I came home or where I'd find her. Once she drove to Albuquerque without any ID or money. She got pulled over for running a red light and spent the night in jail. Even though we aren't married, I pay for the insurance that keeps her at the hospital. His eyes, usually a translucent green, had gone dark.

Callie wasn't often at a loss for words, but his explanation wiped out whatever other questions she might have asked. She was close to making that call.

Her current stay in Durango was having an unexpected effect on her. The other times she'd come home between jobs, she'd been chomping at the bit to get out of town. That was what Callie Meeker did—she followed the music. This time she'd become inexplicably comfortable. She hadn't planned that either. Perhaps Hanna's absence contributed. Her sister had always disapproved of Callie's lifestyle and, without that disapproval, she'd relaxed. Even teaming her nieces and nephew around wasn't all that bad. They were good kids, spoiled and definitely lazy, though being a mother herself had improved Lexi.

As the last customers left the dining room, Callie was packing up her music, fitting the guitar into its case, hoping the rain hadn't turned to snow. She hadn't been able to afford snow tires for the truck.

"Hungry?" Saul was close behind her, his hands lightly at her waist, instantly spreading warmth through her limbs. She was pretty sure he wasn't just talking about food.

"Maybe some of that apple cobbler."

Pulling her hair aside, he kissed the back of her neck, "Anything else?"

She let herself lean against him, felt his breath on her skin.

*Yes. Definitely yes.*

"Your call."

As he moved away and headed for the kitchen, she called.

Saul possessed an erotic combination of gentleness and strength that none of her other lovers had possessed. Callie's first husband had been young and lusty—sex as a physical pursuit. Her second husband had usually needed a substantial amount of alcohol to fuel his passion and, once it was sated, he slept for the next eight or nine hours. Nothing romantic in that.

Saul, however, knew where they were going and how to get there. He took his time, touch-by-touch coaxing Callie to the brink before backing off, then letting his hands and lips expertly bring her back to that brink, until she thought she'd explode. Where had this man been all of her life?

Later, lying beside him, not quite touching, she allowed her mind to wrap itself around what had just happened to her. It was more than sex, more than mere attraction.

It was—a deep caring. She hadn't experienced that gift before.

She must have slept for a while. When she woke, he was lying on his side, watching her, the green eyes capturing hers. Without a word, she began kissing him, maneuvering him until he was on his back. Then she climbed on top.

Because Saul had to be in the restaurant at noon, Callie drove to Durango, picked up enough clothing to last the weekend, and left a note for the kids, who were flying home that evening. She didn't specifically mention where she was, only that she'd be home Monday. She wanted to keep this sweet secret to herself for a day or two.

It was after six when Brooke found Callie's note under the *Read This* magnet on the refrigerator door. Their flight had been delayed in Denver, trapping them on the tarmac for over an hour, so Marie was at her cranky best by the time they picked up Lexi's car in Durango's long stay parking lot.

As soon as they unlocked the house, Lexi slipped Marie into the bouncy chair while she heated a jar of sweet potatoes and some green beans.

Brooke dropped the note on the table. "Callie won't be back until Monday. I thought she was working this weekend."

"No idea," Ryan switched on the thermostat near the stairway. "It's freezing in here."

Brooke was searching the refrigerator shelves. "It's scrambled eggs or nothing. Why is there never any food in this house?"

"Because we expect it to magically appear by itself." Lexi felt as cranky as Marie, promising herself not to take her daughter on a plane again until Marie was big enough to have a seat of her own. The trip would have been much easier if Kyle had been with them. Kyle with his strong hands, his soft laugh. So steadying. Being an adult was not nearly as much fun as she'd imagined when she was eighteen. There were moments when she empathized with Hanna's frustration.

Once she had Marie settled, she'd write Kyle an email. They weren't scheduled for a Skype visit until Sunday night.

Even though she'd been married twice, Callie had never had a honeymoon. When she married Billy, they'd immediately gone into rehearsals in New York and, the second time, she and Damian were performing in L.A. so they spent the day at Venice Beach and appeared with the band that night.

The weekend with Saul felt like a honeymoon. When they weren't in the restaurant, they were upstairs in his two-room apartment, enjoying what they were discovering about each other. In addition to all things sexual, she learned he preferred sleeping on his stomach. He discovered she needed to brush her teeth before they had sex in the morning. Breakfast for Callie was juice and toast, for Saul, the works. He was a good cook, often filling in at the Grub if one of the line cooks was out sick.

He delighted in pampering her, bringing her coffee in bed. And for the first time in her life, Callie let herself be pampered. At some point, the independent Callie would probably return but, for now, she was drifting in a soft haze. Young love in middle age.

She headed back to Durango early Monday afternoon. She and Saul had spent most of the morning in bed, delaying breakfast till almost eleven. Leaning against Callie's truck, his hands framing her face, "Stay tonight."

"Tempting. But I shouldn't. I need to check that the children got home in one piece."

"Parenting?"

She knew he was teasing. "I'm turning into my sister. Not a good sign."

"I rather like that side of you. Soon?"

She smiled into the green eyes. "Absolutely."

*Absolutely.*

When Callie parked in Hanna's driveway, only Lexi's car was there. Ryan was probably at one of Walt's jobs, and Brooke had morning classes at the college. Easier to face Lexi first.

In her high chair, Marie was exercising her lungs, impatient that Lexi was still warming the jars of baby food in a saucepan. The sprinkling of Cheerios on the high chair tray was not enough to pacify her. She quieted for a moment when she saw Callie, then resumed her high-pitched protest.

"Hey Maria, you've got a set of lungs. I predict a singing career." Callie lifted her out of the chair and walked her around the kitchen, trying to quiet her. "Your Mama's working as fast as she can."

"Good luck selling that. She's been fussy all morning. I think she's teething." Lexi turned the burner off. "You can put her back. Maybe she'll quiet down if she has food in her mouth."

Once Marie was focused on her lunch, Callie sat at the table with a cup of coffee that had been kept warm too long. "How was Thanksgiving?"

"Not too bad but I'm guessing yours might have been better."

Callie felt her face flush. "Good guess. How are the newlyweds?"

"They seem happy. Of course Sheri caters to Dad's every whim. But I—well—I sort of like her. I probably shouldn't tell my mother that. I'm not so sure what my father will do with a crying baby in the house, however. According to Mom, he never wanted to deal with the messy stuff when we were little. Refused to change diapers." She wiped a glob of squash off Marie's chin. "Good girl. She loves squash. The spinach won't be as easy. Not her favorite. So just what have you been doing this weekend? Or should I ask who?"

No sense dodging the question. "Saul."

"I was right. Brooke said it was Walt."

"Walt's carrying a torch for your mother. Has been for thirty years."

"Care to share?" Lexi grinned at her aunt, pretty sure that wasn't going to happen.

"Nope, you're too young and innocent." Callie washed her cup in the sink and picked up the overnight bag she'd taken to Saul's.

"Going back?"

"Yup. I'm allowed sleepovers."

Lexi laughed, "Bet sleep wasn't on the agenda—" she stopped. "Sorry. I miss Kyle. Do I get to tell the other two?"

"Sure."

Callie dropped a kiss on top of Marie's head and went upstairs. In truth there hadn't been much sleep. Maybe she'd take a nap before she checked to see whether there was something in the house for dinner.

*Good Lord. I really am turning into my sister.*

Wrapped in a unique—for her—sense of well being, Callie floated through the rest of the week, counting the hours until she would see Saul on Friday. He called every night after closing, talking about nothing and everything. Yes, the sex had been eleven on a ten-point scale but what she thought about most was the color of his eyes. The way he held a cup of coffee. His laugh. How intensely he listened.

She'd fallen hard.

# CHAPTER 14

ZOEY FLEW BACK from Atlanta on Sunday night and hit the ground running. By Monday afternoon, Hanna had four new jobs on her calendar; fortunately, nothing was scheduled for the Sunday of the 10K run. When Hanna asked Zoey about her trip and her time with Stephanie, all she got was *Fine*. Though *fine* didn't sound fine at all. And quite unlike Zoey, she didn't ask about Hanna's holiday.

On Friday, Lexi sent Hanna a short email with a new picture of Marie in a bright red sweater.

We survived Denver, even enjoyed ourselves, though Ry might not agree. He and Dad were closeted in the kitchen Friday morning. No idea about the outcome. Ry looked so thunderous that I was afraid to ask. What did you do on Thanksgiving? Love, Lexi and Marie.

Poor Ryan. He'd never been able to stand up to his father when it came to major issues. Whether he should play football or soccer. Attend the U of Colorado or Boston University. Initially, Ryan had his sights set on attending an East Coast university, but Michael wasn't willing to pay out-of-state tuition. If she were a betting woman, she'd put her money on Michael getting what he wanted—a son to follow in his legal footsteps. If she'd stayed in Durango, would she have been able to run interference for Ryan? Probably not. She'd never been good at standing up to Michael either—except when his infidelity sent her in search of the best divorce lawyer in Denver—and worth every penny.

Two of her new decorating jobs were small holiday weddings—a week apart so some of the decorations could be reused, cutting down on the shopping. The freeways and stores were already crowded with holiday shoppers. She was trying to find time for her own Christmas shopping. Though she was firm about not going home, she was not ignoring the holiday altogether, looking for mailable gifts for the family, especially Marie. Her granddaughter's first Christmas. Old enough to be captivated by the lights on the tree and maybe old enough to rip the paper off her gifts. When Hanna thought about Marie, her heart softened. A grandmother didn't get the first Christmas back.

She was sure she wanted to stay in Del Mar until the half marathon but had no idea what to do about Duncan, who was increasingly attentive. Hanna was fairly sure that, if she gave even the slightest encouragement, they'd take their friendship to the next level. Not an entirely unpleasant prospect. Actually, she was curious what it would be like to have someone other than Michael make love to her. The idea of having sex again began to preoccupy her. As a potential lover, Duncan was less the issue than the sex itself. She'd always believed that women needed to love the men they had sex with. In this case however, she knew she didn't love Duncan and doubted he loved her, but she did want to have sex. It had been a long dry spell.

The Holiday 10K Fun Run was the second Sunday in December. Three times during the preceding week, she and Duncan had done practice runs on the course, so Hanna was confident she'd be able to finish. Because he'd have a better finish time if he didn't stay with her, they agreed to run separately.

He'd warned Hanna that he would have his daughters that weekend. They were in the back seat when he picked Hanna up at 7:00 a.m. Since the race began and ended in Balboa Stadium, Paula could read and Sam could stare at her phone while they waited.

When Duncan introduced them to Hanna, the tension was palpable. Sam, very blonde and a bit overweight, gave a reluctant "Hi." Paula, almost too thin, was reading whatever was on her Kindle and merely nodded. Not an auspicious beginning. If Hanna's own kids had ever pulled that kind of behavior with someone they'd been introduced to, she'd have called them out right then and there. *What did you say?* They'd quickly have found their manners and corrected with *Nice to meet you.* Otherwise, there would have been trouble from Hanna later. Even Michael expected them to be polite.

But Duncan was silent. Either his daughters had him cowed or he didn't know how to discipline them. Hanna turned in her seat and asked, "Do you run?"

Sam looked up briefly and made a face; Paula shook her head, "No way," and kept reading.

Early on, Hanna and Michael had made a habit of taking their three to good restaurants and theater performances, teaching them how to behave in public. How to ask questions of a waiter. How to respond to adults other than their parents. A day with these two girls was not going to be pleasant. Duncan was planning to take everyone to breakfast after the run. Undoubtedly, there'd be hostile silence all round.

After Duncan parked the car and settled the girls in the stadium, he and Hanna went to check in. At least the morning clouds would keep the temperature down. They helped each other pin on their race numbers and began stretching.

"Nervous?" Duncan asked.

"Nothing to be nervous about. I'm not trying to make a certain time."

He checked his watch, "I'll see you at the finish line," kissed her cheek, and went closer to the front, where the better runners were. She was on her own now.

Everyone was upbeat, glad to be out on a cool morning. Before the starting horn, a girl who was probably no more than ten was beside her. A man in his sixties or seventies was in front of her. The young girl quickly left her behind, and the older man fell behind Hanna. After three miles, she grabbed a cup of water at one of the tables set up along the route. The sun had come out and she was beginning to sweat. Running in the midst of these strangers was energizing. Here she was, a thousand or so miles from home, participating in a race, planning to eat breakfast with a man she'd known only a couple of months, working at a job she'd never imagined having. So much had changed. She'd changed. More confident, less stressed, even when one of Zoey's jobs proved difficult. She liked the new layers in her life—liked herself better.

She checked her watch. She'd been running twenty-five minutes.

When Hanna crossed the finish line, Duncan was waiting. He hugged her enthusiastically. "Good time, congratulations."

She returned the hug. "What was it?"

"Seventy-four minutes. Very respectable for your first competition." He kissed her lightly on the lips.

"What was your time?"

"Thirty-five minutes."

The first thing Hanna did after Duncan dropped her off at Zoey's house was run a hot bath, add lavender-scented bubble bath to the steaming water, and soak. Though she wasn't exactly stiff or sore, the water soothed both mind and body. Looking back on the morning, two things stood out: first, she just might be capable of completing the half marathon in January, even if she had to walk part of the course. And second, she did not like Duncan's children. Did not. She wasn't particularly proud of her reaction to Sam and Paula, but it was what it was.

After breakfast—the girls had insisted on IHOP so they could have Belgian waffles—Duncan drove them to the zoo entrance, where they were meeting their aunt and cousins. As soon as Paula spotted their relatives, she yelled, "Stop." Both girls jumped out of the car, with only a quick "Bye," and vanished in the crowd.

Duncan didn't seem bothered or surprised by their swift exit. "They love the zoo."

"Evidently." She regretted the sarcasm, but he seemed not to notice.

On the drive back to Zoey's, they didn't talk. Hanna had no idea what Duncan was thinking, but she was scripting mother-like dialogue she wished she'd delivered within the girls' hearing. *At least thank your father for taking you out to breakfast.* It was always so easy to be eloquent after the fact.

Once they were parked in Zoey's driveway, Duncan apologized. "I'm sorry the girls weren't more talkative at breakfast. They've always been shy with strangers."

Hanna almost said *That wasn't shyness, that was sulking*, but stopped herself just in time. He had no idea his daughters were probably punishing him for making them attend the race and spend time with her. And she'd thought Michael was terrible at reading his own children.

"Do you ever have conversations with your daughters?" A neutral entrance into the deep and mucky parenting waters.

He shook his head. "I never know what to talk about. If I ask about school or their friends, I'm interrogating them. If I try to share their interests in movies or TV shows, they just clam up. Like I'm the idiot of the century."

"Do you ever take them grocery shopping? If nothing else, you can talk about food, plan what to buy for dinner. Or take them to play miniature golf. There are plenty of things to talk about when someone makes a good shot or misses. Let whatever the three of you are doing generate the dialogue. Doing something and talking works better than forced talking." At least it usually did with her kids.

"They never seem interested in doing anything with me."

They had definitely defeated him. Hanna's patience disappeared. "Oh for heaven's sake." Too late to back off now, "Don't give them a choice."

"But—"

"And make them leave their electronic toys behind. It's too easy for them to tune you out." Brooke hadn't had a smart phone until she graduated. Just a phone phone to use in emergencies. She'd thought she was the most abused teenager on the planet, but at least she couldn't stare at it in lieu of looking at her mother when they were talking.

Relaxed after her long soak and a nap, Hanna was fixing herself a grilled cheese sandwich when Zoey got home around five. Another of her ten-hour workdays. Hanna was beginning to worry about Zoey's constant exhaustion.

"Want me to fix you one?"

"Thanks, yes." Zoey took a can of Sprite from the refrigerator. "I never did get lunch. Not sure about breakfast for that matter. This was one of those days when everything went out of its way to go wrong."

Hanna slid the first sandwich onto a plate, put it in front of Zoey, and began slicing more cheddar. "I realize I know nothing about the cooking side of your business, but can I help in some additional ways, like answering phones? You're running yourself ragged."

"Pre-Christmas is always this way. Well maybe busier this year. Word of mouth has upped our bookings by ten percent."

"Without hiring more staff?"

"I did bring in another pastry chef last week, and I probably need to get Kit an assistant."

Hanna laid the second sandwich on the grill. "You're working awfully hard."

"Yeah." Zoey took a bite of her sandwich. "Umm not bad. I like the mustard."

"Didn't you say you had inquiries from a potential buyer?"

"A month ago, but it didn't come to anything."

"If it's happened once, there must be others out there."

"Could be. But what else would I do? The company has kept me busy," she paused, "kept me from missing Jonathon so much. Sometimes it's like he's still here with me." She stopped. "Let's not talk about that. How was your race?"

"Race good, time spent with Duncan's daughters not so good."

"Brats?"

"Too old to be brats. Downright rude. They treat him like he owes them."

"Because of the divorce?"

"Maybe. Whatever it is, they're making him pay. And I picked the wrong moment to turn back into a mother."

"What did you do?"

"Just made a couple of suggestions."

Zoey shook her head and then laughed. "You always did have trouble not saying what you were thinking. Did you have an argument?"

"Not exactly. He said that leaving my children on their own is not a qualification for criticizing his children and his parenting."

"Oops."

"Yeah."

The dry spell probably wasn't going away anytime soon.

Walt's family had moved from Alamosa to Durango the middle of his junior year. The first day in Home Room, he chose the seat next to Hanna because she was the prettiest girl in the room, her smile genuine. "You're new."

"Yes." He was *new* every few years because the Highway Department kept transferring his father. He smiled at Hanna. This time, being in a new school looked more promising.

"I'm Hanna."

"Walt."

The half hour in Home Room quickly became the best part of his day because, for the rest of the day they were in different classes and had different lunch breaks. Hanna was taking Advanced Placement classes, on track for college, preparing to take the SAT in a few months. Walt, on the other hand, had always struggled in school, happier in shop classes because his Dyslexia made subjects requiring large quantities of reading and paper and pencil tests difficult. He spent his after-school hours with tutors that worked with at-risk students. His counselor told him straight out that taking the SAT probably wasn't a good idea, even if he was allowed extra time.

By the beginning of their senior year, they were a couple. Because his grades weren't good enough to allow him to play a sport, he didn't have a sweater or a ring to give her. After exploring other possibilities, he carved a tiny rose out of a scrap of rosewood and had it made into a pin that he gave to her at the Christmas dance. *Hanna, will you go steady with me?*

Looking back at the gangly innocent he'd been made Walt wonder how he'd had the nerve to ask Hanna if she'd sleep with him. He wanted her to agree beforehand, afraid if he surprised or rushed her, she'd be gone forever. Hanna's "Yes," sent him in search of condoms, and then he waited another month until his parents were in Farmington for the day. Even thirty plus years later, he remembered the sweetness of that day, the joy of discovering each other.

But graduation had changed everything. Hanna was enrolled at U C Boulder. Instead of accepting a job that required only a high school diploma, Walt signed up for the Peace Corps. He and Hanna made solemn promises to each other, but letters traveling between Colorado and Africa moved slower than their new lives.

# CHAPTER 15

CHRISTMAS WAS TEN days away. To take her mind off not being able to get Skype time with Kyle until Christmas day, Lexi went looking for her mother's Christmas decorations stored in plastic boxes in the garage annex.

One by one, she carried the three plastic containers to the living room, carefully unpacked the fragile glass balls that had been her grandmother's, and began untangling the strings of lights. Now she needed a tree, but getting her siblings together to go tree shopping was probably impossible. Brooke was taking her last final, Ry was putting in long hours because one of Walt's jobs had a Christmas deadline and, since Thanksgiving, Callie had been at Saul's almost every night. She and Saul were, however, planning to spend Christmas day at the house. He'd even volunteered to cook dinner. The whole Callie/Saul thing had moved with lightning speed. Lexi was noticing a new softness in her aunt, an aura of contentment. She wondered what her mother would say about the relationship. Hanna usually made negative references about the number of men in Callie's life, stopping just short of suggesting her sister was promiscuous.

As soon as Marie woke from her morning nap, Lexi snapped her into the car seat and headed for the Christmas tree lot adjacent to Home Depot. Hopefully, someone at the lot would help her tie the tree to the roof of the car.

The tree was still on the car roof when Callie got home early Monday afternoon. She'd left Saul's earlier than usual—earlier than Saul wanted her to leave—because she'd found a voice mail message from her on-again/off-again agent Jeremy and didn't want to have the conversation where Saul might overhear her.

*Hey Cal. Got a job for you. A good job. Call me ASAP.* He rattled off his cell number.

Her initial response had been elation. A job. Finally. Her second response was how would accepting a job affect this new relationship with Saul. A sharp reality check that tied a knot in her stomach even before she returned the call.

When she pulled into Hanna's driveway—why did she never think of this house and driveway as half hers—she turned off the truck's engine and made the call.

Jeremy answered on the first ring.

"What took you so long? I thought you'd call me last night."

"No reception at the restaurant." Not entirely a lie. She'd turned her phone off.

Thankfully he didn't ask where she'd gone after she left the restaurant.

"*The Wild Geese* need an acoustic guitarist. They're about to go on tour. Two days ago, their regular guitarist smashed his left hand in a car door, really smashed it. Healing is going to take a while and he'll need lots of rehab before he's able to play again. Eric Layton asked for you specifically. Seemed to know you weren't with Leo anymore."

"Every musician in the country knows that. Where are they now?"

"Frisco. They'll begin rehearsing December 27$^{th}$ and leave for Vancouver, B.C. in early January." He explained the pay—far better than what Leo had paid her—and laid out the contract details. "You need to be up there on the 26th." He gave her the names of the rehearsal hall and hotel, and the confirmation number of an e-ticket that had already been purchased in her name. "Any problem?"

She'd never said no to a job in her life. But this time, there was a new set of complications. Well, just one.

Saul.

She took a deep breath and gambled on Saul understanding why she was accepting the offer. "No. It's fast, that's all." She searched for the notepad in her purse. "Give me the confirmation number and the flight number." She added the name of the hotel. "I have to give notice here." *I have to tell Saul. How do I do that? It's been years since my actions impacted someone else, especially someone who could turn out to be the love of my life,* Such a cliché. She'd laughed at Hanna when her sister had once said that about Michael. And here Callie was—thinking the same thing.

"So give it." The connection went dead.

Saul.

She needed to talk to him face-to-face. Not something that could be done on the phone. Not after the last two weeks. The job sounded like a dream come true. *The Wild Geese* were at the top of their game; their last CD was up for a Grammy. It had been a long time since she'd been part of such a high profile group. Refusing the job would send the wrong signal within the music rumor mill. *Did you hear that Callie Meeker turned down a chance to play with Geese*? But taking the job meant leaving Saul for at least two months. She didn't want to be without him that long. There were moments when she wondered whether what she felt was love; she didn't trust herself when it came to emotional attachments to men. She'd chosen badly too many times. The list of those bad choices was long and embarrassing.

Saul didn't feel like a bad choice.

Not bothering to go inside to tell Lexi that she was driving back to Saul's, she reversed into the street and headed for the highway. She felt as wired as if she'd had a dozen cups of coffee.

Halfway to the Grub, she pulled over to call Saul's cell phone.

"I need to talk to you."

"I'm working in the kitchen."

"I'll be there in a few minutes."

"What's wrong?"

"I'll be there soon."

"Cal, you're scaring me." But she'd already broken the connection.

When she arrived, Saul was standing in the restaurant's parking lot where the cold sun was slowly melting the mounds of snow that had been scraped off the asphalt. His heavy sweater wasn't warm enough, but he hadn't stopped to look for a jacket. As soon as her truck stopped, he was at her door, opening it even before she'd pulled the key from the ignition.

He kissed her. "Come inside. It's freezing out here."

Once they were in his office at the back of the dining room, he poured both of them coffee and sat beside her on the leather couch. "What's going on?"

She loved the intensity of his eyes reaching into her. Almost handsome, he had a strong jaw, a nose that had once been broken, and a smile that could make her catch her breath.

At this moment, he wasn't smiling.

*Say it quickly.* "I've received a job offer."

He didn't respond.

"It's a group called *The Wild Geese*. Have you heard of them?"

He nodded.

"Their guitarist wrecked his left hand, and they're about to go on tour."

Quietly, "Do you have to audition?"

"No. The job's mine. They know my work. I have a ticket to fly to San Francisco the day after Christmas."

A week away. Not much time for either of them to adjust.

His face darkened. Not with anger, more with disappointment. Softly, "How long?"

"Two months or so."

He couldn't think of anything to say.

Neither could she.

Both knew that, if he asked her to stay, asked her to turn this opportunity down, she might come to resent her sacrifice. But if she went, she might not be back anytime soon. Sometimes one job led seamlessly to another. And people took different roads.

"I need to give it a shot." She reached for his hand, "Do you understand?"

"Yes." Understanding was different from accepting.

His arm drew her close, his face resting against her hair. Finally, gently, "I'll miss you."

"Me too—you."

A long silence.

With effort, he shifted gears, "Are you coming back tonight? Right now that's what matters most."

She nodded, not sure her voice would be steady.

Quietly. "I ordered a goose for the Christmas dinner with your family."

"A goose!" She pulled away, laughing. "Even before you knew about *The Wild Geese*. What a crazy man you are."

"Agreed. You'll love it."

She was pretty sure Hanna's kids wouldn't. They didn't do strange foods very well. Their loss.

She was so thankful Saul wasn't trying to talk her out of taking the job. His generosity only made her love him more.

*Yes,* she admitted to herself, *it's love*.

Callie told Lexi about the job as they were wrestling the Christmas tree into its red metal stand—an impossible task for one, almost impossible for two.

"Why is my idiot brother never around when we need him?" Lexi grumbled.

Callie screwed the third bolt into the tree trunk. "Probably a law of some kind. Is it straight?"

"No. Let the last screw out a bit."

Callie complied.

"Stop. That's good enough. Once the decorations are on, no one will notice that it leans a little."

"Or care."

"So, is this a good job?"

"Yes. Or I wouldn't bother."

"Does Saul know?"

"Yes." The memory of his reaction made tears threaten. "He was happy for me. Not so happy otherwise."

Lexi picked up a string of the tiny colored lights and began weaving them through the tree limbs. "You guys got serious fast."

"At our age, we don't have time to waste."

"Will you come back here when the tour's over?"

"I hope so."

"But if you two are—"

"Things can change. He might rethink our relationship and, let's face it, I've never stayed in one place for any length of time. I honestly don't know if I'm a candidate for settling down."

Always the romantic, Lexi asked, "Do you love him?"

A long pause. "Could be." She wasn't ready to admit the power of her feelings. Superstitious perhaps.

"If I had to choose between a job and Kyle, Kyle would win every time."

"That's because you are you. And that's what makes you happy. A man has never made me as happy as music has. Different experiences."

"I guess." Lexi wasn't convinced.

Callie wasn't convinced either.

By the time Brooke and Ryan came home, the tree was trimmed and the packages Hanna had sent via UPS—one for each of them and four for Marie—were under the tree. The room looked more festive than any of them felt.

Ryan listened to the news about Callie's departure without comment, but Brooke immediately shifted into drama gear.

"You're going too! How are we going to manage? It was bad enough when Mom left. What is it with everyone?" She grabbed her backpack and stomped upstairs.

"Jeez, Brooke. Not everything is about you." Ryan headed for the kitchen. "Is dinner ready?"

"No. Fix yourself a sandwich." Weeks ago, Callie had begun to sympathize with Hanna's desire to escape parenting.

Hanna and Zoey were planning to spend Christmas day at Zoey's sister's house in San Diego. Christmas Eve day, Hanna would be working into the early afternoon. A brunch for a large family reunion at a home on top of Mount Soledad. The week before Christmas, Duncan had invited Hanna to spend Christmas Eve afternoon with him and his girls. He had matinee tickets for the Old Globe's annual production of *How the Grinch Stole Christmas*. She'd been surprised by the invitation. After their 10K run, there had been a week of being uncomfortably polite with each other because of his response to Hanna's unsolicited advice. And now he was going to put them all together again? She wondered whether he was so uncomfortable with his children that he was using her as some kind of buffer.

"I don't think I'll be finished with the brunch in time." She was glad she had a solid excuse.

Since the 10K race, she'd begun to look at her relationship with Duncan more realistically. Though she enjoyed his company, she was increasingly wary. Taking part in his life would mean taking on his daughters. Why would she want to do that? More parenting she did not need. Especially step-parenting. She'd come to Zoey's to get away from her own responsibilities. She wasn't proud of leaving her children and someday, maybe soon, she'd have to confront what she'd done. But she wasn't willing to compound the problem.

Being with Duncan's family looked less and less like a good idea.

The lie had come easily. "And I already have plans later in the day with an old friend who'll be visiting San Diego." She didn't know she could lie so effortlessly. Nothing to brag about.

"Too bad," he was definitely disappointed. "I already bought you a ticket."

"Perhaps one of your daughter's friends would like to go."

No answer. They finished their run in silence—they'd been doing that a lot lately. And didn't stop for coffee. An admission that they didn't have anything more to talk about.

Being in California had given her a chance to test herself, to spread her wings in ways she hadn't in Durango. This revised version of Hanna trusted her own abilities and, other than taking responsibility for jobs at Zoey's, didn't owe anyone anything—for now. Independence was giving her chances to explore pieces of herself she'd neglected. She had begun drawing again and was planning to buy a few tubes of watercolor paint the next time she was near an art store. There were other more visible changes. She'd lost almost fifteen pounds. Mostly because of her running but also because she was eating healthier, not cooking for children who wanted sweets and carbohydrates. Her hair was shorter. Not quite touching her shoulders and she'd let the young woman who cut it talk her into a few highlights to help hide the gray strands.

She was eager to face each new day and, so long as she didn't let her mind wander to what Walt or her kids were doing, she was fine. More than fine.

# CHAPTER 16

WALT HATED INDECISION. In his customers, his family, and especially in himself. Ever since it was clear that Hanna wasn't going to come home anytime soon, he'd been debating a trip to California. The debate was disrupting his sleep. The *Do Not Go* side argued he'd look like a lovesick fool. What made him think he could encourage her to come back? For him. He was well acquainted with her stubborn streak. In high school, she refused to go out for the cheerleading squad even though she'd have been a shoo in. She was pretty and athletic and popular. Instead, she went out for the track team, preferring to hang out with the jocks. *Why would I subject myself to all that gossiping and competitive dressing?*

The *Get Your Butt to California* side argued that he'd already wasted too much time. He needed to tell her he loved her. He'd never actually said those words—not even when they were sleeping together during their senior year. Dumb kid that he was, he'd assumed that making love said he loved her, that the words which seemed corny and trite when he was seventeen weren't necessary.

But of course they were.

He'd figured that out too late. At least he'd had the brains to say those words to Lily—and mean them. By then, Hanna was long out of his life and engaged to a law student.

If he didn't go to California, go after her, perhaps that guy Ryan mentioned—Duncan somethingorother—would be wise enough to say the right things and, once again, Walt would be left behind.

The remodeling job with the Christmas deadline actually finished early and, at the last minute, his aunt announced she was coming from Farmington to spend Christmas with his mother. Suddenly, he had nothing to keep him in Durango.

Except fear.

Three days before Christmas, he booked a seat to San Diego via Phoenix. The layover in Phoenix would be longer than the total time in the air. When he called Hanna's house, Callie answered.

"I need Hanna's address in California."

"Took you long enough."

"Yeah. I deserve that."

"Just a minute." When she returned, she read off the address for Seabrook and for Zoey's house. "Are you driving or flying?"

"Flying. This time of year the roads between here and Phoenix can be problematic if a storm moves in. I'll rent a car when I get there. How far is Del Mar from San Diego?"

"Not far, half an hour north, depending on the traffic. It's been a while since I played San Diego."

"How's Saul?"

"Good. We're good," she paused. She was pretty sure Saul had told Walt about her new job. "I suppose he told you I'm leaving next week."

"He did." It had been a long time since Walt had seen Saul so depressed.

"I know I'm upsetting the apple cart." Another stupid cliché. What was happening to her? Love was not an apple cart.

"I don't even have a cart to upset. Have a good Christmas."

It was late Christmas Eve morning when he checked into the Sheraton on Harbor Island and asked the concierge for a map of the

San Diego area. He left his overnighter in the room and headed for the parking lot. His heavy white sweater was definitely too warm for the weather. No matter. He'd turn on the car's air conditioning. Now that he was here, he didn't want to waste time changing clothes.

Before he started the car, he took a quick look at the map. According to the notes he'd made while talking to Callie, he needed to find I-5 north. Seabrook Catering was just off Del Mar Heights Road. He'd try there first.

The set up for the Mount Soledad brunch was simple because the house itself was so beautifully decorated that Hanna only needed to do the tables. Bright red, a touch of orange and white. These days she was able to cope with the set ups by herself. As she was loading the empty boxes into her car, a pretty blonde teenager came running from the house and handed her a large box of See's candy. "My mother says to thank Mrs. Seabrook for everything."

"How nice. I will. Thank your mother," a client who'd been easy to work with. Over these months, Hanna had learned to appreciate the easy ones.

Twenty minutes later, as she unlocked the back entrance to the Seabrook kitchen, she heard voices in the reception area.

She stacked the empty boxes on the shelves near the door and grabbed the box of candy. Zoey was seated on one of the couches talking to a man whose face Hanna couldn't see but, as she pushed through the swinging door, she recognized Walt's voice.

Here.

She stopped, suddenly disoriented.

Zoey looked up, "Here she is. You have company, Hanna."

Walt stood and smiled hesitantly.

Hanna was accustomed to seeing him in his work clothes stained with whatever he'd been working with. Today he was wearing stylish denim slacks, polished tan loafers instead of the usual work boots, and a white sweater that must have been uncomfortably warm. Very nice indeed.

She smiled.

He closed the gap between them and kissed her cheek. “I hope you don’t mind that I didn’t call ahead.” *I didn’t want you to tell me not to come.*

“What brings you here?”

“You,” he paused, “I didn’t know what to get you for Christmas so I brought myself.” He didn’t want to sound too serious.

What a lovely speech. Walt wasn’t usually given to pretty speeches. Hanna wasn’t sure what to say. She knew she was blushing.

Zoey pushed herself off the couch and picked up her purse, intending to get out of their way. “Where’d you get the candy?”

“Oh, sorry. It’s for you or the clean up crew. From Mrs. Simons. A thank you.”

“Nice lady. I’ll leave it in the kitchen. I need to go home and wrap presents. My sister hates it when I just shove gifts into brown paper bags.”

Uncertain what should come next, Hanna moved to one of the couches and sat down. Sitting across from her, Walt was no more certain than she was. Their entire relationship had been confined to Durango and environs. On so many levels, this was untested territory.

He couldn’t read her expression. “Do you mind that I came to see you?”

“No, of course not. It’s just a surprise. I’ve been working all morning; my brain is stuck in work mode.” *And you’re the last person I expected.* “When did you get here?”

“This morning. I took an early flight to Phoenix and then to San Diego. I’m staying near the airport.”

Hanna had never before had trouble talking to Walt. Suddenly she was tongue-tied, and he wasn’t helping.

*Try the obvious.*

"Have you had lunch? I'm starving."

He looked relieved. "Is there a restaurant close by?"

Hanna locked the front door, and they walked across the parking lot to Sammy's Woodfired Pizza and Grill. A notice on the door warned that the restaurant would close at 5 p.m. It already felt closed. Only one other table was occupied.

Walt held her chair, "Guess no one eats out on Christmas Eve."

"Everyone's supposed to be at home with family—"

"And friends," he finished her thought.

She smiled. "Yes, friends. It's nice of you to come all this way. What about your mother? What will she do tomorrow with you here?"

"Aunt Agnes is sitting in Mom's living room right now. They'll gossip, play bridge with Mom's cronies, and have Christmas dinner in the retirement community dining room. They were glad to get rid of me."

The waitress brought two iced teas and took their order. Walt drank some of the tea, "Cold tea at Christmas. At home, they'd look at us like we were crazy."

"There don't seem to be food or clothing seasons out here; no one worries about whether you're overdressed or underdressed so long as you're not undressed."

He folded his arms on the table. "Are you happy here? You look happy." If this place made her happy, how could he suggest she go back to Durango? Where she hadn't been happy.

"I am."

"Are you going to stay in California?" *Please say no.*

She shrugged slightly. "Not sure."

He cautioned himself to back off. "What do you do at Zoey's?"

A safer topic. She gave him the abridged version. By the time their food arrived, she was telling him about the 10K run and the January half marathon, appreciating how easy it was to talk to him.

Around a slice of pepperoni pizza, Walt said, "It's like you're back on the track team."

"Sort of."

He wanted to ask about Duncan, get a sense of that relationship. But as was his way, he didn't. Instead, "Good pizza."

"How long are you staying?"

"I have an early flight the twenty-sixth. If you have plans for tonight and tomorrow, don't worry. I can entertain myself. I just wanted to see you, make sure you were okay." *And tell you what I should have told you a long time ago.*

"I don't have any major plans."

"Ry mentioned something about a guy named Duncan."

"He's with his daughters this weekend. *And fortunately my lie about a visitor is no longer a lie.* Zoey and I are invited to her sister's for dinner tomorrow. You can probably come too. Her sister has three teenagers. Adding another plate is normal."

"Check with Zoey first."

"Of course. Let's go over to the house when we're finished eating. I'd like to get into more comfortable clothes, and I want you to see where I'm living."

It was beyond strange having Walt here—old and new worlds colliding. He was waiting in Zoey's living room when Hanna came downstairs, more relaxed in a pair of black yoga pants and a long-sleeved white t-shirt. She found a couple of clean wine glasses, retrieved what was left of a bottle of Sauvignon Blanc and they went onto the deck. The air was damp but not too cool yet. The surf high and loud.

"You're right on the beach. Amazing." He took the bottle from her and poured wine into their glasses. "Does Zoey want to join us?"

"She's knee deep in wrapping paper right now. She's not bashful. If she feels like it, she'll be down."

They sat sipping the wine, letting the sound of the waves fill the space between them. He was probably expecting her to ask about her family. Open Pandora's box.

"How's Callie doing with my brood?"

In the dim light from the living room, she saw him smile. "No lives have been lost. A few bumps and bruises." He recounted the washing machine story and Ryan's grudging acceptance of the job. "To his credit, he kept working even after the machine was fixed."

"Is he a good employee?"

"After a slow start, yes. Took him a week or two to stop falling all over himself."

Hanna was relieved. "He just hasn't found direction." And here she was making excuses for him. That *mother gene.*

"I doubt he wants to stay in construction. My guess is he's getting ready to go to law school. He drove over to Colorado Springs to take the LSAT right after Thanksgiving."

Hanna sighed. "Michael finally got to him. Lexi mentioned they'd talked at Thanksgiving."

Reading her mind, "It's not your fault, you know. Ryan qualifies as an adult."

"You don't—" *understand* hung in the air.

"I do. My mother is still trying to mother me. I call it the umbilical cord curse."

Hanna laughed. She'd missed Walt's practicality and humor. "It is a curse. I've tried to stay below the radar since I left, but it's impossible to stop being a mother."

An opening. "Why did you leave?" *Not even a phone call.*

She poured herself more wine. "I'd been thinking about it for a while, about taking a trip as soon as Brooke was settled at the university. I figured Ry would be off somewhere. Lexi was in California."

"Freedom."

"Temporary freedom. Then everyone was back at the house. When Callie showed up, it wasn't as though I was leaving them entirely on their own. As crazy as Callie's life has always been, she wouldn't let them fall apart completely. I suspect she'll give me an ear full the next time I see her." A pause. "I'm sorry I didn't call you. I was afraid I'd lose my courage. Once I told them I was leaving on vacation, I had to get out of there. I was gone the next morning before they got up."

Walt reached between their chairs to take Hanna's hand. She didn't resist. "Did Lexi tell you that Callie's seeing Saul White?" He omitted the fact that Callie would be leaving in forty-eight hours.

"Callie always has a fella. When we were in high school, some of them started out as my fellas."

"I remember."

"You were my fella."

"Yes, I was." *Still am.* "They're pretty good kids, you know."

"I do know. I just needed something—for me. Just me." Not a politically correct attitude.

"Has this worked?"

"I think so. Thanks to Zoey's generosity." She retrieved her hand. "Enough of my neurotic behavior. How are you, how's business?"

He let her change the topic. "After the holidays, I'm starting on the lobby and dining room of the Silver Hotel in Silverton, and I've begun renovating a house out on the Animas River. It's a long-term project. I'm fitting it in between other jobs."

"Those houses aren't all that old."

"This one was badly treated, but it's sound. I bought it at a foreclosure auction. I should be able to make a profit eventually or live in it myself." He didn't add *with you,* but that had been his reason for buying it.

They talked and talked. About her kids, Callie and Saul, his mother, Zoey and Seabrook, the differences between California and Durango. The latest Durango gossip. Like a very long Tuesday lunch.

When it got too cold to stay outside, they moved into the kitchen where they found Zoey, who was soon telling stories about catering disasters.

And suddenly it was midnight. Zoey raised her wine glass. “Merry Christmas, my friends. It’s been fun but I’m wiped. See you later today.”

Walt stood up too. “I need to find my way back to the hotel. On Durango time it’s one o’clock.”

Hanna walked him out to the car. “Dinner isn’t until three. What would you like to do tomorrow?” *It would be nice to spend time with him.*

“Surprise me.” He grinned, leaned over and kissed her thoroughly, very thoroughly. She was having trouble catching her breath.

“I’ve missed you.” His eyes were holding hers in much the same way his mouth had been holding hers. “I’ll call you as I leave the hotel in the morning.”

# Chapter 17

Hanna slept soundly, not waking until her cell phone rang.

"Merry Christmas, Mom."

Lexi.

"Merry Christmas, darling."

"Were you still asleep?"

"Yes." She glanced at the bedside clock. 7 a.m. "It's an hour earlier here."

"Oops. Forgot. Marie wants to talk to you." There were various unidentifiable noises, then, "It's your Nana."

Baby babbling.

"Hi Marie. Was Santa Claus good to you?"

More babbling.

Lexi interrupted. "She thinks she's really telling us an important story. Very cute. I'll send a video to your phone."

"Did she like her bear? There's a store here where you can build the bear to your specifications."

"Before she woke up, I took it out of the box and set it under the tree. She went for it immediately. And I love my necklace."

"I'm glad." Hanna had found it at the Indian Market in Old Town.

"I'm sorry we didn't get you anything."

"It's okay." *Not really. Punishment for leaving town?*

An uncomfortable silence. "There are stacks of Christmas cards here. Do you want me to send them to you?"

"No. They'll keep. I didn't send any this year."

Easier than explaining what she'd been doing, where she was. When it came right down to it, she didn't feel much of a connection with most of the people from her discarded existence. Some she hadn't seen for years. Parents of her children's friends, a few couples she and Michael had socialized with and who'd sympathized with Hanna when Michael's infidelity became public. Maybe she'd never send cards again. Less was required when you were a runaway. Rather exhilarating to ignore convention. Once again Callie came to mind.

"Where are Brooke and Ryan?"

"Haven't seen Brooke this morning. I think she's with Dennis. Ryan's asleep, and Callie and Saul are already banging pots and pans in the kitchen. He's fixing a goose."

"You're kidding."

"No. I'm told he's a very good cook."

"Walt showed up on my doorstep yesterday. He told me about Saul and Callie."

"They're really into each other. I'm surprised she agreed to go on tour."

"She's leaving?" That could be a problem. Hanna was not ready for problems.

"Early tomorrow."

In the beginning, Hanna had been afraid Callie would take off but, once she had the job at Mountain Grub, it looked like she might hang around. Reducing Hanna's guilt. For less than a second, she wondered whether she should go home—then stopped herself. *Why would I do that?* Callie's departure would simply be Stage Two of getting the children to take care of themselves. Potentially a good thing. But only potentially.

By the time Hanna showered and poured cold cereal into one of Zoey's orange bowls, Walt called to say he was on his way. Fifteen minutes later, Zoey wandered into the kitchen in an old pair of sweats, opening the sliding glass door to let the ocean in. "Gorgeous day. Merry Christmas. Have you and Walt decided what to do until dinner?"

"No." Hanna rinsed her bowl and made room for it in the dishwasher.

"Believe it or not, the zoo is open today. You could spend some time there."

"At the zoo?" Odd choice for Christmas.

"The animals don't do holidays. It won't be crowded. It'll give the two of you time to walk and talk."

"You think we need to talk?"

"He didn't come for the sun and surf."

*Yeah. That occurred to me too.*

"My guess is the man has something on his mind. He seems like one of the good guys."

"He is. Always has been."

"But?"

"It's been mostly me holding back."

"Why?"

"I don't know if I want another committed relationship. It's too painful when they fall apart. I'm going through a selfish phase."

"What about Duncan? You two have spent a lot of time together lately."

"Are you into matchmaking?"

Zoey emptied the last of the coffee into her cup and perched on one of the stools at the counter. "Not I. Just being a nosy roommate."

Uneasy with the turn the conversation had taken, Hanna busied herself with making a fresh pot of coffee. "Duncan's fun to be with, but remember that his daughters hate me. I already have three children I'm trying to unparent. I'm not a good candidate for being a step-parent."

"Do you want to get married again?"

Hanna shrugged. "What about you?"

"I'm not looking. Jonathon would be hard to replace."

"Understood."

"And Walt is—?"

Hanna wasn't sure she could answer that question.

A friend. Absolutely.

Her first love thirty years ago; both of them naïve about life and love.

Hanna was pretty sure she was afraid to trust her heart/her life to anyone—even someone as trustworthy as Walt. Not his fault.

Michael's fault.

Why in heaven's name was she letting Michael wreck any more of her life than he already had? Time to unload that baggage.

Wandering around the zoo on a warm Christmas morning—the thermometer pushing eighty degrees—Walt felt as if he were in a parallel universe. A polar bear slipping into the water and a tiger yawning as it stretched itself awake. No Santa Claus or Christmas songs. And thankfully no snow.

He'd chuckled when Hanna suggested the zoo. "If people ask how my Christmas was, instead of the usual *fine*, I can say *wild*."

Hanna laughed. He noticed she laughed more easily than she had in her last months in Durango. This Hanna seemed younger, lighter; perhaps it was the haircut or the bright colors in her blouse. He resisted the urge to kiss her.

Instead, he held her hand. Most of their conversation was about their surroundings. Was it difficult to be a flamingo, always standing on one leg? The cleverness of the walkway threading through the monkey forest, the view from the Skyfari. Neither mentioned the family she wasn't spending Christmas with.

Just before three o'clock, the GPS in Walt's rental car guided them to Zoey's sister's house on Hortensia in Mission Hills. A quietly affluent enclave of craftsmen homes above Old Town State Park. Luckily, they'd found an open liquor store and bought two bottles of wine for their hosts. An enjoyable meal with Carol, Zoey's sister, her husband Ron, their three sons, and their neighbors, a Federal judge and his wife, who was still teaching at the neighborhood elementary school. Since one of the neighbors' sons was in the Peace Corps in South America, Walt was soon telling them some of his African adventures.

Back at Zoey's, they fixed hot chocolate and sat out on the deck. The warmth of the day was gradually being replaced by a cool dampness. All day, Hanna sensed that Walt had something on his mind, something that lay just beneath their casual conversations. When would he get around to telling her? Was he dating someone?

His feet were propped on the deck railing in front of his chair. "Do you think there'll be fog in the morning? My flight leaves at 7:10."

"Maybe, but unless the fog is really thick, it shouldn't be a problem. Do you have a lot of work waiting at home?"

"Nothing pressing, mostly paperwork and phone calls. Very little will happen until after New Year's. What about you?"

"We have a busy week. The holidays are Seabrook's busiest time."

"Do you like working for Zoey?"

"Yes," she hesitated, "but I'm pretty sure she's going to sell out if she can."

Besides, Isabel would be back the second week of January. Either way, Hanna wouldn't have a job much longer.

"Could you work for the new owner?"

"I don't know—perhaps." Hanna had avoided thinking about not working at Seabrook. She had been avoiding thinking about a number of things, Walt being one of them. Stepping beyond where she was today would require decisions she wasn't ready to make. Until these last months, she'd always been pretty good at making decisions. Now she was on hold.

"Are you ever coming back to Durango?" His voice was deeper; the mood had shifted.

"I suppose. Sometime."

Her answer didn't help him segue into confessing his feelings. He was holding his breath, preparing to bungee jump off an emotional cliff. Slowly, he let out the breath. "What would bring you back?"

She moved over to the railing, staring into a darkness that held no answer.

"Would you—come back—for me?" The words hung in the evening air.

It seemed hours before she answered, "I don't quite understand."

He went to stand beside her. "Would you come back because I ask you to?" A minute or two more, then "I love you, Hanna." Three words so long coming, "I've loved you for a long time. I miss you."

Hesitantly, she turned to face him. He was serious. Maybe a little frightened. Strange since Walt always seemed so sure of himself.

"I've been waiting for you to get over the divorce," he left out *patiently,* "but now you're here, living a whole new life. I'm afraid I'm losing you."

Very gently, Walt folded her against his chest and kissed her, not the way he usually kissed her. This kiss began slowly, softly, gradually escalating to an urgency that pushed her mouth open, tangled their tongues. Little by little, Hanna felt herself disappearing into him, his hands in her hair, holding her as he moved his mouth to her neck. She let out a soft moan.

He stopped, as though he was afraid he'd gone too far, and briefly brushed her lips with his fingertips. "I don't expect an answer now." He was very still, looking into her, all the way into her, silently telling her things she hadn't known he felt; then he moved away, walked through the living room, grabbed his windbreaker off the couch, and let himself out.

Not sure her legs would hold her, Hanna sat down.

Stunned.

Confused.

Thoughts racing in all directions.

When the wind turned cold, she picked up the empty cups, took them into the kitchen, and climbed the stairs to her room. She was glad Zoey wasn't home. Zoey had a penchant for asking uncomfortable questions, and Hanna was already uncomfortable enough.

Her relationship with Walt had made a 180 turn. There was no way to go back to just friendship. He wanted more. She hadn't thought she wanted more. But maybe it was time to stop hiding from her emotions. She'd certainly kissed him as though she wanted more too.

Across the waiting room outside the United Airlines departure gates in Phoenix, Walt spotted Callie, her guitar case propped against the seat next to her. He moved the guitar over one seat and sat down. "Happy day after Christmas."

She turned, her eyes red and a little puffy, as though she'd been crying, "Hey Walt. Back already?"

He shrugged. "I said my piece and got out of there before my heart got stomped on. How was Christmas with the young Sheridans?"

"Except for Brooke staying away, good enough. Having a baby around helps. Saul fixed a goose."

"Brave man."

"In more ways than one." Because he believed in her, believed she wasn't leaving him permanently. "How was your day?"

"We went to the zoo, then had dinner with Zoey's family."

"And how is my wayward sister?"

"Happy, I think." He didn't want to talk about Hanna. The last forty-eight hours were still too tender. Though her response to his kiss was encouraging, he was afraid to get ahead of himself.

"Wow. Both Meeker girls happy at the same time and both leaving their men alone."

The attendant at the gate called his Durango flight. He picked up his carry-on, "Call in once in a while. Let us know where you are."

She nodded, her eyes filled. It was hard to ask: "Take care of Saul for me."

"Will do."

Walt didn't get into his emails until the next day. Among the messages was a note from Ryan Sheridan, giving Anders Construction his notice, effective immediately. No reason. Just quitting.

# CHAPTER 18

THE WEEK BETWEEN Christmas and New Year's, Hanna did her training runs by herself. No sign of Duncan and no message on her voice mail.

In the meantime, Walt's *I love you* speech was giving her plenty to think about while she was running. She would never have guessed Walt would show up on Zoey's doorstep. When she'd decided to escape, she wasn't running from him, hadn't thought about the effect on him, that he'd be collateral damage. Her children and her sister were the intended targets, though they'd probably missed the message.

Over four months in California.

The half marathon was suddenly only ten days away. With or without Duncan, she planned to run the thirteen plus miles. Besides, she'd already paid the $95.00 entry fee.

And after that?

She still had half a dozen jobs to do for Zoey; then she'd turn her records over to Isabel, and Isabel would reclaim her job, or Zoey might sell the business and perhaps the house. At that point, Hanna would have to regroup. If she followed up on Walt's declaration and kiss, she'd have to go home. But if she went back, she might lose what the last months had given her—and that hypothetical gate would slam shut.

Delivering Ryan's final paycheck gave Walt a good excuse to drive over to Hanna's. The sky was threatening snow, charcoal clouds clustered over the mesas above town. Durango had only had snow once this season, just after Thanksgiving.

Callie's truck and Lexi's car were in the driveway. In the dull winter light, the house looked rather forlorn surrounded by its winter-brown lawn and skeletal trees.

Wearing worn cords and a faded USMC sweatshirt that was too big for her, Lexi answered his knock. "Hi Walt. Ry's not here."

She looked so much like Hanna.

"I just came to drop off Ryan's final paycheck. Can I leave it with you?"

"Sure. Come in. Marie is having a long sleep this afternoon, so I'm catching up on laundry." She studied the check Walt handed her. "He quit?"

"According to the email he sent the day after Christmas."

"That explains his shopping trips to the mall and the sudden urge to clean his room. Would you like tea? I could use a break."

He nodded. "You're one of the few people who remember that I prefer tea."

"Today feels like tea. It's supposed to snow later."

"You didn't know Ryan was planning on quitting?"

She ran water in the battered copper teakettle that had been her grandmother's and set it on the front burner. "No one's sharing much around here these days."

"Any guess what he's going to do?" It had taken three months to turn Ryan into a fairly decent employee—at this point Walt hated to lose him.

"I'd guess law school. He's run out of excuses for my father, who hasn't been happy about Ry working for you. Well not you specifically, but working construction."

"Not a fan of manual labor, I take it?"

The kettle whistled. Lexi dropped a tea bag into each mug, poured the water over them, and handed one to Walt. "Something like that. My father doesn't approve of Kyle being a marine either. If it's not a white collar, six-figure job, it's not worthwhile. He's a snob."

*And he hurt Hanna,* Walt added silently. "Are you going to be all right financially without Callie and Ryan's checks?"

"And without Brooke's. She's moving out too."

"When did that happen?"

"I only found out this morning. She and Dennis rented a one-bedroom apartment near campus. Though how they're going to afford it, I don't know. Dad's only giving her money for tuition and books." Lexi brought her mug to the table and sat down across from him. "It's ironic. I move back here because I don't want to be alone while Kyle's deployed, and I've gone from living with four people to being on my own with Marie." Her voice wavered.

"Are you going to tell your mother?"

Lexi shook her head. "Not on your life. In this family, tattling always backfires. They're going to do what they're going to do. And Mom sort of lost any influence she might have had when she left. How is she, by the way?"

"Good." Callie must have told her he was going to California. He stirred sugar into his tea. "Subtle changes. More peaceful than the last time I saw her. She's changed her hair style and is getting ready to run a half marathon."

"Was your visit worthwhile?"

*If only I knew.* "Results aren't in yet. But we had a good time. Warm weather on Christmas reminded me of Africa."

"Do you think she's planning on coming back? I mean, all her stuff is here, her family's here, well most of it. I still don't understand why she left, though I'm not upset about it like Brooke is."

Walt pulled his keys out of his jacket pocket and stood up. "Think of it this way. Are there days you wish someone would take care of Marie so you could go to the mall by yourself or see a movie?"

Lexi looked down for a moment, then met his eyes. "Yeah."

"Imagine twenty-five years feeling that way. Topped off by your father's affair and the divorce."

She searched his face for a few moments, then "You love her."

He smiled. "Always have."

"Does she know?"

"She does now."

"And?"

"As I said, the results aren't in. Let me know if you need anything—that includes money."

"Thanks, we're okay, and Kyle only has another six or seven weeks. We're almost there."

It snowed through the night, giving the Durango snowplows plenty to do. Brooke spent the morning filling boxes with her winter clothes and the textbooks she'd bought for the spring semester. The furnished apartment she and Dennis were renting was so small that there wasn't room for much of anything other than the essentials. She was even leaving her skis behind. Lift tickets were not in the budget anyway. Between the pots and pans Dennis's mother was giving them and what Brooke borrowed from her mother's house—two sets of sheets and several bath towels—they'd have enough to get by.

The apartment was two blocks from campus—less driving—a three-story complex mostly occupied by college students. The rent was reasonable but would still be a stretch. At least they could finally spend more time with each other and have some privacy. Brooke had already put in for more hours at the restaurant and cut back to nine units at the college. She didn't intend to tell her father about taking fewer classes or that his Christmas check had gone toward the deposit on the apartment. Since Thanksgiving, he'd returned only one of her calls and, despite Sheri's talk about reconnecting as a family, she'd also been silent. No need for Hanna to know about the apartment either. Since both her parents were busy living their own lives, she and Dennis should be allowed to live theirs.

It wasn't hard to leave this house; she'd only lived here four years. The house and bedroom she really missed were the ones in Denver. That bedroom had French doors opening onto a tiny balcony overlooking the swimming pool and garden. Her world before her parents' divorce. This house had never felt like home. It would forever be her grandparents' house, a bit dated and seriously drafty in the winter.

She wondered whether her mother felt the same way about the house, making it easy for her to take off for California. Brooke hadn't thought about her mother's departure as anything but selfishness, but maybe there was more to it. Maybe she missed their old house and life in Denver too. There was, however, no point thinking about her mother. It was time to concentrate on this adventure with Dennis. She could start a new life too. She taped up the box full of her shoes and went to clean out the bathroom.

Tomorrow, *The Wild Geese* and Callie were scheduled to fly to Vancouver, B.C. for their first performances. They'd been rehearsing and rehearsing ever since Callie arrived. Two intense weeks submerged in learning the arrangements, fitting herself into the sound the band was known for. A steep learning curve, even for Callie.

She hadn't had the time or energy to call Saul as often as she should have. Nevertheless, he was planning to fly to Vancouver to catch the opening. Though she was eager to see him, she worried that their feelings for each other might have cooled since she'd kissed him goodbye at the Durango airport. It had happened to her before.

She'd also put off calling Hanna. As different as their lives and interests had always been, being in Durango with Hanna's children had given Callie a better sense of who her sister was, what Hanna's life was like. The last four months had also uncovered parts of herself she'd never paid attention to. She rather liked playing at the restaurant, liked spending most of her spare time with Saul and Hanna's kids, being part of something besides strange cities and nondescript hotel rooms. And the applause at Mountain Grub was all for her.

It was after ten in the evening when Hanna answered her cell.

"Han, it's me."

"Where are you?"

"San Francisco. Tomorrow, the band flies to Vancouver. We'll be there five or six days."

"Lexi told me you had a new job."

"Yeah. It was too good to pass up. Great money. I should have been the one to tell you."

"Not a problem."

"The kids will be okay, you know."

"Hope so." Hanna didn't sound convinced.

"I hear Walt paid you a visit."

"We spent Christmas day together."

"Our paths crossed at the Phoenix airport the day after Christmas." Callie skipped the part about having given Walt Zoey's address.

"Good timing."

Silence.

"Are we okay Han? I mean about my leaving?"

"Yes. Always. Break a leg."

A dial tone.

Callie wasn't sure the *always* was true but, for the moment, she'd take it.

The Monday before the marathon, Duncan was once again waiting at Zoey's deck when Hanna left the house. A cold morning by California standards, so she was wearing a sweatshirt.

She was glad to see him, "Hello, stranger." She had missed the discipline of running with him. "Ready to run?"

"I should have called to explain. Paula had an emergency appendectomy. And since she needed care and the college was on break, she's been recuperating at my place. Sam stayed at her mother's."

Why hadn't his ex taken care of her daughter? Asking was certainly not a good idea. Hanna was silently relieved he hadn't asked for her help. A healthy Paula was difficult enough. "How is she?"

"Back in school as of today." He sounded relieved.

They began the ritual of stretching.

"Not much of a holiday for either of you."

"Got that right. How was your Christmas? Did your friend come?"

"He was here two days."

"Did you have a good time?"

Good and emotionally confusing, but she wasn't about to discuss the confusing part with anyone, not even Zoey. "Yes. We spent Christmas day at the zoo."

"Does he live in Durango?"

"He owns a construction company there."

"Known him long?"

"Since high school." She needed to get Duncan off the subject. "Let's do this." Hanna pulled her sunglasses out of her pocket and they set off.

Two days before the race, she and Duncan drove up to Carlsbad so she could get a first hand look at the route the half marathon would follow. Leaving Duncan's car in the shopping mall parking lot, they walked west along Marron, then onto Carlsbad Boulevard, which paralleled the coastline. Between miles six and seven the route doubled back on itself, finishing at the mall where it began. A mostly level run that didn't look all that hard.

When they finished, Duncan suggested an early dinner at a European market and deli near Palomar Airport. “They have a great Reuben sandwich.”

They placed their orders at the counter and were lucky enough to snag a booth just as a family was leaving. Duncan brought their water glasses to the table and sat across from her.

“Nervous about Sunday?”

“Not really. I’m looking forward to it. This race is one of the first things I started working toward when I arrived.”

“So what’s your next goal?”

She shrugged. “No idea. But running makes me feel good, and it’s stripped off some of the weight I had when I arrived.”

“If I’m being too nosy, don’t answer, but are you going to stay out here?”

*The mega-million dollar question.*

The waitress brought plates piled with fries and huge sandwiches.

She dipped a French fry into the pool of catsup on her plate. “Don’t know. Isabel has decided to wait another couple of months before she comes back to work. She doesn’t want to leave the baby so soon.”

Hanna was looking at Isabel’s delayed return as a cushion, extra time to decide what to do next. She couldn’t stay with Zoey forever. When she’d left Durango, she assumed that, by now, she’d have found a new path. Admittedly, she’d found a new confidence, she was in better physical shape, less stressed. But beyond those things, nothing to report.

# CHAPTER 19

DURING THE HALF marathon, somewhere around mile nine, Hanna felt her cell phone vibrating against her butt. Duncan had tried to talk her out of putting it in her back pocket. *You need to run as light as possible.* But she couldn't quite bring herself to leave it at the Gear Check area. She wasn't usually worried about something being stolen, but a new phone wasn't in her current budget.

She was running on Carlsbad Boulevard four miles from the finish line, and now someone was calling her! What were the odds? If she slowed her pace long enough to check the screen, she'd lose her rhythm. She'd been running smoothly and strong, better than she ever had. Not a winning time, but very respectable for her first long race. She voted to ignore the phone.

As she reached for a cup of water from one of the roadside tables at mile ten, the vibration returned. It certainly wouldn't be Zoey or anyone at Seabrook. They knew today was race day. It wouldn't be Duncan. He was ahead of her, maybe even at the finish line by now, and he didn't have his phone with him.

The third time, at mile eleven, Hanna pulled the phone from her back pocket and looked at the screen. Not easy to run and read at the same time.

Lexi.

Lexi had called three times!

The *mother gene* kicked in.

Something was wrong.

Holding the phone to her ear while half running and half walking, she returned the call.

Lexi answered on the first ring. "Mom?"

Hanna could tell her daughter was crying; she could hear the tiny half hiccup, half sob Lexi'd had since childhood.

"What's wrong?"

The only sound was Lexi crying.

Hanna worked her way to the side of the road, letting runners go around her, and stopped. Her heart was pounding.

"Lex, is it Marie? Is she okay?"

More tears.

"Lex. Talk to me." In her panic, Hanna was almost shouting. Several of the runners who had just passed her looked back.

"It's—Kyle—he's—"

"He's what? Lex—words, please."

"—hurt—really badly."

As Hanna was processing *badly*, she began shaking. Walking a few steps to lean against a tree took all her strength.

"How badly?" She realized tears were on her own cheeks.

Gradually, Lexi's hiccups subsided. Hanna waited, afraid of what she'd hear. Her imagination catapulted to all the worst-case scenarios: missing limbs, burns, only hours to live. Effectively terrifying herself. When Kyle had gone from his ROTC unit at the university to active duty, he'd tried to prepare Lexi for the risks a marine would face in a war zone. But no amount of preparation could soften the reality that Lexi was living through now.

Waiting for her daughter's voice to return, Hanna began walking toward the finish line, staying out of the way of the other runners. Everything felt surreal. All the months she'd worked toward this day, hours and hours of running. This half marathon had been an important goal, a test of her new independence, yet now all she wanted was to get back to Duncan's car, to hold her sobbing daughter.

California was slipping away from her.

Finally, "Mom, you still there?"

"I'm here." *But I need to be there. Oh God, what made me think not being there was a good thing? I'm sorry, Lex. My bad.*

"I hear people talking; where are you?"

"In the middle of a race. Tell me about Kyle."

"A bomb went off in the building where his crew was processing incoming replacements. They weren't even fighting."

"How bad?"

"They wouldn't give me any details. Just that he's alive." The tears returned, then, "I'm flying to Frankfurt tonight. The Red Cross got me a ticket. Someone will meet me when I land. Mom, I'm so scared. Can you take care of Marie?"

Of course she could. That's what she did—take care of her family. What had made her think she should do something else?

"Lex, I doubt I'll be there before you leave. I'm going to call Walt to see if his mother will come to take care of Marie until I get home. You can't leave her with Brooke."

"She's not here anyway. Neither is Ry."

"Where are"—she stopped herself— "not important."

"I don't know Walt's mom."

"She's a very nice lady, and she can certainly manage Marie until I get there. I'll call you after I talk to Walt."

A shaky "Okay."

"I love you, Lex. We'll figure this out."

"Okay."

But nothing was okay right now.

Once Hanna ended the call, she checked her watch: only 9:35. As she punched in Walt's number, she realized she was short of breath. A sure sign her nerves were on high alert. The call went straight to his voice mail, so she left a message, hoping he would hear the urgency in her voice.

She tried to calculate how long it would take her to drive to Durango—maybe thirteen or fourteen hours if the roads were good. That figure also assumed she'd be able to stay awake. She'd never driven that far all at once. Flying was probably a better choice. She needed to be at Zoey's so she could get online to buy a ticket.

As she reached the finish line, she saw Duncan standing to one side, waiting for her. He waved, smiling, probably assuming she'd given up running and had to walk the last of the race.

"How'd it go? When did you start walking?" He was carrying the t-shirt he'd qualified for by finishing the race.

"Mile 11, after my daughter called. I have to get to Durango as quickly as I can." Briefly she filled him in on Lexi's call.

He was instantly solicitous. "What can I do?" As a parent, he understood.

"Walk with me. My legs are wobbly. I don't think it's from the running; it's nerves. I know we planned to celebrate after the race, but I really need to get back to Zoey's."

"Will you fly?"

"I think so. It's too far to drive all at once. For me, anyway. And if my car were to give out, there's not a lot of civilization once I leave Phoenix."

"Let's pick up our stuff and get on the road."

He stayed with her while she searched for a flight. Having him there helped keep her from flying apart. He double-checked her itinerary, helped fill in the information, and proofread her credit card numbers as she typed them in.

She found a 6:30 a.m. flight to Phoenix, then one into Durango. She'd be home around noon tomorrow. By that time, Lexi would be in Germany. She'd never been that far away from home on her own, facing the biggest crisis of her life. And her mother couldn't go with her. Until now, Hanna had managed to keep the guilt about leaving her children conveniently buried. Now it was fully resurrected.

Duncan left around one o'clock, promising to drive her to the airport in the morning, "I'll pick you up at 4:15. That'll be plenty of time."

"What about getting to your first class?"

"No problem. Anyway the first day of classes is mostly reading roll sheets and handing out syllabi. A no brainer." He hugged her—a friendly hug. Nothing more.

As though Walt had been waiting for Duncan to leave, Hanna's phone rang just as Duncan's car drove away.

"Hanna, what's wrong?"

She outlined the problem. "Would your mother mind staying with Lexi until her flight and then sleep over with Marie? I can be there around noon tomorrow."

"I'm in Silverton right now, but I'll call Mom. She'll be glad to help. Hanging out with the over seventy crowd is boring her to death. What's your flight number?"

She told him. "I can catch a cab."

As though he hadn't heard her, "I'll try to be there. What else can I do?"

"I have no idea. But thanks."

"Isn't today your big race?"

He remembered.

"Yeah."

"Did you finish?"

"Sort of. Lexi called about two thirds of the way through."

"Try not to worry."

"Fat chance."

She called Lexi back.

"Walt and his mom should be there before you leave. Do you have enough money?"

"There's an ATM at the airport. How do I get Euros?"

"If the Red Cross is meeting you, they can show you how. You need to call your credit card companies and the bank that has your ATM card. Tell them you'll be in Germany so they don't put a hold on your cards because you're using them out of the country. Zoey had that happen to her."

"What else?"

Hanna could tell Lexi was calmer, paying attention.

"You do have a passport, don't you?" She should have asked that first.

"Yes. I got one when Kyle and I went to Acapulco last year."

"Good. Once you're packed, make a list for Mrs. Anders. What Marie's schedule is, what she eats. I'll need that too." She had no idea what her granddaughter liked, when she took her naps. Probably Marie wouldn't remember her. *So whose fault was that?*

"Be sure to take your laptop." When the *mother ge*ne got going, it was hard to turn it off. "What time is your flight?"

"Six fifteen. I go to Denver, then JFK."

"How are you getting to the airport?"

"A taxi, I guess."

"I'll call your cell before you take off."

The rest of Hanna's day was crowded with the mechanics of packing and turning her remaining jobs over to Isabel, explaining everything to Zoey.

"Do you mind having my car parked in your driveway? I don't know when I'll be able to get back to pick it up."

"No problem. Just leave me the keys."

Zoey's cell rang. "I need to take this. I'll catch you at home and I'll bring dinner."

Tears stung Hanna's eyes. Everyone had been so kind. Duncan, Walt, Isabel and Zoey. Taking care of her. It was nice to be taken care of. No wonder her children had trouble leaving the nest.

Though it took Walt's mother more time than he could have imagined to pack one overnight bag, she was looking forward to taking care of Marie. Walt, on the other hand, realized that, as much as he'd longed for Hanna to come back to Durango, she wasn't coming because he'd asked, because she loved him. Once again he was dancing attendance. Being useful was not the role he had in mind.

He was tired of being alone. He'd been single for a dozen years now. Talking to the walls was getting old.

The flights to Durango gave Hanna plenty of time to worry and feel sorry for herself. The two emotions battled each other. Hearing her daughter so distraught had sliced into Hanna's heart. Lexi's life would never be the same, even if Kyle recovered completely. Lexi had had to grow up yesterday.

And Hanna's life was also changing faster than she'd planned. So much for plans. This morning, she was back to being a mother whether she was ready or not. And then there was Walt. Once the plane took off from Phoenix, she closed her eyes, hoping for a few moments of sleep. Today had started way too early.

When Hanna left the baggage carousel, she saw Walt leaning against the wall, waiting. Thank goodness he hadn't listened to her about not picking her up. He opened his arms and she walked in to them. He felt so good, his heavy jacket rough against her cheek. She let him hold her until she could talk without choking up. When she felt calmer, she pulled back. "Sorry, thanks for coming."

"I needed to come into the office to sign some documents anyway." He reached for one of the two suitcases she was pulling. Slowly they walked to the parking lot through the slush that was last night's snowfall.

Hanna shivered. The jacket she'd bought in California was no match for Durango's winter temperatures. And she needed her boots. How quickly she'd forgotten what winter felt like, looked like. Everything was gray and dreary. Nothing uglier than dirty snow.

They didn't talk on the drive into town. Walt couldn't think of anything that would help. Hanna looked exhausted, dark smudges beneath her eyes. The calm, happy woman he'd spent Christmas day with was gone.

Irene Anders had the kitchen door open by the time Hanna was on the porch. "Hanna, dear child." She kissed Hanna's cheek. "Marie's just finished her lunch."

Across the kitchen, Marie was staring at the new arrivals. Still wearing her bib, she was holding a small bottle filled with juice. She was so much bigger than the last time Hanna had seen her, eight months old now, "Hi sweetheart." Hanna touched Marie's cheek, not wanting to move too fast. After all, Marie hadn't seen her for five months.

Irene closed the door behind her son. "Sit down. I have some mac and cheese on the stove. A good day for comfort food."

He unzipped his jacket, but didn't take it off, and sat at the table watching as Hanna stood in front of Marie, talking quietly. Finally, Marie smiled at her grandmother and offered her the juice bottle.

Hanna took it. "Thank you, darling," and then offered it to Marie, who quickly grabbed it.

"Hanna, eat some lunch. You're going to need it. This is a busy child. She's crawling and she's quick."

Hanna took off her jacket and sat across from Walt, who was already working his way through a large plate of macaroni and cheese.

"Irene, don't give me that much. I'm not very hungry."

"Have you heard from Lexi?"

"Not yet. If the flights were on time, she's probably with whoever met her. It'll be a few more hours before she can get in touch."

Marie let out a tiny squeak and stretched out her arms in Irene's direction.

Irene went to get her out of the high chair. “I’ve learned that sound means pay attention to me *now*.” She settled Marie on her lap. “The next stage gets noisier.”

Hanna took a few more bites of her lunch, then pushed her plate aside and held out her arms for Marie.

“Let’s see if she’ll let me hold her.”

It took a few minutes, but Marie finally snuggled against Hanna and closed her eyes.

Irene smiled. “She remembers you.”

Hanna hoped so. “Or she’s just ready for her nap.” She hadn’t realized how much she’d missed holding her granddaughter.

# CHAPTER 20

It was raining when Lexi's plane landed in Frankfurt just after midnight. She'd been in the air nearly seventeen hours, in addition to a three-hour layover in JFK and two in Denver. Pretty close to a full day of traveling.

Right now, the only thing that mattered was getting to Kyle. As she walked through the green *Nothing to Declare* door into the crowd waiting to greet the passengers, she spotted a woman in a dark blue raincoat, holding a sign that had Alexis Jorgenson printed in large black letters. Lexi stopped in front of her. "I'm Lexi—Alexis."

The woman smiled and held out her hand. In heavily accented English, "Welcome to Germany. I am Hilda Mueller, with the German Red Cross. How was your flight?"

"Long."

"Did you sleep?"

Lexi shook her head. She'd tried, but she was too terrified about what she'd find when she got to the hospital. A clock tightly wound.

"We have reserved a room for you at a hotel near Landstuhl Hospital."

"I want to see my husband first."

"There are no visiting hours in the middle of the night. You will feel better if you can have a shower and change your clothes. Then I promise we will go straight to the hospital."

Lexi considered protesting, but she didn't have the energy.

The hotel was scrupulously clean. A no-frills room with white walls, a feather comforter inside the navy blue duvet covering the bed. A flat screen TV mounted on the wall, a small dresser and a nightstand. An upholstered chair by the small double-paned window. At least the shower had hot water to loosen some of the tension in her shoulders and neck. She washed her hair, rinsing the grubby feel of the plane down the drain and, for a few moments, she almost felt human.

By the time she was dressed in wool slacks and the white cowl neck sweater Kyle had given her Christmas before last, the soothing effects of the shower were already wearing off, and the unfamiliar spacey sensation was returning—making her feel as though she were walking in a dimension separate from the real world. She could open doors, get in an elevator, but she felt like a puppet being controlled by some invisible power. This must be the jet lag everyone had warned her about.

Hanna received Lexi's brief email message late Monday: *Arrived after midnight. Really, really tired. I have Euros and I've been loaned a cell phone that will work over here. I'll call. I can't see Kyle until nine o'clock.*

Hanna was thankful Lexi had arrived safely. But the hard part was yet to come. The young woman who'd been afraid to stay alone with her new baby was being severely tested. Hanna wished she could hear Lexi's voice to measure how she was holding up. In the meantime, Hanna hit reply and typed: *Thanks for letting me know. I love you. Mom*

If she were religious, this might be the perfect time to pray—maybe it would be acceptable to pray anyway. She wasn't sure how God felt about people like her, people who preferred to rely on themselves or other people instead of trusting a power she couldn't see.

Since Marie was safely asleep, Hanna took a shower and crawled into Lexi's bed, relatively certain the sheets needed to be changed, but she was too tried to care. In seconds she was asleep.

Marie woke before six, rattling her crib to get attention. Once Hanna figured out where she was and what the clatter was, she changed Marie and took her downstairs, putting her in the high chair with a handful of Cheerios on the tray. After consulting the *What Marie Eats* list, Hanna turned on the teakettle to heat water for the cream of wheat and a bottle, then measured out coffee and began emptying the dishwasher. Just the way she always did. Things should be different. She'd seen the ocean, almost run a half marathon, yet here she was measuring coffee into the same coffeepot.

In Durango.

Moments later, her cell rang, making her stomach tighten, a sure sign she was afraid of what she'd hear.

Lexi's voice—barely audible, "Mom?"

"Yes, darling. Are you okay?" An unnecessary question. Hanna knew the answer. Mothers always knew.

"Everyone is being very nice and helpful."

"How is he?"

"Well—" Her voice disappeared into tears. Hanna waited—and waited.

Eventually, "At least he's alive. They weren't sure he—" a deep breath. "They operated two days ago." A pause. "They amputated the lower part of his left leg—midcalf. Oh Mom, he looks awful, so white, almost shrunken. They're keeping him sedated."

"Does he know you're there?"

"I think so. But he hasn't said anything. He just looks at me and then goes back to sleep."

"What do the doctors say?"

"That he'll recover, but he'll probably have to leave the Marine Corps. He loves being a marine." More tears.

"Lex, have you called his parents?"

"The Red Cross called them before I got here. They're coming."

Hanna was grateful Lexi wouldn't be completely alone. Kyle was close to his parents.

"How's Marie? Did she remember you?"

"Right now, she's devouring Cheerios." Hanna pulled the whistling teakettle off the burner. "I think she remembers me. She didn't cry when I put her to bed last night. Is there anything I can do for you?"

"Just take care of my baby."

"Call when you can."

"Okay."

"I love you." Hanna turned the phone off and stood staring blankly out the window. The picture of Lexi all alone in a strange hospital, sitting beside her young husband, tugged at her heart but there was nothing she could do but wait.

She'd never been much good at waiting.

By eight o'clock, Marie had been fed and was happily bouncing in the chair someone had bought while Hanna was in California. She was at sixes and sevens with herself. This was the second day she hadn't been able to run, and her calves already felt tight. It was probably too cold to run even if she hadn't been caring for Marie. Though the furnace was on and she'd found the fleece pants and top she usually wore around the house in winter, she was chilled through. She might have to lay a fire in the fireplace.

She missed California. Missed the other Hanna. Probably no way of getting her back.

She'd forgotten to ask Lexi where Brooke was, where Ryan was. For that matter, where Callie was. In August, they'd all been here—cluttering up her space. Today there was just Marie. In California, it hadn't seemed strange to be without her children, but in Durango it did.

She checked Brooke's room. Clearly, her daughter wasn't living at home. The sheets had been stripped from the bed and there was no makeup in the bathroom that the three children shared. Brooke was never far from her cosmetics. In other circumstances, Hanna would have been upset that her daughter hadn't told her where she was living. Of course Brooke could argue that Hanna had moved out first. Hanna didn't intend to let Brooke put her on the defensive. Right now, Brooke was undoubtedly in a class or at work with her cell phone turned off.

So she called Callie.

On the fourth ring, "Jeez, Han. It's early." No question her sister had been asleep.

"I know, sorry. There's a family emergency."

Callie's voice was instantly awake. "What emergency?"

"Kyle. He's been badly injured and Lexi's in Germany at the hospital."

"When did all of this happen?"

"Two days ago. I'm at home with Marie."

"Oh my God. How bad is it?"

It was surprisingly good to hear the warmth of Callie's concern. The tears Hanna had not shed when talking with Lexi, made explaining about Kyle's leg take longer than it should have.

When Hanna finished the story, "Do you know where Brooke and Ryan are?"

"Ry's in Denver with Michael. I don't know the details. He drove to Denver sometime after I left Durango; Walt told Saul that Brooke and Dennis are living in an apartment near campus."

"I guess I shouldn't be surprised—but I am."

"You did say you wanted them to stand on their own two feet, didn't you?"

Hanna did not need to be reminded. "Touche."

"You okay?"

"Worried. Out of sync. I'll figure it out, I guess. Where are you? How's the job?"

"Job's great. Minneapolis not so good. A huge snowstorm hit two days ago so we had to cancel one performance. Saul was scheduled to fly in yesterday, but his flight was cancelled." Hanna could hear disappointment in Callie's voice. Her sister was serious about this guy.

"He's your groupie?"

"Yeah. I love it. He came to Vancouver for our opening."

"How much longer is the tour?"

"Five weeks. We play Chicago next, then New York, New Orleans, and close in Los Angeles."

"You sound happy."

"Yeah. Good music, good money, and a good man. Can't beat that combination."

"Guess not."

"Keep me posted."

"I will."

Callie's unabashed happiness only served to depress Hanna even more. Callie was once again off doing Callie things and Hanna was in Durango. She stopped short of adding *unfair*. Being AWOL had been strengthening, but being home was quickly erasing the pleasure she'd found at Zoey's. Once again, she was the support system; add to that the guilt of having walked away from her family—and Walt.

Ryan was in his father's clutches, and Brooke had turned to Dennis. Could Hanna have prevented those choices? Did it matter? Maybe not. Even before Hanna left, Brooke had chosen Dennis over CSU, and Michael had been putting pressure on Ryan for months.

The phone interrupted her ruminating.

Walt.

"Any news about Kyle?"

Hanna repeated Lexi's information, managing not to cry. Men hated crying females.

"Are you okay?"

"Not particularly. Do you by chance have Brooke's address?"

"She and Dennis are at the Vista Apartments. Don't know which number."

"Thanks. How's the hotel job?"

"Wonderful and complicated. I don't remember if I told you that I'm staying in Silverton until the job's finished, using one of the hotel rooms."

No, he hadn't.

Walt had moved away—if only temporarily.

Callie had already moved on.

So had Brooke and Ryan.

Michael had made his move nearly four years ago.

Lexi and Kyle were being forced to move into a different life.

And Hanna was back to square one. There was a message in here somewhere. Undoubtedly the wrong time to throw a pity party. Lexi and Kyle had to come first. She was gradually coming to understand that, once you became a parent, you could never come first again.

How had she not known that?

While she was waiting to hear from Lexi, she should probably track Brooke down. Time for *mea culpa* number one. Instead of trying Brooke's cell, Hanna called the restaurant to ask about her daughter's work schedule. Easier to find a way to talk to her at *Steamworks* than when she was on her way to a class. And even if Hanna had the apartment number, suddenly appearing on Brooke's doorstep might be an invitation to have the door slammed in her face.

The girl who answered the restaurant's phone told Hanna that Brooke was working the lunch shift: 11 to 2.

Going anywhere with a child under two is hard work, especially when the temperature is close to freezing. Hanna dressed Marie in her hooded jacket, leggings, boots, and bright red mittens, then struggled to remember how the buckles worked on the car seat. Whoever had designed the seat should be forced to use it. Marie was close to tears when the second buckle successfully snapped into place. Next came putting the stroller into the trunk of Lexi's car. By the time Hanna started the car, she questioned the wisdom of the errand.

She parked half a block from the restaurant, settled Marie into the stroller, and bribed her with a cookie. Hanna had rarely bribed her own kids. Hopefully, there were different rules for grandmothers.

Brooke saw them the moment Hanna pushed the stroller through the front door, surprise and a frown crossing her face. There was something different about Brooke though Hanna couldn't quite put her finger on specifically what was different. Maybe more mature.

Since she wasn't a customer, Hanna didn't want to push the stroller into the dining room, so she waited until Brooke handed menus to three customers at the window table and walked reluctantly into the foyer. She stooped to kiss the top of Marie's head but made no move toward Hanna.

"You're back."

Brooke's tone of voice and body language said this conversation was not going to be easy. Hanna had disappointed her, and Brooke was always slow to forgive.

Fair enough.

"I flew in yesterday."

"Because?"

Hanna took in a steadying breath. "Kyle's been injured."

Brooke's expression changed to concern.

"Lexi's in Germany with him. She has no idea how long she'll be gone or where Kyle will be sent for whatever comes next in his recovery. I'm taking care of Marie." *And at some point may be taking care of Marie's father.*

"How serious?" Brooke didn't know Kyle all that well. A few holiday celebrations, the wedding.

"They amputated the lower part of his left leg."

"Oh my God." Tears filled Brooke's eyes. "What—how?"

"I have no idea. I talked to Lexi this morning. The Red Cross loaned her a cell phone that will work over there. It's an eight-hour time difference. We just have to wait until she gets in touch again. She has her laptop. You could email her."

"I'll write her on my break."

"Good."

"Does Ry know?"

Hanna shook her head. "No, I started with you,"

"Don't bother to call him until dinnertime. He's clerking in Dad's office."

"Thanks for the warning." So far, so good. Hanna risked a more personal question. Neutral tone, no judgment. "How are you and Dennis doing?"

The defensive Brooke returned. "I have to get back to work." She was at her customers' table, order pad in hand, before Hanna could think of something else to say.

Before she could apologize.

Perhaps it was too early for an apology.

Since she and Marie were already dressed for the cold weather, Hanna stopped at City Market before going home. At least Marie was now big enough to sit in the shopping cart seat, but she was getting fussy because it was past her lunchtime. Time for another cookie bribe. Shoppers did not need Marie at full volume.

As Hanna was standing in the check out line, she heard a voice she recognized. "Why Hanna, I didn't know you'd returned from your trip."

Hanna turned. Sonja Cahill, the wife of Brooke's high school biology teacher was in line behind her. A tall, rather austere woman who thrived on gossip and was always a bit overdressed for any occasion.

"I have." Hanna didn't intend to share Kyle's story with anyone else. In a small city like Durango, the news would spread like wildfire. She wasn't willing to cope with other people's interest or compassion right now. Sympathy could get messy.

"So did you enjoy yourself out there, where was it, California?" Sonja and probably everyone else in Durango knew perfectly well where she'd been.

"Yes, I did."

"Was it *fun*?" Subtext, did you meet a man while you were being a bad mother?

Fortunately the cashier started ringing up Hanna's purchases. But Sonja was not deterred. "I hear Brooke and her boyfriend are living together."

"Yes." Hanna kept her eyes on the cash register screen as each item was added to her total.

"Did you give her permission? Seems a shame. Such a good student."

Hanna ran her debit card through the machine and punched the necessary buttons. The cashier laid Hanna's receipt in her hand. "Have a good day."

Without answering Sonja's question, Hanna pushed the cart toward the door.

And so it had begun.

The fallout from going AWOL

# CHAPTER 21

LEXI FELT LIKE she was a hundred years old. For two days, she'd been sitting in Kyle's hospital room, watching him sleep, worrying as she listened to the beeping monitors attached to various parts of his body. Amazed that there were no visible signs of the blast on his arms or face. What remained of his left leg was wrapped in bandages and raised in a sling. She tried not to look at it, but what wasn't there was all she could see.

The surgeon had explained to Lexi that he was keeping Kyle sedated for the pain. Maybe tomorrow they'd begin weaning him from some of the medications, letting him wake up so he could begin to move around. The physical therapist outlined the stages of Kyle's recovery, how long the physical rehab would take and where it would take place. So much information so quickly, none of it easy to process or accept. Right now, her life and Kyle's were defined by this impersonal room. Even when she returned to the hotel at night, the sounds and smells of the hospital followed her.

She hadn't called her mother again for fear she'd totally break down if she talked about—everything: what Kyle's leg looked like, how strange it was to watch him without being able to touch him or talk to him. The first day in Germany, she'd wondered if she was dreaming. The second day she knew she wasn't. So she sent brief emails that talked about everything else:

The food in the hospital cafeteria—much of which was new to her.

Another marine wife—Laura—whose husband was in a coma.

What the hospital room looked like.

The shuttle bus that ran between the hotel and the hospital.

The weather. Worse than Durango's.

Reading what Lexi wasn't saying, Hanna kept her own messages upbeat, detailing Marie's antics—*I've been sketching her*—the Durango weather, the phone conversation with Ryan.

Ryan had answered with "Hi, Mom. How's California?"

"It was great. However, I'm back in Durango."

Unlike Brooke, Ryan didn't sound as though he wanted to punish her. But then Ryan had always accepted things and people at face value. Not necessarily looking for the best in others, like Lexi did, or creating drama, like Brooke. Michael had once observed that Ry was their matter-of-fact child. Today she was grateful for that quality. She was in no mood for more guilt.

"I'll email Lex as soon as we hang up."

"She needs all the support we can give her. Brooke said you're working for your father."

"Not directly. I'm doing research in the contracts department. It pays enough for me to give George half the rent. I don't want to stay at the condo with Sheri and Dad."

"Do you like the job?"

"It's cleaner than working for Walt."

He hadn't answered her question. "And?"

"And I'll start law school in the fall, I guess."

*I guess?*

Ryan didn't sound any more sure of what he wanted to do than he was before she left, but she now understood his uncertainty better. She was in the same boat. Making life choices wasn't nearly as tidy as others would have you believe—as she had believed. Ryan was only twenty-two. What he wanted out of life would undoubtedly change and change again. Law school could lead to other kinds of jobs, not just being a lawyer, regardless of what Michael might believe.

The same for Brooke. Living with Dennis didn't—in today's society—mean they would stay together forever. Hanna did hope Brooke was on the pill. She'd broached that topic as soon a Dennis entered the picture a year ago but had been stonewalled.

Her cell rang.

"Mom?" Lexi. And she was hiccupping.

"Yes, darling. How are you?"

"He yelled at me. He's never ever yelled at me."

*He* was undoubtedly Kyle. At least he was alert enough and strong enough to yell. In Hanna's view, good news. In Lexi's, probably not.

"He told me to get out of the room."

In her calmest tone, Hanna asked, "Why did he want you to leave?"

"The nurse came to change the bandages on his leg. I wanted to watch so I'd know what to do if I have to change them sometime."

*Good for her.*

"Maybe he didn't want you to see the wound."

"He didn't have to yell." A hiccup.

"Maybe he doesn't want to look at it either. Yelling might help him."

Silence. Then, "I never thought about that."

"Give him some time. All that medication is probably affecting his behavior."

"It's just so hard. He only wants me to tell him about Marie, and he won't talk about what happened or what we're going to do when he gets better. Actually, he doesn't talk much at all. It's like he's really angry with me. I don't know what I've done wrong."

"I doubt he's angry with you. He needs your patience. Everything's going to be different for a while."

"How long, do you think?"

*Possibly forever.*

"No idea." *A mother lie.*

"The physical therapist said that in about ten days, they'll transfer him to Walter Reed, in D.C. to fit him with the first prosthesis and begin his rehab. After that, they'll send him home."

"Home?"

"Durango. We don't have any other home right now. He'll get long term rehab at Mercy Regional."

*Long term?* In her initial concern for Kyle, Hanna hadn't thought about the recovery stage, which was about to take place in her house—for a long time.

Not entirely good news.

"Will you go to D.C. with him?"

"No. They're sending me home day after tomorrow. I don't have an itinerary yet. Oh, wait. I've got to go. The nurse just left the room."

Dial tone.

Hanna stared at the dark screen. Was there no end to the number of ways her family could require her services?

For a fraction of a second, she fantasized about buying a one-way ticket to San Diego, but of course leaving Marie wasn't an option. The *grandmother gene* was even more powerful than the other one.

As she was talking to Lexi, snow had begun to fall, soft fat flakes that would cover the dirty patches left from last week's snowfall, decorating her yard with white icing. She'd planned to go to the ATM, get groceries, and stop for gas. Probably too messy to venture out with Marie. Maybe tomorrow.

Opening her laptop, she emailed Callie, then Brooke, because her daughter wouldn't answer her calls. And Ryan, reminding him to keep his father in the loop. Michael needed to contact his daughter.

While she waited for Lexi's return, Hanna cleaned and cleaned. Effective therapy when life descended full force. Like now. She started with the kitchen, then moved on to the bathrooms. Had anyone in her family noticed the dirt? Of course not. Lexi's room was the only one that was fairly clean. She purged her own room of what Callie had left behind, clothes and a couple of cardboard boxes, burying them in the back of Brooke's closet.

The next day, she started on laundry. Several loads of sheets and towels. She put fresh sheets on all the beds and finished with a load of Marie's clothing. Busy hands.

In the few days that Lexi had been gone, Marie's crawling speed had increased; the time had come for baby gates at the top and bottom of the stairway and locks for the kitchen cabinets. It wouldn't be long before she would be walking.

Lexi's flight from Denver was due to land just before three on Friday. She'd been in Germany twelve days. Hanna had been home eleven days, though it seemed much longer. Yesterday, Zoey'd called to report that she had a firm offer from an L.A. catering company to purchase Seabrook Catering. "It went into escrow three days ago."

The door to California slammed shut.

"Do you know what you're going to do?"

"Yes and no. First, I thought I'd bring your car to you, weather permitting, or will I be in the way?"

Hanna's heart lifted. Something to look forward to. Having Zoey in the house would be good for Lexi too. "Please, please come. Kyle will be at Walter Reed for a while. Stay as long as you like."

"Is the skiing good?"

"So I'm told. You can use Brooke's gear." She could hear Brooke's protests. Sharing had never been easy for her youngest.

To meet Lexi's flight, Hanna had dressed Marie in a red corduroy jumper, white t-shirt and white tights. Her hair was finally long enough for a tiny ponytail. When the plane emptied, they were waiting at the luggage carousels, Hanna holding Marie in her arms so Lexi could see her baby right away. "Remember to wave at Mama when she comes through the gate." But Marie wasn't interested. She much preferred chewing on the old cloth diaper that was her constant companion.

As Lexi hurried toward them, Hanna could see how hard the last twelve days had been for her daughter. She'd lost weight; her face was drawn and pale, as though she were the patient instead of Kyle. Lexi lifted Marie out of Hanna's arms. "Hi baby girl, it's Mama." Marie studied Lexi for a moment and then waved.

Hanna laughed.

"What's funny?"

"Now she decides to wave. A bit late."

"She's beautiful." Lexi was holding her so tightly that Marie started to squirm.

"Let's put her in the stroller and I'll take your suitcase."

On the drive into town, Lexi rode in the back seat, talking to Marie, making her giggle. "At least she didn't forget me."

"It's only been two weeks. She remembered me after five months."

"Such a smart baby." Lexi leaned over to nuzzle Marie's neck. "Mama promises not to leave you ever again." If Brooke had said that, Hanna might have suspected a reference to Hanna's extended vacation. But Lexi wasn't given to cheap shots.

"I bought baby gates this morning, and we need to see if we can install the cupboard door locks." Better to talk about something other than Kyle right now. Let Lexi have a soft homecoming.

"She'd just started crawling when I left."

"She's fast and can disappear instantly." Hanna chose not to confess that last night Marie had made it from the kitchen to the foot of the stairs before Hanna realized she was gone.

Though Lexi was clearly exhausted, she insisted on feeding, bathing and putting Marie to bed. "I've missed doing this. I love being her mother."

Hanna had fixed Lexi's favorite comfort food, spaghetti and meatballs, but Lexi didn't eat much and was too tired to carry on a conversation. By eight o'clock, she was in bed, leaving Hanna alone in the kitchen to sift through her own thoughts, some of which she didn't care to deal with.

How would Kyle manage in a two-story house? Would there be physical therapists at the house or would he go to the outpatient rehab at Mercy? Fortunately there was a shower in the downstairs bathroom. They'd need a bed—a hospital bed probably—in the dining room. How long would it take before he was able to function on his own? What would his state of mind be? Would he and Lexi and Marie be living here indefinitely? Hanna shoved her selfish reaction to this scenario away. No one had a choice in this.

Not only had she been unable to finish running the half marathon, she hadn't been able to finish enlarging the borders of her tent.

*Get over it.*

This was going to require a different kind of mothering.

Thank goodness Zoey was coming. Hanna would have someone to confide in. Because her mind wouldn't shut down, it was after midnight before she slept, only to be awakened by Marie's crib rattling at half past six. Hanna hurried to pick her up before she woke Lexi.

# CHAPTER 22

THE THIRD WEEK of February brought a false spring that lasted long enough for Zoey to make the drive to Durango. The day after she arrived, winter returned, dumping a foot of snow on the mountains.

She was ecstatic. "Deep powder! Where are Brooke's skis?"

"In the back of her closet."

Zoey brought fresh energy into the house. Lexi was already in better spirits, and Hanna felt herself looking forward to each day. Zoey was good medicine.

"It's strange not having an office to go to." Zoey was washing the breakfast dishes while Hanna was cleaning out the refrigerator. A task several months overdue.

"Did you close everything down at Seabrook?"

"Not exactly. It's being gradually rolled into the Los Angeles company that bought me out. The owners are trying to break into the San Diego market and will use Seabrook's name for a while, then transition to their own. They're upgrading the kitchen and promised to keep all my employees. That was a major issue for me because the staff has been incredibly loyal."

"Did you get a good price?"

"Yeah." She grinned. "Even after paying off my creditors, I'll have enough to live on for quite a while. I think Jonathon would be okay with the terms of the sale."

"So what are you going to do? Travel?"

"At least to Atlanta to tell Steph I sold the company. I need to do that face-to-face, though she may believe I'm dishonoring Jonathon. And the day after I accepted the buyout, I was offered a chance to teach."

"Really? Where?"

"At the American Culinary Institute. A class on catering. They have schools on both coasts. It'll take me a month or two to put all the information together. I'll give the class a dry run at their San Diego campus during the summer quarter. I'm ready to try something new."

As soon as the highway to Purgatory was open, Zoey invited Lexi to go skiing. "My treat."

"But my skis are in storage in California."

"Then I'll rent a pair, and you can use Brooke's. You and I both need a day in the fresh air."

And Hanna needed to see Walt. He'd been working in Silverton for almost a month, calling a couple of times to ask about Kyle. She was pretty sure he'd been in Durango once or twice to look after things at his office but hadn't come by. He was either giving her space or intentionally distancing himself. Perhaps because she hadn't responded to his Christmas confession.

It took half the morning to get everyone put together; then she delivered Lexi and Zoey to the Purgatory lift area. "Call when you're ready to leave. I'm only twenty minutes away."

With Marie singing to herself in the back seat, Hanna drove north to Silverton, hoping Walt would have time for lunch with her. She was uneasy about suddenly showing up at his job site. Normally, she wouldn't look for an excuse to go see him, but his *I love you* speech had changed things. She'd spent a lot of time tiptoeing around the implications of that night on Zoey's deck, reliving the way he'd kissed her, the way the kiss had made her feel, yet unable to figure out how Walt should fit into her life or how she would fit into his. Undoubtedly she was over-thinking the situation.

Hanna hadn't been to Silverton since high school. The plows had cleared the streets, piling mounds of snow along the curbs, so it took careful maneuvering to find a place to park. The Victorian buildings lining the streets were well cared for, not just as a museum of the mining days but as a year-round tourist destination. Art galleries, boutiques and restaurants. The frame false-front structures were painted inviting colors: orange, yellow, turquoise. Splashes of brightness against the gray day.

Built of the local red sandstone, the hotel was on Greene Street. Walt's pickup, half buried in snow, was in the uncleared parking lot. Rather than just walking in the front door unannounced, she called his cell before she got out of the car.

"Anders."

"Walt, it's Hanna."

A slight hesitation. "Hi. Everything all right?" Clearly, he was accustomed to things being wrong in her life. That was a little embarrassing.

"I dropped Zoey and Lexi off at Purgatory. Do you have time for lunch? Warning, I have Marie with me."

"Sure." Papers rustling. "Where are you?"

"Just down the street."

"Come along. We can walk to the diner that's over on Blair."

Pushing the stroller on a sidewalk with slushy snow was tricky. Fortunately, Walt met them at the door because she wouldn't have been able to hold the heavy door and get the stroller inside. "Let me help with that."

"Thanks. These new strollers are three times the size of the ones my kids had."

Once the stroller was inside, they were faced with the uncomfortable silence born of all the important topics they were avoiding. To take the edge off the moment, he leaned over and lightly touched Marie's hair. "Hi young lady. You're not skiing yet?"

The awkwardness backed off a little. "Given her crawling speed, I imagine she'll be a downhiller soon enough. Are you sure I'm not interrupting something?" He was wearing work boots, his usual faded Levi's stained with whatever oil he'd been using, and a much-washed blue flannel shirt. Since he'd met her at the Durango airport, he'd let his beard grow. She liked the look. "How's the job going?"

He picked up his parka and slipped it on as he glanced around the lobby. "Definitely a work in progress. I'm almost finished rebuilding the check-in area. The worst job was stripping the wallpaper, then priming the walls for the new paper that will go up tomorrow. It took hours to find paper with a similar pattern."

"You like doing this." It showed in his voice, in the way his face lit up.

"Absolutely. I've never done a building this old before. But getting it right takes a lot of research and that slows me down. Gail has enough on her plate with running the office." He reached for the stroller handle. "Let me. The sidewalks keep melting, then freezing over."

By the time they got to the restaurant, Marie was entering complaint mode. Hanna reached under the stroller for the bag filled with baby supplies. "Do you suppose I can get them to heat some water to mix with the formula?"

"Sure. They aren't all that busy when the roads have been closed."

Walt chose a table where the stroller could be pulled alongside, then took the empty bottle and the packet of formula into the kitchen. She could hear him laughing with someone. He probably knew the staff. When he returned to the table, he was carrying two menus under his arm and two glasses of water. "It'll only take a minute. Will Marie want something else?"

"So long as there are a few French fries, she'll be happy. She had a big breakfast. Zoey loves playing aunt and manages to get more cereal down her than I can." Having Marie to look after and talk about gave them a neutral zone, taking away some of their discomfort.

"When did Zoey arrive?"

"Four days ago. She sold her business and decided to deliver my car. I was wondering how to manage getting it here."

"And so Hotel Sheridan is back in business?"

"Pretty much, but having Zoey here helps."

After they ordered, he asked about Kyle and Lexi. That topic occupied most of their lunchtime. "Will he be able to negotiate stairs?"

"No idea. I'm thinking of putting a hospital bed in the dining room if he can't. Lexi has a list of the equipment we should have in the house and where to obtain it. She came home with all kinds of paperwork. She seems okay with taking the responsibility for this. I'm proud of her courage. I've been trying to let her get back into her own routine with Marie and find ways to have some fun, like skiing today. But we also need to prepare the house for Kyle's arrival. Once he's home, a lot is going to be required of her."

"And you."

She nodded.

When they were back at the hotel, Marie lost her fight with sleep and, while Walt was talking to one of his workers about the light fixtures that were being installed, Hanna took the time to explore the lobby. On a plywood table supported by sawhorses were the pictures of what the dining room and lobby had looked like the day before Walt's crew tore it apart and a picture of what it looked like when it was built in 1897. The new owner wanted the lobby to resemble the original as much as possible and yet appeal to today's visitors.

A few minutes later, Walt was looking over her shoulder. "The next step is finding carpeting that represents the period but will hold up under heavy foot traffic. I've got Gail going through catalogs to narrow down the possibilities."

"It's going to be wonderful when you're done."

"Hope so."

Hanna's cell vibrated. She reached into her coat pocket.

"Hi Lex." Listening. "Sure, in about half an hour. Can you find a place to stay warm until I get there? Good." She ended the call.

"I'll walk you back to your car and help get Sleeping Beauty settled."

"Simple things, like getting in and out of a car, aren't simple with her."

Again Walt took charge of the stroller. Rather sweet. She'd never pictured him pushing a stroller. Had never seen him with children. They walked in silence, avoiding the one subject that was on their minds. Walt longed for an answer; Hanna was afraid to give one.

At the car, she opened the back door, "Would you like to have me help with the carpet research? Now that Lexi's home and Kyle is still in the hospital, I have some free time."

Once Walt had the sleeping Marie buckled in, he backed out and turned around. "That would be a big help."

"I'd enjoy the challenge. I miss creating the designs for Zoey's clients. This will let me keep my artistic hand in."

"You're sure you want to do this?"

"I am." She was surprised how much she wanted to get involved. "I'll give Gail a call tomorrow."

They stood beside the driver's door, Walt's hands jammed into his jacket pockets, removing the possibility of a hug or a kiss on the cheek. Like the old days.

"I'm glad you're home. I know you don't want to be."

She heard his sadness. Knew he was disappointed in her.

Sidestepping his comment, "It's not easy for anyone right now. Thanks for lunch."

She got in and opened the window. "Next time you're in town, let me know. I'll fix dinner."

For the first time since she'd walked through the hotel door, he smiled. "I'd like that."

Walt watched Hanna's car drive away, unsure whether to be encouraged by her visit or not. When he'd heard her voice on the phone, he felt a leap of hope, which he struggled to hide once she was sitting across the table from him. She'd kept her hair short and lighter. He remembered touching it when he kissed her at Zoey's. Wanted to touch it again, touch her. It was probably too soon. To make sure he kept his distance, he resorted to pushing the stroller, keeping his hands occupied. He didn't trust the emotions she stirred.

Yet the longer it took her to respond, the less certain he was of her answer.

What if she turned him down? Since he couldn't let his thoughts go there, he called Gail to tell her Hanna was going to help choose the rug.

Lexi and Zoey were full of their afternoon on the ski slopes. "Mom, you should see Zoey on skis. She puts everyone else to shame."

Hanna laughed, "Now you know why I didn't join you. I was put to shame by her ability years ago."

Zoey pulled off her knit hat and ran her fingers through her hair. "Surfing keeps the same muscles in shape, but I could tell it's been a while. Lexi's pretty good too."

"Michael had them on the slopes when they were three years old. Because Ryan is the one who has no fear of speed or danger, he's gone into snowboarding."

As they rounded the corner onto their street, Lexi exclaimed, "Hey, that's Brooke's car."

Hanna's stomach clenched. Her last meeting with Brooke hadn't gone well. And since that meeting, Brooke hadn't come near the house. She'd invited her sister to have coffee with her the day after Lexi returned. Tempting as it was, Hanna hadn't tried to debrief Lexi. And Lexi hadn't volunteered whatever she knew about Brooke's living arrangements or what she and Brooke talked about. The mother was out of the loop.

Lexi carried Marie up to her crib while Zoey and Hanna stashed the ski equipment in the garage.

Zoey took note of Hanna's frown. "You and Brooke are—what?"

"On very different pages. She's mad and not ready to discuss my crimes."

Zoey laughed. "Maybe she and Stephanie should start a support group for children whose mothers have screwed up."

And that observation was why Hanna loved having Zoey in residence. A little humor never hurt.

# CHAPTER 23

THE DAY BROOKE was born, Hanna would never have imagined she'd be afraid of her own daughter. But today, standing in the door of Brooke's bedroom, Hanna was pretty sure she was afraid of Brooke's unyielding judgment. So far, neither Lexi nor Ryan had given any sign that they were especially angry about her leaving. But Brooke was angry enough for all of them.

On the mother level, Hanna wanted Brooke's good opinion, her love.

On a more personal level, she didn't regret the months in California and really didn't want to apologize. She'd needed the change so badly that Brooke's present snarkiness was not going to tarnish her memories of those months. All the self-help books, Hallmark cards, and time-worn platitudes about the joys of being a mother couldn't alter the fact that she'd simply gotten tired of day-to-day care giving. And since no one had noticed that she too needed some TLC, she'd given herself a mothering break. Though she wouldn't have chosen to be back in Durango just yet, she was coping because she now knew that leaving was a possibility. She hadn't known that before.

All Hanna could see was Brooke's back, her unruly curls held back with a wide pink headband. "Can I help you find something?"

Startled, Brooke turned quickly. "I didn't hear you. I thought it was just Lexi and Marie coming upstairs."

"We were together. What do you need?"

"My skis. They were in the back of my closet. Dennis scored a couple of free lift tickets for next weekend."

"We left your ski gear in the garage. Lexi and Zoey were at Purgatory today. Lexi used your skis."

"Mine?" Her face flushed as she straightened up. "She used *my* skis! She has her own. What is *wrong* with this family?"

She walked past Hanna and thumped down the stairs.

As Brooke reached the kitchen, Hanna heard Zoey's cheerful, "Hi Brooke." The only answer was the slam of the back door.

Rehearsing all the things she wished she'd said, Hanna made her way down to the kitchen.

Zoey was sitting at the kitchen table with the morning paper turned to the daily crossword. "What happened up there?"

"Bad timing. She was looking for her skis. Brooke's not good at sharing her toys and, even worse, she was trapped into talking to the wicked mother."

"How long will it take before she calms down?"

Hanna shrugged. "Maybe never." She looked at her watch. "I think I'll make meatloaf for dinner. I need to keep busy."

"How did your lunch with Walt go?"

"A bit awkward in spots. I know he's waiting for my answer."

"Answer to what?"

"At Christmas, he told me he loved me—asked me to come back home." Hanna hesitated, "For him. Though he didn't specifically say it that way."

"Wow. You never mentioned that."

"Still processing."

"If you have to think this long, the answer is probably no." Zoey always preferred getting to the bottom line. A skill Hanna sometimes envied.

"Not really. I'm pretty sure I do love him, but I don't want to commit to anything until I'm comfortable with me, with who I am.

He deserves a complete person, not someone who's still dissatisfied with her life. And now Lexi and Kyle are—will be here."

"Parenting is never simple. I wish someone had explained that to me when I was young." Zoey picked up her pencil. "What's a three letter word for a tall conical cap?"

"Is that a *New York Times* crossword?"

"Yes."

"Those are way too hard."

"You'll note I do them in pencil and rarely complete one."

"That's a relief," Hanna began chopping cloves of garlic. "It's so good to have you here."

"Nice to be here. This seems to be the year we need each other's houses. You needed to stretch, and I need to catch my breath. The sale went faster than I expected."

"Your house was more peaceful than mine is."

As if on cue, "Hey, Mom." Lexi was at the top of the stairs.

"Yes?"

"Dad just called my cell. Sheri had her baby this morning: six pounds, nine ounces. Michael Nicholas, Junior. Both of them are fine, but Dad sounds a little rattled. Sheri made him stay with her for the whole time. That's all I know. I need to finish giving Marie her bath."

Hanna tossed the garlic into the bowl and started chopping a white onion. "I bet Michael hasn't had an easy day." She should be ashamed of the pleasure that gave her. "He's never handled pain and blood well. When Lexi was born, he raced out of the delivery room to throw up and never returned. When Ryan and Brooke were born, he adamantly refused to be there. Sheri must have greater powers of persuasion than I had. At least he finally got his junior. He wanted Ryan to be junior, but Michael's dad had just died so we bowed to his mother's wishes that the baby be named for his grandfather."

"I always wondered where the Ryan came from."

"Maybe Michael will be a more hands-on father this time. With our three, he was always working." *Stop talking about it.* "Was Jonathon a good father?"

"Yes. Stephanie adored him. If she was afraid at night, she always called for him, not me. Since his death, I think she sees herself as parentless."

"There's a peculiar no win aspect to parenting. Even if you think you're doing a good job, you probably aren't—at least as far as your children are concerned."

"We should drink to that." Zoey pulled two wine glasses from the cupboard.

Lexi had left her laptop with Kyle so he could email her when he felt up to it, and she could send him pictures from her mother's laptop. Since she'd been back in Durango, she'd written him everyday and sent photos of Marie—in her high chair, in her snowsuit. But he hadn't answered anything. She wasn't as worried about his physical condition—the doctor had assured her his leg was healing—as she was about his mental state. Since the attack, he'd become a stranger, giving one-word answers to her questions. There was no give and take between them. Not even a smile. He had such a great smile. She didn't know how to reach him, and the lack of privacy in the hospital hadn't helped.

Though she'd asked whether she could accompany him to Walter Reed, she was actually glad that the doctors told her she should go home. *He'll be in rehab every day. There won't be anything for you to do.* But, if she had been allowed to stay with him, they might have begun to erase the distance between them. She was afraid that, when he came to Durango, they'd be even farther apart. At some point, she'd have to warn her mother about his state of mind. After one doctor had mentioned possible depression, she'd gone online to read up on the various problems that returning, wounded military personnel faced. What she read scared her even more. She wished she had someone to talk to who'd experienced what she and Kyle were facing.

Writing a daily diary for him was a way to pretend they were the same couple they'd always been. It kept the fear at arm's length.

Hi Darling: As of today, I have a half-brother. Dad and Sheri's baby, Michael Nicholas, was born this morning so now Marie is older than her uncle. So weird.

I went skiing with Mom's friend Zoey—the one she was staying with in California. Zoey drove Mom's car here for her and will stay with us for a while. She's fun. I haven't skied since we left Colorado.

How was your day? Do you know when you're leaving Landstuhl?

We love you so much.

The next morning, there was a brief email message from the hospital. Kyle was being transferred to Walter Reed in two days. A phone number and the name of the rehab center were included.

But there was no message from Kyle.

She did her crying before she went down to breakfast.

As soon as Lexi told Hanna that Kyle was on his way to D.C., Hanna spent some quality time with a calendar. Based on the paperwork Lexi had brought with her, Kyle would probably be in Walter Reed for two to three weeks. That date would dovetail with the end of Callie's tour. Walt's joke about Hotel Sheridan was no joke. Once again, she might have a full house. Lexi and Marie in Lexi's room, Zoey in Brooke's room, Kyle—well, the whole hospital bed issue needed clarification. If Callie came back to the house, she'd have Ryan's room or, if Kyle could negotiate stairs, he'd be in with Lexi or use Ryan's room for a while, putting Callie back on the pullout downstairs. And if Brooke and Dennis broke up—

*Don't borrow trouble.*

*Think about the rugs for Walt.*

As she'd promised, Hanna spent two mornings with Gail, looking at available carpeting suitable for a Victorian lobby and dining room. Once they'd chosen five possible patterns, it was time to show the samples to Walt and the hotel owner. Around noon the third day, Hanna decided to drive to Silverton. She packed up the photocopies and catalogs, in case he didn't like their choices, and made the hour drive north. Hotel Sheridan could get along without her for the afternoon.

It had begun raining by the time she passed Mountain Grub and, as she pulled into Silverton, her windshield wipers were on high.

Gail had called ahead to tell Walt that Hanna was bringing him the rug samples. No element of surprise this time. In spite of the rain, the hotel's front door was wide open. Hanna laid the catalogs on a folding chair just inside the door and propped her dripping umbrella against a chair. "It's freezing in here."

On his knees, rubbing oil into the check-in counter with a soft towel, Walt looked up and smiled. "I need to get rid of the chemical fumes." He stood up, rubbing his hands on the towel. "Carlo's allergic to one of the oils I'm using. I gave him the day off."

"The wood is beautiful. What's the color?"

"Cherry, though the label on the can has a more elegant name. With two coats of stain and three coats of this oil, it should look beautiful. Gail said you have some rug designs that might work."

"We do. Where can I spread the catalogs?" He looked around. Except for the floor there wasn't an available flat surface. "How about the kitchen?" He picked up the stack of catalogs. "Gail said you hadn't had lunch yet, so I ordered cheeseburgers from the diner."

"I do love cheeseburgers." It had been a long time since she'd had one and, in that moment, Hanna felt they were at least friends again.

While they ate, they studied the catalogs spread out on the kitchen prep counter. Gail had sent along enlarged photocopies of the best rug candidates so they could study each one separately. When they finished eating, they carried them around the lobby and dining room, holding them against the new wallpaper, the new counter, and the refinished hardwood floors. Working on the decision was fun; Hanna was surprised how much she was enjoying herself, enjoying Walt. This afternoon, Walt reminded her of the young Walt, who used to tease her, who laughed easily. It had been a long time since she'd seen young Walt. But of course young Hanna hadn't been around either.

Two hours later, sitting on the bottom step of the stairway, they were debating the two best rug possibilities, one with a predominately dark red background covered with intertwined flowers, another a lighter rose background with a geometric pattern.

"These stairs are what the guests see first." Hanna stood up and arranged the photocopies on the steps. "Look at the samples from this point of view. In the lobby or dining room, the rugs will be competing with the furniture. But here, the rug is the major focus. They stood facing the stairway for a few minutes; then Walt walked out the front door and reentered the hallway.

He didn't hesitate. "The red one."

Hanna nodded. "It's stronger."

"Of course it's the most expensive."

"Should we run it by the owner?"

He shook his head. "Once I told him I had a designer working on the problem, he said he'd trust our decision."

"You didn't. I'm not a designer."

"Yes, you are. That's what you were doing for Zoey."

He had a point. "Sort of."

"Anyhow, we get to make the choice. I'll call Gail so she can put the order in tonight. She has all the measurements." He went looking for his phone in the kitchen.

When he finished the call, "Gail says 550 is closed."

"But it's not snowing."

"There's a huge rockslide on this side of Molas Pass. It'll take most of the night to clear the boulders and put up protective netting." He paused, "I know this is rather sudden, but it looks like you're spending the night with me."

There were so many ways to read that statement.

"Since it's the only road between here and Durango, I guess so, but I need to call home so they know the slide didn't fall on me." She pulled her phone from her purse.

Lexi answered. "Where are you?"

"In Silverton with Walt, looking at rug samples for the hotel. There's a big rockslide on 550. The highway's closed, so I'm stuck up here until they get it cleared."

"And you're staying at the hotel? With Walt?"

"Yes."

Her daughter giggled. "Have fun."

"Lex—" but Lexi had hung up. Hanna hoped she wasn't blushing.

"What'd she say?"

She wasn't about to tell him.

Alone in the hotel—all night. The possibilities were unsettling.

She needed something to occupy herself—them. "Is the kitchen functioning?"

"Yes, but the only food in the refrigerator is beer, which of course isn't food. The owner cleaned everything out of the cupboards when we started work because we'd be using a lot of strippers and glues that might contaminate food."

"Is the Silverton Grocery still down the street?"

"Yes, it's pretty much the only game in town."

"Let's cook dinner." If she and Walt were going to be here tonight and maybe tomorrow, she needed something to distract her from all the possibilities her mind was exploring.

They walked the two blocks in the rain. He'd produced a golf umbrella that easily covered them so long as they walked close. The weather was bent on throwing them together.

Only a few customers were inside the store. Walt pushed the trolley over the pine plank floor, letting Hanna make the decisions. "I'm assuming the kitchen has a grill."

"A very large grill, state of the art."

She picked out two rib eye steaks, took her time choosing what would go in the salad, added two baking potatoes, salad dressing, sour cream and butter, then eggs and bread for breakfast. Coffee of course. It felt like they were playing house.

When they reached the wine department, Walt chose a bottle of red, a Chardonnay, and a Sauvignon Blanc. "To ward off the cold." He surveyed the cart, "Dessert?"

"Your choice."

"Ice cream." He stopped in front of the freezer and surveyed the choices. "If I recall, your favorite is Pistachio."

He remembered that about her, yet she had no clue what ice cream he liked. "I'm afraid I don't remember what your favorite is." She did know which ones her children preferred. Even what Michael preferred.

"Strawberry." He added a pint of each flavor to their purchases.

It was nearly six o'clock when Hanna unpacked their food in the hotel's kitchen and began looking for a salad bowl small enough for two servings.

"This is the most elaborate kitchen I've ever cooked in. It feels like we're trespassing and someone will come chase us away."

"Even Saul is envious of this kitchen in spite of redoing his two years ago."

Walt busied himself opening the Chardonnay and pouring a glass for each of them while Hanna scrubbed and pricked the potatoes, finally figuring out how to turn the oven on. She washed the lettuce and started on the salad. Walt set the table with the hotel's elegant gold-rimmed china. They worked silently, easily anticipating what the other needed, yet they'd never cooked together before, not even when they were younger.

By the time the grill was ready for the steaks, the rain had increased, lashing at the windows. The kitchen felt cozy, safe with the smell of potatoes and sizzling steaks.

Once everything was on the round, wooden table in the kitchen—probably where the staff took breaks or ate their meals—Walt switched off the harsh fluorescent lights, leaving just the fixture above the table. Candles would have been a nice touch, but that was perhaps suggesting too much. The steaks were perfectly done, medium for him, medium-rare for her.

As they ate, Walt told her about what still needed to be done at the hotel—at least another two or three weeks of work. About the grand reopening the owner was planning just before Easter. She told him about the prognosis for Kyle, about her encounters with Brooke. Listening to him and having him listen to her, she relaxed, probably the wine. Not once this evening had she thought about California.

The heat from the oven and grill warmed the kitchen but, when they went into the lobby with their wine, it was at least twenty degrees colder. They ended the evening sitting on one of the new sofas, wearing their jackets, drinking the last of the red wine, and watching the 10 o'clock news on KOB. "It's like camping out in the best hotel in town. Is there heat upstairs?"

Walt shook his head. "We turned the furnace off while we were tearing things apart. When I stay over, I use a space heater I brought from home."

Just one heater.

For the two of them.

# CHAPTER 24

WHEN HANNA WOKE the next morning, her first thought was that her nose was very, very cold. Why wasn't her house warm? She didn't need to have a problem with the furnace; it was practically new.

Her second thought was that her head hurt. A lot. The kind of pain that usually came from too much wine. Especially a mixture of red and white wines. Then she remembered she wasn't in her own house. She was in Silverton. With Walt.

Keeping her eyes closed against what little light the red velvet drapes let in, she attempted to sort through what had happened the night before, dimly recalling a discussion about a space heater—and t-shirts. Trying to ignore the throbbing behind her eyes, she pushed herself up onto her elbows and slowly opened her eyes. She was in a four-poster bed, wearing a faded gray t-shirt with L.L Bean printed across the front.

Carefully—so it wouldn't fall off—she turned her head.

Beside her, Walt was sleeping on his back, snoring softly, the thick white duvet that covered both of them pulled up to his chin.

She was in bed. With Walt.

Wearing what was undoubtedly his t-shirt. Yet she was still wearing her bra and underpants.

Perhaps sensing she was staring at him, he rolled onto his side and opened his eyes, pushing the pillow under his head. His eyes lingered on her face. "Good morning. How nice to find you in my bed."

What did he mean by that? And how had she gone from wearing her coral fleece pullover and wool slacks to the t-shirt?

Her "Good morning" was understandably tentative. Just what had they done last night? She couldn't seem to remember and asking would be embarrassing—to say the least. But she did need to know whether they'd had sex.

"How's your head?" Evidence that Walt knew she'd drunk too much.

"Not good. I'm—fuzzy about—well—everything." She'd often given Callie grief about waking up in strange beds. So much for older sister superiority.

He waited a moment, apparently enjoying her confusion, then grinned. "No, we didn't."

That explained the underwear.

*Why hadn't they?*

Answering her unasked question, "I have a rule against ravishing women who've had too much wine," his eyes were teasing; "when the ravishing does happen, I want you to remember it."

*Ravishing*? Not a word she'd imagine Walt using. This Walt was not the steady, solid Walt she was used to. This one was definitely much sexier. They'd slept in the same bed. Actual sleeping, not the other sleeping. In spite of her headache, she was acutely aware of his physical presence.

"Probably a good rule."

"Would you like a couple of aspirin?"

She must look as bad as she felt. "Please."

He pushed the duvet off. He was wearing flannel pajama bottoms and an old white t-shirt. Watching him walk barefooted into the bathroom was surprisingly intimate. Maybe it was his bare feet. Or his beard. He brought her a glass of water and an aspirin bottle, turned the space heater on, and crawled back into bed. "It'll take twenty minutes to get the temperature into the sixties. It's pretty efficient."

Hanna swallowed the two aspirin tablets and slid down under the duvet, closing her aching eyes, hoping the pills would know enough to go straight to her head where they were so desperately needed.

The next time she woke, her head had returned to its normal size, and her nose was warm. She looked at her watch, nearly ten o'clock. And no sign of Walt. She made a dash for the bathroom, diving back under the duvet just as he opened the bedroom door. He was dressed for work in the same stained Levi's and a heavy green sweatshirt, his hair still wet from the shower, a mug of steaming coffee in his hand.

"Good morning again. Feel better?" He handed her the mug.

Taking a sip before committing herself, "Ummm, tastes good. I think I may live. How much did I drink last night?"

"Not all that much, really. But you got sleepier and sleepier. It was all I could do to get you up the stairs before you conked out."

"I shouldn't drink red and white in the same evening. Did I—undress myself?"

His smile said no.

"Oh."

"Keep in mind, if we go back thirty years, I have—"

Before he could finish with *seen you naked*, she changed the subject. "Any news about the road?"

"I called the highway department. They hope to have at least one lane open this afternoon. When you've showered, come have breakfast. You need something non-alcoholic in your stomach."

Even though the hotel was without heat, at least there was plenty of hot water. Hanna stood under the shower, wishing she'd thought to buy a toothbrush at the grocery store. Between the aspirin and the coffee, her head was almost clear by the time she dried off.

Her reaction to Walt this morning kept disrupting her train of thought. She wasn't sure what had changed to make her wish they'd had sex. But given her condition last night, she wouldn't have remembered. And after his discussion about ravishing, she was pretty sure she didn't want to miss the experience.

As she was coming down the back stairway into the kitchen, she met Carlo carrying a mug of coffee. He couldn't hide his surprise at seeing her but wisely didn't comment.

Busted. Though they hadn't had sex, it certainly looked as though they had.

Trying to cover her discomfort, "Is the road open already?"

"Yeah. They have one lane cleared."

In the kitchen, Walt was making himself a cup of tea.

"I just met Carlo. What about the fumes?"

"I'm done working with the oil that was bothering him the most. But just in case, I'm keeping the front door open."

"He said the road's open so I can drive home." She was a little sorry that she could.

"It is." Walt took a plate of toast out of the warming oven. "The omelet is ready. I added some of the tomatoes and scallions from last night."

"I didn't know you could cook." Clearly there were many things she didn't know about him. "Lexi said Saul cooks too."

"Very different. He's been to culinary school. I cook to keep from starving." He cut the omelet in half and slid the two portions onto plates. "I fixed lots of toast. It'll settle your stomach."

She sat at the table. "Thanks for taking care of me last night."

He chose the chair across from her. "My pleasure. I was rather hoping the road would stay closed another night."

She felt her cheeks flush. "I'd have to skip the wine."

*Oh God, she was flirting with him.*

In the midst of breakfast, Carlo called for Walt to look at one of the front windows. "It leaked last night. There's damage to the new wallpaper underneath the sill."

Hanna finished eating, then washed the dishes, hoping Walt would return. When he didn't, she put on her jacket, found her purse and the catalogs and went outside. Time to make a graceful exit, though it might be too late for the graceful part now that Carlo had caught her coming down the stairs.

Walt was on a stepladder, trying to determine where the water was coming in. When he saw her, he came down, "Sorry to leave you on your own. Looks like we may have to re-caulk the window."

Reluctantly, "I should go home." Not her first choice, but wiser.

He walked with her to the car, took the keys from her hand, unlocked the car door, and held it open. "Be careful."

"I will."

"I enjoyed last night."

"I enjoyed what I remember."

With his thumb, he touched her lips lightly, then kissed them. "Until next time," and walked back to where Carlo was waiting.

*Next time.*

She felt the ground shift ever so slightly.

Instead of an hour, it took two hours to get back to Durango. Most of the debris had been removed from the highway, and steel netting was being hung over the road cut to protect the pavement from further damage. Half of the outside lane had vanished into the canyon below.

Hanna barely noticed her surroundings. She was preoccupied with the memory of Walt in his bare feet. Walt lying alongside her all night long without her knowing he was there. Walt going to California to tell her he loved her. Those memories were different from all the other times when Walt was listening to her problems, helping her, picking her up at the airport. Walt the helper. Right now, she was thinking more about Walt the romantic. Walt the ravisher. She laughed out loud. Such a delightfully archaic word. In the last twenty-four hours, their relationship had been turned inside out.

Only Zoey was home when Hanna arrived. She gave Hanna an evil grin. "Don't tell me any lies Hanna Sheridan. Truth please."

Holding off the inevitable interrogation. "Where's Lexi?"

"The local hospital called. Kyle's due to be transferred from Walter Reed on the twentieth. She hurried over to talk with the social worker and bravely let me take care of Marie."

"Well, you did raise a daughter."

"Marie's going to have her legs under her in a month or so. Watch out."

"Fed? Sleeping?"

"Yes'm. Now back to Walt."

That's what Hanna was afraid of.

"Nothing to tell."

"Sure, sure. Separate rooms? Separate beds? Same bed?" She was watching Hanna's face. "Ah, in the same bed."

"How do you do that? How do you read me that way? It's really annoying."

Zoey laughed. "I had your number the day we moved into the dorm. Okay, now that we've sorted out the sleeping arrangements, what happened?"

"We did not have sex."

"Okay, why not?"

"Red wine, white wine."

When Zoey stopped laughing, "You haven't learned not to do that to yourself?" Zoey had often played wine watchdog during college parties.

Hanna shook her head. "Wasn't paying attention. And not because of what you're thinking. Just not paying attention. We shopped for groceries, fixed dinner, watched the news and, after that, I remember nothing."

"Headache?"

"Big time. Fortunately he keeps aspirin on hand."

"Okay, no sex, then why do you look lit from within?"

Hanna took her time answering. "I'm seeing him from a very different perspective, he's—"

"In love with you. That can be very appealing."

"I've known that for almost two months. No, this is—me responding to *him*, not to what he said." She repeated, "To *him*."

"Sexually, right?"

"Oh yeah."

Zoey and Hanna were fixing dinner when Lexi got home. As soon as Hanna saw her daughter's face, she knew the interview at the hospital had been upsetting. Instead of asking, Hanna simply put her arms around her, and Lexi let herself be comforted, mumbling into Hanna's shoulder. "This is going to be so hard."

"I know, darling. Let's go into the living room." Instantly in mother mode, "Would you like some tea?"

"Sure."

Zoey waved them out of the kitchen and began filling the teakettle.

Lexi curled up at one end of the couch, so Hanna took the other end, facing her.

"What did they say?"

Lexi took a breath, letting it out slowly in the tiny relaxing puffs she learned in Lamaze class. "He'll fly here with a corpsman and go straight to the rehab center at the hospital and begin the therapy schedule."

"Probably standard procedure."

"That's not all." Lexi's voice caught. "They think he has symptoms of post traumatic stress disorder, and so he's also going to have regular appointments with a psychologist or psychiatrist—I forget which. Anyhow, they're worried about his state of mind. He's having nightmares, wakes up screaming, thinking he's in Afghanistan. And he's still not talking much, like he was with me in Germany. I thought it was mostly shock and he'd get over it." Tears were running down her cheeks. "I don't know if PTSD means he's crazy or dangerous. And how do I handle it with Marie? I don't want her to be frightened by him." She took a breath. "I'm supposed to meet this psychologist sometime next week."

Zoey brought a mug of tea and the sugar bowl. "In case you want sugar."

"I do, thanks."

Zoey set both on the coffee table and left them alone. Hanna waited while Lexi sipped at her tea. Though the tears had stopped, her daughter looked like she had when, at age four, she was afraid to get in the swimming pool with Michael so he could teach her to swim.

Hanna let several minutes go by, then gambled on a mother solution. "Before Kyle comes home, why don't you go to Denver for a few days. You and Marie can meet the new baby. It'll give you something else to think about."

Lexi caught her lower lip in her teeth, considering the idea. "I'd like that. I really would. Sheri and I can compare baby notes. But I need to get things ready for Kyle being here."

"I can get started on it. Leave me the instructions they gave you."

Lexi was quiet, then "Let me call Sheri, make sure it's okay."

When Hanna carried the sugar and empty mug into the kitchen, Zoey was putting the finishing touches on a green salad. "Lexi okay?"

"She's calling Sheri. I suggested she take Marie to Denver before Kyle comes home. She seems to like her stepmother." Hanna was uneasy about sharing Lexi with Sheri, but she couldn't make Lexi dislike Sheri in the same way she did.

"Looks like you're losing all your house guests at once. The real estate agent called to tell me the escrow on Seabrook closes in two days. I need to show up in person to sign tons of paperwork. I made a plane reservation for tomorrow morning."

An empty house. Unexpectedly good timing.

The perfect time to cook Walt the dinner she'd promised him.

Before she got cold feet, Hanna left a message on his cell, asking whether he'd be available for dinner tomorrow, then went up to her bedroom and closed the door. She didn't regret leaving the message, but she needed some quiet time to understand why she had and acknowledge what would happen if he accepted the invitation.

Because the invitation wasn't really about dinner.

While she was in California, she'd been expecting some sort of life changing epiphany. Which never occurred. She'd enjoyed herself, stretched herself. No question. But running races and working for Zoey, even spending time with Duncan—nothing helped answer the profound question that had pushed her out of Durango. Even before Lexi's emergency, Hanna had begun to wonder if looking for greener pastures had been a fool's errand. Nothing had jumped up and said *Stay in California; here's where you belong.* But Durango hadn't said anything either.

Then the unplanned night in Silverton with Walt. Oddly enough, it felt like that hotel room was where she was supposed to be. With him. A quiet answer she couldn't have predicted.

Among the other epiphanies that hadn't shown up was how the children would fit into the Walt equation. She'd learned that her children would always be in her life. She was back on mother duty, waiting for whatever parenting would be required when Kyle returned. There was no way to compartmentalize her life because children slopped over into everything. Establishing boundaries was impossible. No baby gates for adult children.

Walt called an hour later. "What time?"

No turning back. This was the way she'd felt as she was driving to California.

Fortunately, Zoey and Lexi's late morning flights were close enough so that Hanna could drop them off at the same time and then go grocery shopping. She decided on lasagna. A green salad and crusty bread. She bought only white wine, promising herself not to drink more than one glass. Instead of ice cream, she stopped at *Bread Durango* for toffee brownies.

While the lasagna was baking, she sorted out the house, changed the sheets on all the beds, pretending this was a normal laundry day, not just that she wanted clean sheets on her bed. And she saved time for herself. Took a leisurely bath, washed her hair—she needed to have it cut—and found underwear that could almost be classified as lingerie.

She was nervous. What if she was rushing into Walt's arms simply because she didn't see anything else, except parenting, on her horizon. Last summer, she hadn't wanted to settle for what Durango offered, yet here she was, taking steps toward settling.

And it was okay.

A lot okay, actually.

There weren't many events that Walt remembered as significant markers in his life. The day he first saw Hanna in Home Room, the day he arrived in Africa, the day he heard about Lily's death, the day he decided to establish Anders Construction, and the day Hanna returned to Durango.

Perhaps tonight's dinner would be another.

Instead of going to Hanna's back door as he usually did, he went to the front door and pushed the doorbell. When she opened the door, she was almost laughing. "The front door! How very formal of you Mr. Anders," then stopped herself as she saw the bouquet of red roses he was carrying. He handed them to her and followed her inside. "I realized I've never given you flowers." *I want you to know how serious I am about loving you.*

"Oh my." A light film of tears blurred her vision. "Walt, they're beautiful."

Laying the flowers on the kitchen table, she pulled the card out of its envelope and read: *Is this the next time?*

She turned to face him, holding the message against her heart, too moved to get words out, so she simply nodded.

"Good." He folded her into his arms and they stood together, holding on to each other. Not kissing. Movement might break the spell.

Finally she whispered, "The flowers need water." She stepped away. In the back of the pantry she found the tall cut-crystal vase that had been her mother's pride and joy, added a spoonful of sugar to the water, and began clipping the ends. When she was satisfied with the arrangement, she set the vase in the middle of the kitchen table.

Then wasn't sure what to do next.

She couldn't remember ever feeling this nervous with Walt, not even the first time they had sex. "Would you like some wine? I only have white. I've learned my lesson."

"Where's the corkscrew?"

"On the table."

He poured her half a glass and a full one for himself. "This is all you get."

She blushed. "I'll save mine to have with dinner. Shall we eat now or—"

"Now, please." He grinned and she blushed again.

Looking back, Hanna remembered they barely spoke during dinner. Talking might spoil the suspended expectation. But there was plenty of thinking going on. She pushed her dinner around her plate, her stomach too unsettled to cope with food. Walt, however, had two helpings of lasagna.

And they agreed to skip dessert.

# CHAPTER 25

SOMETIME IN THE middle of the night they wandered down to the kitchen.

"How about the brownies we didn't eat and some hot tea?" Walt turned the heat on under the teakettle.

How could he be so wide awake when she was still wrapped in the delicious fog produced by very, very good sex. Tonight she'd discovered that being with Walt had nothing to do with *settling.* Some of the people she thought she needed to run away from were proving themselves necessary to her happiness.

Hanna opened the tin where she kept the teabags. "Brownies and tea will be fine."

Carlo's call woke them around noon. He'd finished repairing the window. Did Walt want to look at it? Walt did, and so Hanna rode along. While Walt and Carlo repaired the water-damaged wallpaper, Hanna strolled around the streets of Silverton, peering in windows, enjoying the cool winter sun on her face. Maybe the weather was due to improve so she could resume running on a regular schedule, one of the California things she wanted to keep doing. The other was her art—exactly what kind she wasn't sure. Maybe she should turn one of her sketches of Marie into a watercolor.

After Walt was finished, they drove back through Durango and southeast to a popular steak house in Ignacio, taking their time over dinner. Since Lexi and Marie wouldn't be back until the next evening, they had the whole night before them.

After Walt left for Silverton the next morning, Hanna, in a burst of energy, began dealing with the list of items Kyle would need. There should be a railing of some kind in the shower. Perhaps a stool too. She studied the downstairs bathroom's shower stall. Not particularly large. A railing was feasible but there was no room for a stool. If he was on crutches, it might not be possible to move from the sink to the toilet to the shower.

An hour later, the burst of energy was buried by all the unknowns. She should have talked to Lexi more. The information Walter Reed had provided talked about doorways to accommodate a wheelchair—was he going to be using a wheelchair? The doorway into the kitchen was probably too narrow. The living and dining room were more open. No problem. The front and back porches had several steps. A ramp perhaps?

Frustrated by what she couldn't do right now, she put on her running shoes and a fleece pullover and went jogging through the neighborhood. Though there was no sun, the streets were dry. After twenty minutes, her left hamstring tightened up, so she walked home, no sense pushing too hard.

She missed Walt.

Lexi's plane came in at 6:20, and since Hanna hadn't heard from Walt, she and Lexi decided to have dinner at McDonald's. Lexi was full of family news.

The new baby was adorable. "They're calling him Nicholas."

Sheri was anxious about losing the baby weight as fast as possible. "About fifteen pounds." Not sure when or if she'd go back to work.

Michael was playing proud father but not changing diapers.

Ryan seemed bored with the work at Michael's office but was dating one of the interns: Celeste.

"She's gorgeous. Her mother is from India and her father's from Mexico. You've never seen such dark eyes. Ry's head over heels."

Walt called Hanna's cell just as they were leaving the restaurant. "I'm still in Silverton. I should probably stay." He didn't sound as though he wanted to. "The countertop for the check-in desk is being delivered first thing in the morning."

"Probably a good idea." Especially since Lexi was back.

"I'd rather be with you."

"Me too."

"I'm guessing you're not alone. Lexi?"

"We're just leaving McDonald's. We've been corrupting Marie with the toys in a Happy Meal, most of which we ate for her."

"I'm guessing it's easier that I'm not there."

"Maybe."

"I'll be back tomorrow afternoon if the installation goes well."

"Call when you're finished."

When they were in the car, Lexi asked, "Who was on the phone? You were sort of talking in code."

"Walt. He's still working at the hotel in Silverton."

Lexi didn't ask anything else until she saw the roses in the kitchen. "Where did these come from? They're gorgeous."

"Walt."

"Really?"

"Really."

"Anything you'd like to tell me?"

"Nothing you can't already guess." She was not going to discuss her new relationship with Walt.

"Okay then, I'm going to bed. Flying with Marie is exhausting."

*The Wild Geese* closed out their tour in L.A.'s Walt Disney Concert Hall. All four nights had been sold out. On the final night, Saul was sitting in the balcony—the only comp ticket available by the time he called to tell Callie he was coming. She was wearing a long orange/yellow filmy skirt, a matching yellow tunic, and leather sandals. Her hair was clipped at her neck with the silver butterfly that he'd given her before she left Durango. He never tired of listening to her play. Tonight she'd had two solos.

When the concert was over, the loudly appreciative audience refused to let the band go, even after each member had been introduced and thanked, and four encore selections played. It was after midnight when the house lights went off and the last of the audience reluctantly left so *The Geese* were able retreat backstage to see friends and family and then go to the after party at a bar on Spring Street.

Callie had faxed Saul a back stage pass so he could find her after the show. Since the door to her tiny dressing room was open, he stepped inside as he lightly knocked on the door. "Hey."

She had her back to him, peering into the mirror, removing her make up. "Hey back. Let me get this cream off my face. I'm all gooey."

He closed the door behind him, "Great finale. Of the three performances I've seen, this was the best."

"The acoustics here are amazing, and the audience really energized us."

She went over to the small sink, washed her face with soap and water, dried it, and turned into his embrace.

"God, I've missed you."

He grinned, "But not while you're performing. I can tell."

"Well, no. When I play, I can't think of anything but the music. But the rest of the time—" Her kiss spent considerable effort convincing him. "When did you get in?"

"A little after six, in the middle of the evening commute on the 405. I stopped for takeout and ate in the car. I didn't want to be late. Can we get out of here or is there a party you have to go to?" When he'd gone to Vancouver for the opening, the after party had lasted until dawn. Not the way he'd planned on spending the night.

"I told Eric you were coming. He understands. I do need to be fed though."

"Room service?"

"Of course. *The Geese* are still paying."

She gathered her makeup and the music. Saul picked up the guitar case. "Anything else?"

"No. Where'd you park the car?"

"I put it in Valet Parking. After all, one of the stars of *The Wild Geese* is my girlfriend. Can't have her walking the mean streets of L.A. at midnight."

"Flattery will get you almost anything."

"I'm counting on it."

At the hotel, while Callie was showering, Walt ordered her a hamburger with everything and fries, her usual after-concert meal of choice. Saul ordered himself a grilled cheese sandwich and a bottle of wine.

When the food was delivered, she laughed, "A grilled cheese sandwich? And you call yourself a chef!" Wrapped in a huge towel, she wandered around the room, eating her hamburger, pulling clothes from dresser drawers, and tossing them into the open suitcase on the floor. She was still wired from the performance, walking off the adrenaline. Walt was stretched out on the bed, watching her. The next time she was close to him, he reached out his arm and pulled her onto the edge of the bed. "Sit a minute. You said you had news. The last time you had news you took off for two months. Should I be worried?"

She escaped his arm so she could stand and look at him. "No."

"Good, because I'm not ready to let you out of my sight for awhile."

"It's a CD demo. You know Sean, the drummer? Well, his agent was at a rehearsal the other day and heard me messing around with one of my own compositions. He liked what he heard and is thinking of maybe a dozen tracks, my guitar, a little percussion and perhaps some keyboard."

"Vocal?"

"Only two pieces have lyrics."

"When and where does all of this happen?"

"Whenever I get everything pulled together. I have a lot of work to do, but I can do it in Durango. No specific date. And I need to raise the cash for the recording session."

"You have to pay?"

"Just for the demo."

"If you need money—"

She shook her head. "No, this is my problem."

He got off the bed to stand very close to her. Not touching her—his face a cross between serious and amused. "If you marry me, you'll get half of my considerable fortune."

She laughed. "I happen to know your considerable fortune is tied up in the restaurant and making sure Diana's expenses are taken care of. Besides, I'm against marrying for money." She finished her hamburger and tossed its wrapping in the bathroom trash. More serious now, "I don't want you to have to support my career."

He took both of her hands in his and slowly lifted them to his lips.

Callie stood immobile, letting the feeling of his lips on her fingers travel to other parts of her body. "Was that *marry me* thing for real?"

"Yes."

She held onto his eyes. "A real proposal?"

He kissed her forehead. "Are you accepting?"

Firmly, "Yes." Followed by a whisper, "I'd love to be your wife." Corny but she loved saying it. *Wife*. So much was embodied in that word. She'd never much liked it until now.

"And I want to be your husband. We'll find the money somewhere."

"I already have a plan."

"You do?"

"I'm going to tell Hanna I want to sell my half of our parents' house." *And she may not be thrilled.*

"You own half of the house?"

"I do. Up to now, Hanna has needed it more than I have. It's free and clear so, if she wants to keep it, she can put a mortgage on it and buy me out. Or we can sell it."

"Will she agree?"

"Don't know. I haven't talked to her yet. But the chance to make a recording of my own work is too good to pass up. And once I have some cash, maybe we could rent a place a little larger than the Grub's attic."

"Maybe." He unwrapped the towel she was wearing and let it fall to the floor. "I've waited long enough to make love to my fiancée."

Saul and Callie drove straight from the Durango airport to the Grub, "Even though I've only been gone two days, I need to make sure everything's okay."

"Hanna parents her kids and you parent the restaurant." She loved that about him. Not much she didn't love, actually.

"It is a bit like my child."

Three days later, she drove to Hanna's late in the afternoon. Hanna was alone in the garage, surrounded by boxes and furniture Callie hadn't seen before. Her sister did not look pleased.

"Hello big sister. Where'd all this come from?"

"Lexi decided to stop paying for storage on their household stuff, and so it's in my garage." *Where else?*

"You don't park in there anyway."

"Not the point," she gave Callie a brief hug, "When did you get back?"

"Monday. The tour ended Sunday night. And, yes, I'm staying at Saul's. You don't need to worry that I'm moving in here."

Hanna's smile confirmed her relief. "In that case, do you want to stay for dinner?"

"If you have enough. Where's Lexi?"

"At the pediatrician's. Time for some of Marie's shots. Let's go inside. No sense my looking at all of this any longer. It isn't going to disappear." She hit the remote on the garage door. "Wine or coffee?"

Callie looked at her watch. "Wine. And before you remind me, I came to pick up the stuff I left here." She found an open wine bottle in the refrigerator and worked the cork out as Hanna handed her a glass.

"You're not joining me?"

"It's a little early. I'll finish the coffee." She sat opposite Callie. "Your boxes and clothes are in Brooke's closet. Probably at the back. Zoey was using Brooke's room so things got moved around."

"When does Kyle arrive?"

"Day after tomorrow. Lexi's a nervous wreck."

"And you?"

"Mostly worried. We don't know how he really is."

"Anything I can do? I'm singing at the Grub on weekends, but I have time during the week."

"Thanks. I have no clue how any of this will go."

"I know." Callie considered broaching the house topic, decided against it, and instead went with, "Saul and I are getting married a week from Saturday," and waited for Hanna's response.

Hanna gave her a long look. "Are you sure? This will be the third time."

"We're both sure."

"You've been sure before."

"Never this sure. This time SURE comes in capital letters."

"What if another job comes along?"

"Saul and I will decide what to do then."

"Where's the ceremony?"

"The Grub. I'd like you to stand up with me. You can wear whatever you want so long as we don't clash. I'm wearing what I was wearing when he proposed. Orange and yellow."

"And?"

"Saul is asking Walt to stand up with him. Judge Arlington will make it all legal. Can you do the flowers?"

"A traditional ceremony. You're full of surprises."

"Life in full of surprises."

# CHAPTER 26

IT WAS DRIZZLING the day Kyle flew into Durango. The hospital's social worker, Rosa Ling, had instructed Lexi to go directly to the Rehab Center instead of meeting him at the airport. A van equipped for a wheelchair would take him and the corpsman directly to the Center, so there wouldn't be room for Lexi.

She'd changed her clothes three times and spent more time on her make up and hair than she had in weeks. Unfortunately, Kyle might not even notice what she was wearing. Her husband had become an unknown quantity.

Hanna dressed Marie in a new blue jumper with a matching t-neck and tights and soft-soled Mary Janes. Marie could easily pull herself up and make her way around the coffee table but, the moment she let go, she sat down hard and then howled at the injustice. Lexi and Marie would go to the Center first. Then when Lexi called, Hanna would pick up Marie and take her home.

Hanna hadn't slept much, her mind reviewing and reviewing everything she needed to do. Tomorrow, one of Walt's employees was coming to install handrails in all the bathrooms and build a temporary ramp at the front porch in case Kyle was using a wheelchair. If he was on forearm crutches, he could probably handle the steps at the back porch. Depending on his progress, he might even be able to get himself upstairs with crutches, so they hadn't rented a hospital bed yet. He'd be at the Rehab Center a minimum of one week, maybe longer.

Lexi had spent all of yesterday unpacking the wardrobe containers with Kyle's clothes, hanging them in Ryan's closet and filling the dresser drawers. Kyle might prefer to sleep in Ryan's bedroom for a while since Lexi's room was full and running over with baby paraphernalia. Hanna had suggested putting Marie in Ryan's room by herself—she should probably have been sleeping on her own weeks ago—but making that transition while Kyle was recovering risked a return to nights of trying to get Marie back to sleep.

Hanna had filled the pantry and refrigerator with Kyle's favorite foods. At the same time, she was helping Callie get ready for her wedding. In the midst of all the chaos, Hanna had only seen Walt the night he came for dinner. At the front door, out of Lexi's hearing, she apologized for neglecting him. Walt kissed her. "I'm not going anywhere. I know how to be patient." She'd really wanted him to stay. Just as they had begun to be—whatever they were—her family had returned to the head of her to-do list.

*Don't go there.*

Having checked that Kyle's flight was on time, Lexi buckled Marie into her car seat. "I'll call when I need you to come get her. I'm so nervous I've been to the bathroom three times since I got dressed."

Hanna hugged her daughter, then watched her drive off to what would be a difficult day. Mothers couldn't run interference on a day like this. Only pick up the pieces.

Lexi called just after noon. "Can you come? Marie's cranky and hungry." Hanna filled a bottle with formula and locked up the house. Since she couldn't help Lexi with Kyle right now, she could do the grandmother thing. Marie's disposition would improve as soon as she was fed. Hanna was grateful Lexi had insisted on buying a car seat for the Civic so transporting Marie was easier. They'd be doing a lot of dropping off and picking up with both cars.

She found a strained, white-faced Lexi in the reception lounge, pushing the stroller back and forth to keep Marie quiet. "Did you bring a bottle?"

Hanna pulled it from her purse.

"Great." Lexi tested it on her finger and handed it to Marie, who stuck it in her mouth instantly.

Hanna waited a few minutes, "Can I ask how he is?"

"Oh sure, sorry." Lexi's thoughts had been elsewhere. "By the time they checked him in, he was exhausted. Now he's sleeping. We only saw him for a few moments."

"Was he glad to see you?"

"I guess." Lexi's eyes filled. "He was more interested in Marie. He took her on his lap for a few minutes while he was in the wheelchair. She wasn't afraid—just looked and looked at him."

"Did he talk to you?"

"Not much. I kissed him but he didn't kiss back. And he's so thin. The clothes I brought will fall off him. But he did smile at Marie, so I guess that's something. I love his smile."

"He probably doesn't want any other company."

Tears were on Lexi's cheeks. "I'm not sure he wants to see any one, not even me. When he was in Landstuhl, he really hurt his parents. They tried to comfort him, but he wasn't having any of it. Wouldn't talk to them either."

Hanna heard a new note in her daughter's voice, perhaps despair. Or resignation. Even the best mothering had limits; her daughter was having to bear her own pain.

Rather than going straight home, Hanna drove to the Grub, grateful that Marie had fallen asleep in the car seat as soon as she'd polished off her bottle. Hanna called Callie's cell. "I'm outside in the parking lot. Marie's asleep so I don't want to disturb her."

"Wise choice. Have you eaten?"

"Yes. But coffee would be nice and maybe crackers for Marie if she wakes up. She's only had milk for her lunch."

"Be right there."

"In faded Levi's and a heavy, oversize sweater that was probably Saul's, Callie quietly opened the car door and handed Hanna a coffee cup, then slid in, holding a baggy of saltines.

Softly, so as not to wake Marie. "How is he?"

"Hard to tell. He did hold Marie on his lap, but he's mostly been sleeping. I worry because he's not communicating with Lexi."

"I imagine that makes everything harder on her."

"She's handling it better than I would have expected."

"Why would that surprise you? She is, after all, your daughter, and you handle difficult things."

"Except when I skip town. Anyhow, if you'll sit here with Marie for a few minutes, I'd like to look at the restaurant's dining room, make some notes about the decorations. Anything you especially want?"

"Just Saul," Callie smiled. "Maybe lilies of the valley—but no gladiolas."

Hanna took her time studying the dining room. Planning flowers and centerpieces was a welcome relief from all the issues surrounding Kyle's homecoming.

Hanna's days were shaped by Lexi's trips to the Center, sometimes with Marie, sometimes not. Kyle's physical therapy started at 7:30 a.m. every day. He was learning to balance himself with and without the temporary prosthesis. How to stand up and sit down. How to take care of what was called his residual leg, wrapping it tightly to keep the swelling down, fitting the socks that helped the prosthesis fit over the still swollen leg. The fifth day, Kyle let Lexi watch him wrap it. A milestone. He was gradually letting her into his new reality instead of yelling at her like he did that day in Germany.

Lexi usually visited Kyle around lunchtime, then took Marie over after dinner. At the end of the week, she brought along one of Marie's favorite books, hoping he would read to her, but he'd had a long morning working on the parallel bars and then an emotional hour with the psychologist in the afternoon. Kyle was tired, so she simply left the book and coaxed Marie into kissing him goodbye. The second night, he was asleep when she and Marie arrived. But on the third night, he was feeling better. Lexi rejoiced in the scene of Marie tucked into his arm, listening to her Peek-a-Boo story and eventually falling sleep against her father.

Kyle touched her cheek. "She's so good." He laid the book on the bed.

"Tonight anyway."

This was the first moment since he'd been at the Center that he actually met Lexi's eyes.

"You've done a good job looking after her. Remember when you didn't think you could?"

He was being nice to her, instead of giving her the silent treatment. A hint that *her* Kyle was still in there somewhere. Lexi fought her tears.

"I've had help from my family. Do you want me to take her?"

He shook his head. "I've missed all the baby things."

"There'll be more."

"Do you think she'll mind?"

"What?"

"That her father is—handicapped?"

"Of course not."

As he stroked Marie's hair, the tenderness on his face touched Lexi's heart. For the first time since that horrible phone call from Germany, she was hopeful.

He looked up and, very quietly, "Do you mind?"

She sat on the bed, shocked by the question. "Oh God, no. How can you think that? I love you. I was so scared I wasn't going to get you back." She couldn't stop the tears.

Marie stirred, woke up and, seeing Lexi's tears, set up one of her famous howls.

"Rats." Lexi picked her up, "Shhhh baby girl. They'll throw us out for making too much noise." She paced the room, wishing she'd brought a second bottle or a pacifier.

Kyle reached out his arms. "Give her back to me."

"Are you sure? She's heavy." He looked so frail in his pajamas.

He held Marie, humming softly as she gradually quieted, gave this new person in her life a tiny smile, and settled back to sleep.

Later, Lexi described the scene to her mother. "It was so sweet. I couldn't resist taking a picture of them with my phone." Lexi showed Hanna the image on her Smart Phone. "I'm going to have a print made and then frame it."

With Marie asleep in Lexi's bedroom, Lexi and Hanna were sitting on the bed in Ryan's room, wondering whether it would serve Kyle's needs. "His therapist says that he can probably negotiate the stairs. But he's having nightmares, wakes up sweating, yelling sometimes. So it's better that he sleep alone for a while. He probably doesn't need a special bed since he's already getting in and out of bed by himself."

"When are they releasing him?"

"The Monday after Aunt Callie's wedding."

As usual, everything was happening at once.

Callie had called Ryan to invite him to the wedding. He agreed to fly down that morning but would go back early the next morning because he had plans with Celeste Sunday night. Brooke was taking the day off; Dennis was on duty at his dad's clinic. Hanna hadn't seen Brooke since the confrontation about the skis. Hopefully, they could stay out of each other's way for one day.

# CHAPTER 27

THE MORNING OF Callie's wedding, spring showed up in southwestern Colorado. Fifty-six degrees, a soft breeze drifting off the mesas and not a cloud in the sky. Though there might still be another snowstorm before winter gave up, today was a gift from the weather gods.

Callie had decided to sleep in Brooke's room the night before the ceremony, laughing at herself for not staying with Saul. "It's not that I'm superstitious or preserving my virginity but, since I'm actually inviting my family to witness our vows, I'm going to play the wedding game."

Hanna left the house before Callie was awake, picking up the flowers from the florist and arriving at the restaurant around ten. Above the entrance was a white banner with bold black letters: **Closed Today for Saul and Callie's Wedding.**

Wearing a white apron over gray sweats, Saul helped Hanna unload the car. "How's my bride?"

"Still in bed when I left."

"That's my girl. Early is not her favorite time." He was holding one of the two elaborate bouquets of peach and white roses. "Where do you want these?"

Carrying the second one, Hanna pointed. "On the edge of the stage—over there." Then she placed the other one about ten feet away. "That should leave enough room for the wedding party. I hope Cal likes them. She said to keep it simple and no gladiolas."

Saul laughed. "Yes, I heard about that."

"She does speak her mind."

"One of her best features." He turned serious. "You don't have to worry. I love her the way she is."

"On most days, so do I." *When had that happened?* "It has, however, taken me a very long time to say that sincerely."

Chairs were arranged in an arc in front of the low stage where Callie usually performed. When the ceremony was over, the guests would move to the tables covered with yellow linen cloths. The florist had used the tiny ceramic guitars Hanna had purchased to hold the lilies of the valley Callie wanted in her bouquet and in the centerpieces.

Hanna had been surprised by Callie's choice. "I wouldn't imagine you'd be a lilies of the valley kind of girl."

"So many things you don't know about me, and I don't know about you. That'll change now that we're living in the same town unless, of course, you head for the beach again."

"I probably won't. Walt made me promise that, if I felt like running away, I'd give him two weeks notice so he could go with me."

Callie laughed. "I like that man more every day. He's not about to let you out of his sight anytime soon."

Hanna had to admit that every day she was learning how special Walt was—had always been.

Except for two of Saul's employees cleaning up the kitchen, Hanna and Walt were the last people in the restaurant. Saul's Aunt and Uncle and Callie's friend Louise were the first to leave. Not long after, the newlyweds set off for Pagosa to spend the next three nights in the Springs Resort Hotel. Saul's assistant would manage the restaurant while he was gone.

Ryan and Brooke left about the same time. Ryan borrowed Hanna's car to meet a couple of friends at one of the sports bars in town. Brooke was going to the library to study. Lexi and Marie planned to visit Kyle and then go home, Lexi admitting she was beat.

Walt brought a half empty champagne bottle to the table where Hanna was taking apart the table decorations; the lilies were already wilting. He poured himself a glass. "Want some?"

She shook her head. "Is there coffee or tea?"

"No, the kitchen crew is anxious to leave, so they've emptied everything." He sat down, stretching his legs in front of him. "A good day."

Hanna dropped the last of the lilies into the trashcan she'd brought from Saul's office. "Agreed. No glitches and no parent/child confrontations."

"When I picked Ryan up at the airport this morning, I got the sense he's changed. Not so bored with everything."

Hanna had noticed the same thing. "He kissed my cheek, asked how I was, and did not mention gas money. A new and improved Ryan."

"All he could talk about was Celeste."

"According to Lex, he's really serious about her. He hasn't had a steady girlfriend since his junior year at Boulder."

"Did Brooke say anything to you?"

Hanna put the miniature guitars into a plastic bag. "No, but at least she didn't advertise her feelings. I half expected she'd chew me out on sight."

During the afternoon, Hanna had watched Brooke from a distance, once again trying to gauge what was different about her youngest. Though it had been only a month since the ski confrontation at the house, the *mother gene* sensed something was going on. Maybe she and Dennis were having trouble. At lunch, Brooke had been sitting at the table with Lexi, Marie and Ryan, laughing when Callie threw the bouquet straight at her. At other times, she seemed preoccupied and, for Brooke, rather quiet.

Without question, it had been Callie and Saul's day. He couldn't take his eyes off her. When he'd repeated his *I, Saul, take thee Callie* the joy on his face lit up the room, and Callie never stopped smiling. Before the judge could say *You may kiss the bride,* Callie was already kissing Saul—making the wedding guests laugh.

Throughout the afternoon, Lexi took snapshots of the wedding party and guests, and Brooke used her cell phone to videotape the ceremony. This time Hanna wasn't in charge of pictures, which meant she might actually be in some of them.

Her son, in navy slacks with a white short-sleeved shirt and a yellow cardigan that Hanna hadn't seen before, looked rather professional. Perhaps the law office was rubbing off on him.

By five o'clock, the celebration was winding down. All the toasts had been given, the gifts loaded into Saul's truck, and his *Opening them will give us something to do this weekend* comment got a bigger laugh than the kiss.

While Saul was taking their bags to the truck, Hanna hugged Callie. "Be happy."

Callie kissed her sister's cheek. "I am. I want you and Walt to be happy too. Don't wait too long."

"We won't."

"We'll be back Tuesday. Saul begins to hyperventilate if he's away from the restaurant too long. It's really sweet. Will Kyle be at the house by then?"

"Yes, he's scheduled to be moved to outpatient status Monday morning."

"May I come by?"

"Of course."

The swinging door between the kitchen and dining room opened, and a young man leaned in, "Mr. Anders, we're leaving now."

"Thanks, Mickey. Please lock the back door, and we'll lock the front." He stood up, taking his keys from his pocket. "What else goes into the truck?"

"Nothing. The guitars and bouquets stay here." She started toward the door, "I'm way past tired." So grateful she didn't have to drive home.

The lights were on all over her house. At the back door, Walt took her into his arms, "I wish that had been us today," and spent considerable time kissing her goodnight.

"Do you want to stay over?"

"Very much but I don't want to creep Ryan out because his mother and ex-boss are sleeping in the next room."

"Tomorrow night?"

"Absolutely."

As much as she craved sleep, Hanna forced herself to stay up to watch the ten o'clock news and wait for her son. When Ryan came home, he headed for the refrigerator and came back to the living room with a can of coke.

"Did you meet your friends?"

"Yeah. Actually two of the guys work for Walt. We used to hang out after work."

"How do you like working in your father's office?"

He shrugged. "Okay, I guess, but I never see what any of my research leads to. On a building site you can see the results of a day's work. And I miss being outdoors."

With that opening, Hanna went after the big question. "Do you really want to go to law school?" She was having a hard time seeing Ryan as a lawyer.

"It's okay for now."

"What would you rather do?"

Another shrug. "Aunt Callie told me that not knowing what I want to do is pretty normal. That it's rare at my age to know what you want to spend your life doing. Of course Dad says he was always sure he wanted to be a lawyer, and Aunt Callie always wanted to be a musician. But she said it's okay to start on a path you're not sure of because there's no law that says you can't change paths if you find something better. So law school might not make me become a lawyer, but it might lead to something I've never considered. I mean, you sort of changed paths for a while—mother to marathoner—so I figured, why not? Clerking pays better than working construction even though I liked working for Walt."

That was probably the longest and most thoughtful speech Hanna had ever heard from her son. And he was quoting footloose Callie.

For the next hour, he talked and talked about Celeste.

Hanna had wanted him to get some direction, and he had. Without her help. Not knowing what to make of that turn of events, she went to bed.

A Scarlett O'Hara *think-about-it-in-the-morning* moment.

# CHAPTER 28

EXCEPT FOR TAKING Ryan to the airport, Hanna spent most of Sunday in the kitchen. Lexi baked Kyle a key lime pie and a double batch of chocolate chip cookies. Hanna prepared three different main dishes, then froze them in individual portions. Flexible meal planning. After dinner, Lexi and Marie made what would be their last evening visit to the Center. Tomorrow was Discharge Day.

Walt arrived at Hanna's while they were gone, bringing a duffle bag of clothing, his laptop, and a bottle of wine. Hanna met him at the door, took the bottle from him and walked into his arms.

Against her hair, "Quite a welcome. I should bring liquor more often."

"I'm so glad to see you." She'd been looking forward to this moment all day.

"And I'm so glad to be here. Are we alone?"

"For the moment."

He proceeded to kiss her thoroughly, pressing her against the wall, his hands sliding under her sweater.

And then Lexi's car pulled into the driveway.

*Of course.*

They stepped apart, and Hanna hurried to the bathroom to straighten her clothes and run a brush over her hair.

When she reemerged, Walt was calmly and rather expertly putting Marie into her high chair. Hanna was pretty sure she looked flustered, but Lexi seemed not to notice.

"How's Kyle?"

"A thousand times better. He has really progressed, except he's still having nightmares." Lexi handed Marie a box of apple juice. "I'm the one that's nervous."

"Will he have a wheelchair or just crutches?"

"Crutches—they want him to use the prosthesis as much as possible. The problem is— it makes his leg hurt if he wears it too long."

She leaned against the edge of the table. "I hope all of this is going to be okay." Hanna put her arms around her daughter. "I hope so too."

Walt woke at first light, enjoying the warmth of Hanna curled against his back, silently thanking the universe for the miracle of having her close by. Such a long time coming.

When he heard Lexi getting Marie up, he went into the master bathroom to shower. Hanna was still asleep when he finished, so he went downstairs. In a pale blue fleece robe, Lexi was cooking cereal for Marie, who was holding onto the cupboard knobs to navigate the kitchen. "There's coffee if you want some. Did we wake you?"

He found himself a cup and poured coffee into it. "No. I'm always awake at first light. Can't seem to break the habit even when I don't have to get up."

"Marie is a first light kid. Come here, punkin," Lexi interrupted Marie's kitchen tour and put her in the high chair. Marie was ready to register her protest, but Lexi was prepared with a spoonful of cereal. "I have to catch her before she goes into howling mode."

"What time do you collect Kyle?"

"Ten o'clock."

"Would you like me to go with you?"

She smiled, "How nice, but no. I don't think he wants a fuss." It had taken all this time for him to let her help him with even the smallest task.

"I understand."

"Don't get me wrong. I'm glad you're here to take some of the pressure off Mom and, if Kyle needs help that Mom and I aren't able to provide, you can step in. He's not comfortable with being dependent on others' help."

"I wouldn't be either. It's a guy thing. I have to be in my office this morning, but I'll swing by after lunch to see how things are going."

Lexi wiped cereal from Marie's chin. "Thanks."

In between chasing after Marie and cleaning up the kitchen, Hanna had stationed herself at the kitchen window, watching for Lexi's car. She was used to taking care of her own children, but Kyle's recuperation was an entirely different situation. She kept reminding herself she was Lexi's back up. *Do not take charge.*

They arrived just after eleven, earlier than Hanna had anticipated. By the time Lexi came around to the passenger side, Kyle had opened the door and turned so his right leg was on the ground. Then, he placed his hands under his left thigh to help move the leg with the prosthesis. Lexi brought him the crutches from the back seat. Using the open door, Kyle pulled himself up and took the crutches from Lexi. Once he slid his arms into them, he began walking to the back porch.

Hanna opened the kitchen door as he was negotiating the steps. She made herself focus on the thatch of blond hair that hung over his forehead. A better look than his Marine haircut. It was wiser to focus on his hair instead of the prosthesis. This young man her daughter had fallen in love with looked much older than the day he'd brought his wife and daughter to stay with Hanna. Being indoors for all these weeks had stolen the color from his face. Lexi was right. His clothes were too big for him.

As he stepped onto the porch, he looked up at Hanna with half a smile. "It takes me a while, but I eventually get there."

Hanna felt relief; if he could see a little lightness in the situation, maybe he was going to be all right.

"No worry. I don't have anything else scheduled." As he stepped into the kitchen, Hanna turned to intercept Marie, who was crawling in his direction. Kyle didn't need to have his daughter use his legs to pull herself up while he was still learning how to walk again. "Look, Marie, here's your Daddy."

Marie held out her arms—her *hold me* signal. When Kyle didn't take her, she looked puzzled and debated crying.

Hanna quickly walked her away—going into the family room where most of the toys were. This morning, Hanna had picked them up off the floor so Kyle wouldn't trip on anything. She set Marie on the floor and found a bright blue teddy bear in the toy box. When she looked up, Kyle was in the doorway.

"Let me get into a chair; then I can hold her."

He made his way to the recliner Ryan favored for watching football and awkwardly dropped into it, letting the crutches fall noisily to the floor. "Hey, baby girl. Can I hold you now?"

Marie frowned.

"Is she mad at me?"

"Not at all. She frowns when she's figuring something out. She's used to people taking her the moment she puts her arms out. She'll learn."

"I'll be able to take her when I get rid of the crutches." He held out his arms. "Come on Marie, come see Daddy."

It took several minutes; then she dropped the bear and crawled to Kyle. He reached over and lifted her onto his lap. "She's heavy, or I'm just that weak."

"Trust me, she's heavy. And strong. Your daughter is one determined kid."

As he kissed Marie's forehead, she reached for the dog tags he still wore, yanking them.

"Ouch. Wow, she is strong."

Marie laughed at his reaction and tugged again. As Hanna went to find Lexi, she heard Kyle laugh too. Marie was going to be better therapy than anything the doctors could prescribe.

The day was easier than either Lexi or Hanna had expected. Walt came by, ostensibly to pick up some papers he'd forgotten, but by then Kyle had managed the stairs—a fifteen-minute climb—and was in Ryan's room taking a nap.

Not until 2 a.m. the next morning, when Kyle woke the household screaming, did the reality of his problems sink in.

The scream was shrill and seemed to last several minutes, though it was probably just seconds—scaring Marie into her own screams, followed by crying and more crying. While Lexi was calming Kyle, Hanna brought Marie into her room, walking her until she quieted and, once the baby nodded off, Hanna laid her between herself and Walt.

"Sorry. Welcome to the joys of family life. I may need to move her crib in here tomorrow."

Walt yawned, "Not a problem," and went back to sleep. Hanna, of course, was wide-awake, listening for sounds from Ryan's room and to Marie's soft breathing. Though her love life had improved, her family life was only marginally better.

In the morning, Walt and Marie were the first ones awake. "I'll take her downstairs with me." He kissed Hanna, who was more asleep than awake. Sometime later, she heard the bedroom door open, then close—too sleepy to open her eyes.

It was midmorning when she finally woke up. No Walt, no Marie. After a shower, she made her way to the kitchen where Kyle was eating his way through a stack of pancakes. Marie was trapped in her high chair with mangled pieces of pancake in front of her.

"Any left, Lex?" Hanna poured herself orange juice.

Lexi spooned more batter on the griddle. "I made plenty. I thought Walt would want some, but he had an appointment. He got Marie up, changed her diaper, and had her in the high chair by the time I got down. He's amazing."

"True, though I didn't know he could change diapers."

With the last bite of pancake, Kyle wiped the remaining syrup from his plate. "That's the best food I've had in months. I'm stuffed."

Lexi looked over at him and smiled, "You need to be stuffed."

"Sorry about the yelling, Hanna."

"Don't be. But I think we should try Marie's crib in my room tonight."

"What about Walt?"

"He's adaptable and can sleep through almost anything. What time do you have to be at the Center?"

"Eleven. Lexi and I appreciate you helping us—this won't last forever."

Hanna leaned over and kissed his cheek. "I know. Good to have you back."

Callie had always believed she could truly be happy only when she was playing her guitar. But Saul had changed that. Now she was happy with or without the guitar. The first three days as Mrs. White had been the happiest of her life.

As soon as they got back to Mountain Grub, Saul headed for the kitchen while Callie worked on rearranging the two rooms over the restaurant so she and Walt could function until they found a larger place. It was time to discuss the sale of the house.

Instead of calling ahead, she begged a couple of salads from Saul's kitchen and headed for Hanna's. She'd been silently rehearsing the best way to present her case about selling the house but, if Hanna dug her heels in, Callie didn't have a back up plan. Legally, Hanna had two choices. Either way, Callie would get her share of the house, but she didn't want to make this a legal problem that might drive a wedge between them. They'd been getting along better than they ever had.

Only Hanna's Civic was in the driveway. Callie knocked on the back door and then walked in. "Hanna. Where are you?"

From the upstairs a faint answer, then feet coming down the stairs.

By the time Hanna entered the kitchen, Callie was opening the salad containers and searching for silverware. "I brought Mountain Grub take out."

"I didn't know they did take out."

"They don't. But I know the owner—rather intimately."

"Nice perk." Hanna pulled two bottles of water from the refrigerator and sat down.

"Many, many perks," Callie twisted the cap on a bottle and drank.

Hanna studied her sister. "You look—bride-like."

"Pray tell, what is bride-like?"

"If you don't know, I'm not explaining." She dribbled dressing over her salad. "Kyle, Lexi and Marie are at physical therapy. Lexi's learning how to help with some of the exercises that he'll be doing at home. They've been taking Marie so she gets used to the way he moves during the exercises. He doesn't want to frighten her."

"Actually, I came to see you."

"So is the salad a bribe?"

"Can't I bring lunch for my sister?"

Hanna gave Callie the *I know you're messing with me* stare.

"Okay, it's a bribe—sort of."

Hanna put her fork down.

No sense tap dancing around the request. "Han, I need cash. Would you be willing to sell the house—or buy my share?" It was harder to ask than she expected.

Hanna's expression was half puzzlement, half resistance. "Why now?" Running through Hanna's head were all the reasons that selling wasn't possible now. Lexi and Kyle needed a place to stay. Actually Hanna needed a place to stay. Walt's one bedroom apartment was small, and they hadn't gotten around to talking about moving in together or—anything permanent. She didn't want to assume too much.

If she wanted to stay in the house, she'd have to put a mortgage on it, and she had no idea whether the alimony payments would qualify as enough income.

What if Brooke and/or Ryan needed to come home? There'd be no home. Would she want them to come home?

Not really. That was what had sent her California.

Callie let Hanna churn through the implications. When she sensed Hanna was calmer, "For the first time in my life, I need that kind of cash. Most of Saul's assets are tied into the restaurant. We'd like to buy something together. The two rooms over the restaurant are way too small. I want to pay my share of the down payment."

No response from Hanna.

"And I need to front some cash for the CD demo I've been asked to submit to Pantheon Music. Except for the house, all I have are my earnings from the tour—a nice nest egg—but not enough. I still have massive credit card debt, and my truck is ten years old with 150,000 miles. At some point, I'm going to need a new one. And I suppose I should pay my bill at the motel in Henderson."

More silence.

"Would you please say something! Throw something."

"I need to think."

"It doesn't have to be done tomorrow—but soon. The real estate market is in pretty good shape right now."

"I never imagined we'd get rid of the house."

"You don't have to, but I'd like my share. You've had the use of it for nearly four years."

"You never wanted to live in Durango."

"I do now." Callie considered reminding Hanna that going to Zoey's had opened the way for Callie to fall in love with Saul. Without the urgent need for grocery money, she might not have gone to work at the Grub.

A great many things might not have happened had Hanna stayed at home. Brooke might not be living with Dennis, Ryan might not be headed for law school. Of course. both of those things might have happened anyway. Playing *what if* served no purpose.

Waiting for Hanna to say something, Callie finished her salad and put the plastic container in the trash. "Let me know. Saul's going to the bank sometime this week to see what kind of loan he can get." And she left Hanna sitting at the table.

Hanna hadn't seen this coming.

Her childhood had been lived here.

Her life as a divorcee had been lived here. Yet she'd walked away from this house for five months with no sense of loss. Her children had no emotional connection to his house. Clearly, Callie didn't.

When Lexi, Kyle and the baby came home, Hanna fixed them grilled cheese sandwiches, opened a bag of potato chips, and listened to what the therapy was like."

Lexi noticed Hanna hadn't made herself a sandwich.

"Aren't you hungry?"

"Callie brought salads."

"How is she?"

"Fine."

"I hear the Callie snarl." Lexi knew her mother too well. "I thought you guys were doing better."

"We are, sorry."

"So?"

"She wants us to sell the house."

# CHAPTER 29

HANNA LEFT LEXI and Kyle in the kitchen and went in search of her running shoes and a sweatshirt.

Her brain seemed to have stopped—like a clock whose battery has run down. Jogging might jump-start constructive thinking. However, after only half an hour, her right calf cramped up, so once again she had to walk back home. She was definitely out of condition and needed a regular running routine like she'd had with Duncan.

The exercise having partially revived her brain, she showered and drove to Southwestern Realty, the office that had helped sell Irene Ander's house a year ago. Procrastination wasn't an option. She needed to ask questions and be given facts and figures before she could deal with all the other ramifications, the human ramifications. Walt, Lexi, Kyle, Callie, Ryan, Brooke.

The agent on floor duty, Terence Ruiz, was patient with what she didn't know and, hopefully, accurate about the value of her house. Two hours later, her head was spinning. She had an appointment with a loan officer the next morning, and an appraiser would be at the house in two days.

Hanna wasn't upset with Callie—her sister had every right to ask for her share of the house—but she was upset about the timing. Kyle had weeks of rehab facing him. Hanna and Walt were still exploring their new relationship, nowhere close to making concrete plans about living arrangements.

Moving—or going into debt—had not been on her horizon. Even though Walt was probably at a job site, she needed to talk to him.

"Anders."

"Hi, it's me."

"Hi, me."

"Can you take a coffee break?"

"Sure."

"Fifteen minutes?"

"I can do that."

Walt was already in the coffee shop when she arrived, a slice of lemon meringue pie in front of him. As she began explaining this new development—she was trying not to think of it as a crisis—Hanna felt herself choke up. Walt laid his fork down and reached across the table. "Give me your hands." She complied, and he folded both of his over them. "Calm down."

His touch made all the difference. He made all the difference. Hanna inhaled, "Callie wants us to sell the house—or wants me to buy her out." After a few moments, she pulled one hand from his grasp and laid the pages of comparable properties on the table. "The real estate agent's pretty sure the house is worth between $350,000 and $400,000. An appraiser will come day after tomorrow."

Walt picked up the papers, studying the pictures of the house sales. "He's probably in the ballpark."

"If I decide to keep the house, I'll have to qualify for a loan to pay Callie. I have an appointment with my bank's loan officer to explore what I can qualify for. But the payments will probably eat up most of Michael's alimony check."

Their coffee came.

"When does Callie want an answer?"

"Soon. She and Saul are looking at condos, and she also needs money for some kind of a CD demo. I was so shocked about her wanting me to sell the house that I didn't ask about the demo."

"I'm not surprised they want a better place. The two rooms he's been living in are no bigger than your garage. When the restaurant was originally built, those rooms were for one of the cooks, so someone would be on the premises at night."

If Terence were right about the value of the house, the mortgage would be huge. "What do you think I should do?"

Walt waited. He wanted her to make this decision without his input. His own feelings for Hanna and his vision of their life together shouldn't influence her right now.

"It's your house, so it's your decision. Just remember that, whatever you decide, I'm with you."

That brought her tears. "Thanks for coming. I needed to talk this out."

"It'll be okay." He smiled.

"I keep telling Lexi the same thing about Kyle. I hope we're both right."

Before she told Lexi about the house, Hanna wanted to have the appraisal figure and the information from the bank. She'd spent hours looking at her current expenses, factoring in what a mortgage might cost. Since neither Brooke nor Ryan was living at home, they could no longer be claimed as dependents on Hanna's income tax. A sizable loss. And if Hanna and Walt were to marry, her alimony would disappear and she'd be financially dependent on him. Back looking for a job.

One of the things she'd loved about her hiatus in California was feeling unencumbered. Just her car, her clothes, her laptop, jobs for Zoey, and running every morning. A wondrous simplicity. No complicated decisions, no responsibilities. And except for Zoey's clients, no one expected anything from her. That simplicity didn't seem possible in the midst of her Durango life.

Every morning, while she was waiting for the financial information to show up, she made herself jog. Exercise helped.

Having Walt at the house every night helped too. But when all the paperwork and the numbers arrived, she knew the house would have to go. The math made the decision for her.

She called Callie.

"I'll be right over."

Callie let herself into the kitchen and, without a word, put her arms around Hanna. "Are you okay with this?"

"No—Yes—Maybe. It all comes down to the numbers. Want coffee?"

"Sure." Callie sat at the table. Looking through the pages of real estate listings lying on the table. "Are these comps?"

"Un huh." Hanna set the coffee on the table and sat down, pushing the appraisal report across the table. "Terence, at the real estate office, thinks the appraisal is a bit low because several of the comps are six months old. He says the market is inching its way up, and so we might list the house for more. Not a lot more. We don't want to scare off the initial buyers."

Callie flipped through the appraisal report, looking for the final number. "Wow. I didn't imagine it would be worth that much."

"Me either."

"So what comes next?"

"We list it. But not until we've sorted out what things we want to keep and what we can get rid of. Otherwise a buyer might show up before we're ready."

"Have you told the kids?"

"No. Only Walt."

"What does he think?"

"He's letting me decide."

"Wise man. Have you thought about where you'll live? I don't want to be responsible for you living on the street."

"I'm more worried about where Lexi and Kyle will live." If worse came to worse, Hanna was pretty sure she could squeeze into Walt's apartment—at least in the short term.

"You might want to worry about Brooke too."

Something in Callie's tone tweaked the *mother gene.* "What about Brooke?"

"She came up to the restaurant two days ago, assuming that, since I've led such a licentious life, I wouldn't give her flack."

"Cal—out with it."

"She's pregnant."

*Damn and double damn. That's what was different about Brooke.*

Hanna shouldn't be surprised. Brooke and Dennis had been having sex for at least a year, so pregnancy was not beyond the realm of possibility. But she didn't want her teenage daughter to start her adult life with a baby. Too late for what Hanna wanted. Too late for many things. And Brooke told Callie, not her.

Payment in full for leaving.

Michael's mother, Sybil, was always talking about trouble coming in threes. On the surface, this seemed to be the third trouble. Kyle's injury, selling the house, and now Brooke. Hanna let Sybil's rule of three wander around in her head for a few moments and then found a light in the tunnel. Selling the house might not classify as trouble. Perhaps selling the house would be freeing. A huge change, but not necessarily a bad change. And though she'd have preferred Brooke finish her education and get married before she got pregnant, Brooke was the one who would have to figure out her own life. None of these things should be allowed to interfere with where Hanna's life was going. Where she and Walt might be going. She was suddenly in awe of that truth.

Callie got up to get more coffee while Hanna gathered up the paperwork on the table. "At least she told someone in the family."

"Lexi knows too. My guess is that Brooke's counting on one of us telling you so she won't have to."

"Has she seen a doctor?"

"Yes. It's due in early September."

"Thanks for the heads up."

Callie added sugar to her coffee and sat down. "What comes first?"

"Choosing what you and I want, then letting everyone else choose. Lexi and Kyle have what they were using at Pendleton. I'm not sure what I want to keep of my own furniture. And I'm not all that fond of mother's French country furnishings, though she had some nice antiques."

"Is tomorrow too soon to start?"

"No. I'll tell Lexi tonight and then call Ryan. Do you want to tell Brooke, since she's talking to you?"

"Sure. Let's give ourselves a week or two before letting them make their choices."

"Only fair. Ryan won't want much. I can't predict what Brooke will or won't want."

As soon as Hanna told Lexi and Kyle, Lexi went online looking for rentals. Kyle was quick to reassure Hanna. "We'll be okay. We've weathered a lot this year. Finding a place to live should be easy in comparison." Every day, Hanna was gaining more respect for her son-in-law. He'd emerged from his injury stronger and steadier, had already begun driving himself to his rehab appointments and was spending extra time in the Center's gym to rebuild his strength. "You've had my family underfoot long enough."

Dealing with Ryan was easy. He'd taken his bicycle and snowboard with him when he drove to Denver after Christmas. "I'll drive down over Easter weekend to pick up the rest of my stuff. I might bring Celeste. Is that okay?"

"Sure." Did that mean one bedroom or two? Undoubtedly one. At least he was ready to share his girlfriend with the family.

As expected, Brook proved to be the most difficult. Hanna left several voice mail messages, all of which Brooke ignored for three days.

When she did return the calls, she began the conversation by complaining: "We don't have enough room for all my things."

"Maybe you should look for a bigger place, something unfurnished." Though what they'd use for money, she didn't know. "You can take some of the furniture from here, certainly your bedroom set. Bring Dennis and take a look."

"But all my clothes, books and scrapbooks—everything needs to be stored someplace." And there was the famous Brooke whine. Hanna wished she'd figured out a way to cure her youngest of that sound years ago.

"Brooke, you need to come look at the furniture. You might also want some of the kitchen utensils. The listing begins next week."

"Why can't you store some of my things in boxes someplace?"

"Because I can't. I don't have a someplace either." At this point, Hanna wasn't sure where she was going to store her own things. "You'll probably need a bigger place when the baby comes."

She wanted Brooke to know she knew.

Two days later, Brooke and Dennis came over to look at the furniture that hadn't been spoken for, and Dennis decided to take most of the tools Hanna's father had left in the garage. "They'll clean up pretty well."

Brooke was beginning to show. Hanna wished they could talk about the pregnancy. Was Brooke happy? Scared? Was the pregnancy an accident? How did Dennis feel? But that conversation wasn't going to happen right now.

As they were loading the tools into Dennis's truck, Brooke asked, "Where are you going to live? California?"

Hanna forced herself not to show how Brooke's words hurt. "Don't worry, I'm staying in Durango."

"I'm not worried. Come on Den, I have to get to work. We can come back for the furniture tomorrow."

In the midst of all the sorting, discarding and deciding who would take what, Walt felt it was time to show Hanna the house along the river.

The day before the *For Sale* sign would appear in her front lawn, he found Hanna sitting in the back yard, staring into space.

"A penny," he leaned over and kissed her.

"Probably not worth even a penny. Just enjoying a peaceful interlude. Ryan and Celeste will be here tomorrow."

Walt smiled, "There's certainly been a lot of coming and going, a lot of bartering. 'If I can have this, I'll let you have that.'"

"Brooke's favorite game, and Lexi lets her get away with it. Fortunately, Lexi is naturally easy going and so happy Kyle's doing well that she doesn't much care if Brooke is manipulating her. My hope is that Brooke's child learns how to manipulate her. Sweet revenge. Rule twelve in the mother code book."

"There's a code book?"

"I wish."

"Do you have time to take a ride with me?" He held out his hand and pulled her to her feet.

"Always."

They drove to the east side of town, a little over a mile from Hanna's, following the street above the Animas River, stopping in front of a white split level house on a large, wooded lot that sloped down to the river. The house had new vinyl siding and mullioned replacement windows framed with dark green shutters.

"Is this the house you bought to renovate? It looks great."

He walked to the passenger side and opened the door.

"I hope you like the inside too."

He pulled a key from his pocket and handed it to her. She studied it for a moment—puzzled that he wanted her to open the door—then fitted it into the lock and the door swung open into a spacious living room/family area with a floor to ceiling native stone fireplace. Beyond was the dining room/kitchen. The whole first floor was essentially one large room with a high ceiling supported by beams of light wood.

Hanna stood in the doorway, "I love the openness. Did you remove the walls or was this the original floor plan?"

"I only removed the wall between the kitchen and dining room. That way when you're in the kitchen, I can still see you and you can see me."

It took a few moments for Hanna to absorb what he'd so casually said. What his giving her the key meant.

"Is this—?"

"Ours? Yes. But only if you like it. I had us in mind when I put in a bid at the foreclosure auction last fall."

Walt watched as the implications sank in. Watched her walk into the kitchen, and look out the window over the sink. "You bought it before you came to see me."

"I did."

"You were that sure."

"Only of me. Not so sure about you at that point."

A simple answer, "I love it."

He felt his life change. Finally.

Very slowly, she walked back to him, placing her hands on either side of his face, smiling into his eyes. "You are a remarkable man, Walt Anders. I love you." She pulled his face against hers and kissed him. "You've kept this to yourself all this time?"

"I wanted you to be sure what you were going to do. We'll have to camp out for a while. I can only work on this job in between the jobs that pay."

"I don't care. I'm not keeping all that much from the house anyway. Most of it will fit into the garage. Can I see the upstairs?"

He kissed her. "Let me show you."

"How many bedrooms?"

"There were four but now there are only two—and an art studio. I combined two bedrooms and put in a skylight. Not only will you have a place to work on your art, but Hotel Sheridan will effectively be out of business."

*Clever man.*

"I wouldn't bet on it."

# CHAPTER 30

THE ESCROW ON the house closed the last Wednesday in July, and the moving van arrived just after nine the next morning. Callie had volunteered to oversee the loading of what was left in the house. Saul was at their new condo and Hanna was at the house on Animas because Walt was starting a job in Ignacio. By two-thirty, the old Meeker house was empty, Hanna's furniture in the back of the van and what Callie had chosen from her parents' possessions in the front. Whatever no one else in the family wanted had already gone to the halfway house in Bayfield or to Goodwill. As soon as she locked up the house, Callie would follow the van to the condo so Saul could get back to the restaurant for the dinner crowd.

Neither Hanna nor Callie had been nostalgic about selling their childhood home though Hanna had been weepy the day she found several boxes of their parents' mementoes: their wedding album, a pressed flower, her father's *Bible*.

Callie's share of the sale price had gone toward paying off half of the equity line of credit Saul had taken out on the restaurant for the down payment on their condo. She'd never before owned much of anything except a series of beaten up trucks and her guitar. Footloose Callie had gone over to the conventional side and was enjoying every minute. Initially, Hanna was putting her share in the Credit Union. She and Walt would need some of it for blinds and flooring once the renovation was finished.

Callie suspected some of Hanna's cash would end up subsidizing the expenses for Dennis and Brooke's baby. Since Brooke wouldn't be attending Fort Lewis in the fall, there'd be no more checks from Michael. Now that Brooke was working fewer hours at *Steamworks,* Dennis was working full time at his dad's clinic, making barely enough to get by. Fortunately, Brooke was still on Michael's health insurance though he was making noises about taking her off since she wouldn't be attending college in the fall.

*Dad can get Sheri pregnant but, when I get pregnant, I'm chopped liver.*

The house sale had displaced Lexi and Kyle earlier than they might have planned. They were renting a two-bedroom house in Bayfield, and Kyle would start teacher training at Fort Lewis in August, his veteran's benefits paying for his tuition and some of their living expenses over the next year. Lexi had already told Brooke she'd be glad to take care of the new baby when Brooke went back to work. *I'm looking after Marie; one more won't be a problem.* Hanna hoped Brooke planned to pay her sister, but they'd have to work it out themselves. Somewhere in this year, Lexi had become a confident mother and Brooke, who'd turned up her nose at the suggestion she should change Marie's diapers, was about to have a huge reality check. Hanna had served notice she was babysitting only in emergency situations. *And I do mean emergency.* An experiment with setting boundaries.

As the van lumbered down the street and disappeared around the corner, Callie locked the front and back doors and left the keys in the lockbox. This chapter closed. A year ago, she was camped on Hanna's doorstep. Today she was married, back singing in the restaurant and, in three months, she'd go to L.A. to do the studio work on the CD.

It took three tries to get her truck started. She really did need new wheels.

Waiting for the van, Hanna sat in her studio, mentally designing where everything should go. She'd been searching catalogs for a drawing table and storage cabinets. It was like having Christmas in mid-summer.

She would always wonder what would have happened if she hadn't gone to California.

Perhaps Brooke wouldn't have moved in with Dennis and gotten pregnant so soon.

Perhaps Ryan would have found the kind of job he wanted instead of giving in to his father. But then he might not have met Celeste.

If Callie hadn't gone to work at the Grub, she and Saul might not have found each other.

And Hanna might still be wondering what it would feel like to get away from Durango, and Walt wouldn't have gone after her.

She had no regrets about running away. And wasn't planning any apologies.